SCENT

Praise for Kris Bryant

Lucky

"The characters—both main and secondary, including the furry ones—are wonderful (I loved coming across Piper and Shaylie from *Falling*), there's just the right amount of angst, and the sexy scenes are really hot. It's Kris Bryant, you guys, no surprise there."
—*Jude in the Stars*

"This book has everything you need for a sweet romance. The main characters are beautiful and easy to fall in love with, even with their little quirks and flaws. The settings (Vail and Denver, Colorado) are perfect for the story, and the romance itself is satisfying, with just enough angst to make the book interesting...This is the perfect novel to read on a warm, lazy summer day, and I recommend it to all romance lovers."—*Rainbow Reflections*

Temptation

"This book has a great first line. I was hooked from the start. There was so much to like about this story, though. The interactions. The tension. The jealousy. I liked how Cassie falls for Brooke's son before she ever falls for Brooke. I love a good forbidden love story."—*Bookvark*

"This book is an emotional roller coaster that you're going to get swept away in. Let it happen...just bring the tissues and the vino and enjoy the ride."—*Les Rêveur*

"People who have read Ms. Bryant's erotica novella *Shameless* under the pseudonym of Brit Ryder know that this author can write intimacy well. This is more a romance than erotica, but the sex scenes are as varied and hot."—*LezReviewBooks*

Tinsel

"This story was the perfect length for this cute romance. What made this especially endearing were the relationships Jess has with her best friend, Mo, and her mother. You cannot go wrong by purchasing this cute little nugget. A really sweet romance with a cat playing cupid."—*Bookvark*

Falling

"This is a story you don't want to pass on. A fabulous read that you will have a hard time putting down. Maybe don't read it as you board your plane though. This is an easy 5 stars!"—*Romantic Reader Blog*

"Bryant delivers a story that is equal parts touching, compassionate, and uplifting."—*Lesbian Review*

"This was a nice, romantic read. There is enough romantic tension to keep the plot moving, and I enjoyed the supporting characters' and their romance as much as the main plot."—*Kissing Backwards*

Goldie Winner *Listen*

"Ms. Bryant describes this soundscape with some exquisite metaphors, it's true what they say that music is everywhere. The whole book is beautifully written and makes the reader's heart go out to people suffering from anxiety or any sort of mental health issue."—*Lez Review Books*

"I was absolutely captivated by this book from start to finish. The two leads were adorable and I really connected with them and rooted for them…This is one of the best books I've read recently—I cannot praise it enough!"—*Melina Bickard, Librarian, Waterloo Library (UK)*

"The main character's anxiety issues were well written and the romance is sweet and leaves you with a warm feeling at the end. Highly recommended reading."—*Kat Adams, Bookseller (QBD Books, Australia)*

"This book floored me. I've read it three times since the book appeared on my Kindle…I just love it so much. I'm actually sitting here wondering how I'm going to convey my sheer awe factor but I will try my best. Kris Bryant won Les Rêveur book of the year 2018 and seriously this is a contender for 2019."—*Les Rêveur*

Against All Odds

"*Against All Odds* by Kris Bryant, Maggie Cummings, and M. Ullrich is an emotional and captivating story about being able to face a tragedy head-on and move on with your life, learning to appreciate the simple things we take for granted and finding love where you least expect it."—*Lesbian Review*

"I started reading the book trying to dissect the writing and ended up forgetting all about the fact that three people were involved in writing it because the story just grabbed me by the ears and dragged me along for the ride...[A] really great romantic suspense that manages both parts of the equation perfectly. This is a book you won't be able to put down."—*C-Spot Reviews*

Lammy Finalist *Jolt*

Jolt "is a magnificent love story. Two women hurt by their previous lovers and each in their own way trying to make sense out of life and times. When they meet at a gay- and lesbian-friendly summer camp, they both feel as if lightning has struck. This is so beautifully involving, I have already reread it twice. Amazing!"—*Rainbow Book Reviews*

Goldie Winner *Breakthrough*

"Looking for a fun and funny light read with hella cute animal antics and a smoking hot butch ranger? Look no further...In this well-written first-person narrative, Kris Bryant's characters are well developed, and their push/pull romance hits all the right beats, making it a delightful read just in time for beach reading."—*Writing While Distracted*

"It's hilariously funny, romantic, and oh so sexy...But it is the romance between Kennedy and Brynn that stole my heart. The passion and emotion in the love scenes surpassed anything Kris Bryant has written before. I loved it."—*Kitty Kat's Book Review Blog*

"Kris Bryant has written several enjoyable contemporary romances, and *Breakthrough* is no exception. It's interesting and clearly well-researched, giving us information about Alaska and issues like poaching and conservation in a way that's engaging and never comes across as an info dump. She also delivers her best character work to date, going deeper with Kennedy and Brynn than we've seen in previous stories. If you're a fan of Kris Bryant, you won't want to miss this book, and if you're a fan of romance in general, you'll want to pick it up, too."—*Lambda Literary*

Forget Me Not

"Told in the first person, from Grace's point of view, we are privy to Grace's inner musings and her vulnerabilities...Bryant crafts clever wording to infuse Grace with a sharp-witted personality, which clearly covers her insecurities...This story is filled with loving familial interactions, caring friends, romantic interludes, and tantalizing sex scenes. The dialogue, both among the characters and within Grace's head, is refreshing, original, and sometimes comical. *Forget Me Not* is a fresh perspective on a romantic theme, and an entertaining read."—*Lambda Literary Review*

Whirlwind Romance

"Ms. Bryant's descriptions were written with such passion and colorful detail that you could feel the tension and the excitement along with the characters."—*Inked Rainbow Reviews*

Taste

"*Taste* is a student/teacher romance set in a culinary school. If the premise makes you wonder whether this book will make you want to eat something tasty, the answer is: yes."—*The Lesbian Review*

Touch

"The sexual chemistry in this book is off the hook. Kris Bryant writes my favorite sex scenes in lesbian romantic fiction."—*Les Rêveur*

By the Author

Jolt

Whirlwind Romance

Just Say Yes: The Proposal

Taste

Forget Me Not

Touch

Breakthrough

Shameless
(writing as Brit Ryder)

Against All Odds
(with Maggie Cummings and M. Ullrich)

Listen

Falling

Tinsel

Temptation

Lucky

Home

Scent

Visit us at www.boldstrokesbooks.com

SCENT

by
Kris Bryant

2021

ISBN 13: 978-1-63555-780-0

This Trade Paperback Original Is Published By
Bold Strokes Books, Inc.
P.O. Box 249
Valley Falls, NY 12185

First Edition: January 2021

Credits
Editors: Ashley Tillman and Shelley Thrasher
Production Design: Stacia Seaman
Cover Art by Deb B.
Cover Design by Sheri (hindsightgraphics@gmail.com)

Acknowledgments

Hands down, my editors deserve all the thanks for getting this book out. Writing during a pandemic is extremely difficult, but Ashley held my hand during the content stage of it until it worked itself into a solid story. And Shelley gave me two rounds of copy edits to catch all the mistakes. My editors are wonderful and I love them for their support and understanding.

Thank you to Rad, Sandy, Cindy, Stacia, Toni, and everyone in front of and behind the scenes. They press on every month and get our books out and into the hands of our readers on time. They make us look good when they deserve all the credit.

Christopher Elbow Chocolates was so unbelievably helpful during the research phase of this book (lucky me, huh?). Gordon took time out of his busy schedule to give me a tour of the warehouse and the store. I have learned so much and have tasted the best artisan chocolates in the world. Go to elbowchocolates.com and see the amazing combinations of flavors and chocolate that are almost too beautiful to eat. Almost.

I couldn't have done this without my friends. Thank you to Fiona for keeping me on my schedule and encouraging me to participate in writing sprints (which help so much!), Jenn, and the beautiful g.s., KB Draper and our socially distancing writing dates, HS, Melissa, Georgia, Sugar, Paula, Cathie, Sue, KC, and for everyone who checks in on me and ensures I'm doing okay. Thank you to Deb for your never-ending support and always coming up with the best covers before I even have a chance to start thinking about what I think will look good.

This is the fourth installment of the sensory series. Thank you to my readers, who have made this series successful and fun to write. You are my cheerleaders and I appreciate every kind word, review, and email from you along the way.

To Nikki

Chapter One

"I'm sorry to do this, but I have to leave for another meeting, and I don't want to be late." I looked at my watch for effect, but I knew exactly what time it was and how long I had to catch the train. Only a few minutes, and I couldn't miss it. Any other day? Sure, but not today. She caught the train only on Thursdays. I stood and nodded at the partners and the sales staff circled around the conference table, all eyes on me and my interruption.

"I'll catch you up, Nico." Trish, my sister and part owner of Tuft & Finley, winked at me from the center chair.

"Have a good night, everyone." I avoided Trish's smirk. She knew what I was doing and why I was in such a hurry. We had no secrets. I grabbed my messenger bag and my phone from my office on the way out the door. My reflection in the foyer mirror showed a slightly flustered woman in desperate need of a haircut, but still attractive. I didn't look my best, but it was the best I could do right now.

I reached the platform with two minutes to spare. I smoothed the creases in my pants, tucked my shirt deeper into my waistband, and adjusted my belt so the buckle lined up perfectly with the buttons of my shirt. It was too hot to wear my blazer, so I carefully folded it over my bag and rolled up my sleeves to look as casual as possible. I was trying to impress a woman who didn't even know I existed. When the doors whooshed open, I slipped into the semi-air-conditioned car, where the pungent smells of exhaust and metal pushed their way in as people rotated out. I caught a whiff of overused cologne from the suit who had just vacated my seat. For a moment, I considered moving, but I wanted to be in the same place I was the last four Thursdays.

It was only a matter of time before she noticed the familiarity of me in the same seat week after week. I adjusted my bag under the bench and pulled out my tablet. I smiled when a book I'd started late last night popped up on the screen. My day had been so hectic I'd forgotten about it. I looked at my watch. We would be at her stop in four minutes, and she would ride it until two stops before mine.

With my first show less than three months away, I needed extra studio time. To say I was nervous was an understatement. One of my pieces had been noticed outside a coffeeshop during a news story about an up-and-coming neighborhood, and suddenly I was the next best artist in the greater Chicago area. I knew my fame wouldn't last, and my family really pushed me to ride the wave while I could. My watch buzzed. I looked at the message.

Have you made contact? Trish's text made me smile.

I picked up my phone and shot off a quick text. *In T-minus thirty seconds.* I added a thumbs-up to show confidence, more for myself than for her.

Maybe this time you should, oh, I don't know, SAY HI???

We'll see.

Ugh. Don't make me ride the train with you next week and force you to talk to her. Because you know I will.

Trish was my champion. She was deliriously happy in her marriage and wanted the same thing for me. This unknown woman was the first one who'd made my heart beat faster in almost two years.

When the train lurched to a stop, her stop, I tensed. I pretended to be engrossed in my book, but truthfully, I was using my peripheral vision to find her in the crowd. When I saw the familiar black heels on the ribbed floor in front of me, I looked up and held my breath. She looked at me. For the first time, we made eye contact. Her eyes were blue, like mine, but lighter. My breath hitched, and my stomach fluttered. Before I could smile, she looked away and took a seat on the same side, but in a different section. I closed my eyes and waited. A sugary scent washed over me, and I smiled as the wave of sweetness carried me back to my childhood when my parents took us to Navy Pier on the weekends, and Trish and I gorged on cotton candy, caramel apples, and chocolate. She smelled delicious. Today it was definitely chocolate. Last week, she smelled like buttercream frosting.

With both hands, she cupped a small white box, held together with a red, silky ribbon as if it were the most important thing in her life, resting on her knees. I glimpsed her through the people who sat and stood in the space between us. Her hair was long and straight and the color of dark honey. She looked cool and calm while I sat fifteen feet away holding my elbows away from my sides for fear of sweating through my shirt. Even though the temperature inside the train wasn't bad, I was nervous because today I was going to talk to her. Maybe. Probably not. I sighed when I saw she was wearing earbuds. Not that I had the courage to talk to her, but it was just another obstacle I could list when Trish asked me if I'd made my move and I told her the same thing for the fifth week in a row.

Is she there yet?

She's wearing earbuds, and about two million people are standing between us. Or maybe I'm talking to her right now, and your buzzing is distracting. I answered Trish's text and waited for the backlash.

That's bullshit. Bawk bawk. I smell chicken. Chicken and egg emojis followed her words.

I don't even know what I'm doing or why I'm trying. I have to stay focused on my art. I don't have time to date.

Total lie. I was busy, but I always had time for love and romance. It had just been too long, and I'd forgotten to make it a priority.

My phone rang. "Well, now for sure I can't talk to her." I answered Trish's call with a low whisper.

"Maybe if I make you sound all important, she'll overhear the conversation, and you can impress her with your knowledge of whatever it is you do at Tuft & Finley."

"You're funny. Talking about myself probably isn't the best way to impress a woman. Tell me what I missed after I left," I said.

Our company was growing, and things were starting to fall through the cracks. We needed to hire more people because we were already spread too thin. Tuft & Finley had started in college as an environmental recycle project that turned into a packaging company. We never thought it would grow into a profitable business. We all had different dreams and goals after college, but it was hard to walk away from its success. We were all at the point where we wanted to sit back and relax a little, but we were working just as hard now as we did back then. We needed at least five new employees to pick up the slack.

"We went over a few resumes and scheduled interviews for a second-shift warehouse manager, two office assistants, and an outside sales rep, since ours decided to get knocked up," Trish said.

I laughed because she was referring to our partner, Anna Finley, who'd just found out she was pregnant with twins. "Come on. You could do that job in your sleep."

"Yes, but that's exactly what I want. Sleep. When was the last time we all had quality time away from the office?" Trish asked.

"Didn't you just get back from Cancun last month?"

"Four days and we never left the room, but I don't consider that a vacation."

The train went silent right as I said, "Stop it. I've heard you have sex before, and my virgin ears are still burning." I glanced at Thursday, fearful she'd heard me. She made eye contact and lifted her eyebrow. She had definitely heard. She and the ten or so people between us. I noticed her earbuds were out. When was it ever quiet on the L? "Shit."

"What?"

The noise level went back up. "The whole world inside this car just heard me, including Thursday." I hated that I was too chickenshit to talk to her and find out her real name.

"Perfect. You have her attention. Now go over there and be wonderful you." Trish had more confidence in me than I did.

"I'll call you later." I quickly hung up and sneaked a peek at Thursday. She was back to being engrossed in whatever was on her phone. When the train stopped again and several people rotated out, I spotted available seats closer to her. I should have made my move, but it would have been ridiculous to leave a perfectly good seat near the door for one right next to her. Then it would have been obvious that I was trying. I sighed and shot off a text message.

Mission aborted. I'll just enjoy the view when she exits the train.

Gifs of people and animals fainting blew up my phone. Even though they made me smile, I felt a ping of sadness. My divorce from Mandy had destroyed me. I used to be confident and knew how to talk to women, but Mandy had ripped my heart and my confidence to shreds. Trish had spent the last eighteen months trying to build me back up. The only good thing that came from my deep depression was my art. It was dark and radiated anger, but heartbreak sold, and I was using that negative energy to create more pieces for my show. Nothing was more appealing than a tortured artist's soul.

TRIP HER! By mistake, I mean. Don't let her fall on her face. Oh, catch her!! How romantic.

I guess today isn't my day. No worries. There's always next week.

I'm coming with you next time. I need to see what you've been working on anyway.

How about you just drive over?

I took the train only because my warehouse studio was in an industrial part of town. After I'd blown out my luxury-sedan tires on nails and sharp metal pieces for the third time, I gave up and started taking the L. My studio was right off the platform. The noise didn't bother me, and the rent was cheap. When I had to transport pieces, I used my 1978 Ford F-250 with wood-panel siding and a beat-up bed. It was an eyesore, but Lucy was still reliable. I'd had her transmission replaced last year and upgraded from an unused eight-track to a satellite radio system. It was probably the most expensive thing about her.

No, thanks. I know about the nail bombs, and I don't want my car stolen.

I inserted an eye roll emoji. *It's not that bad.*

I shared the bottom story of a warehouse equally with three other tenants. The second and third stories were blocked off. We all had our own locked studios but had a common space that housed a worn leather couch, two reclining chairs that didn't match, and two vending machines whose contents were questionable. I swore the same bag of Funyuns was in there for over a year. I'd donated a kitchen table with a bench and a refrigerator.

Ben, the owner of the building, worked on cars. His overhead crane had rails that ran into my studio, and when I needed to lift a piece onto Lucy's bed or a larger flatbed, he helped out. Sometimes we shared tools, but sometimes we wouldn't talk for weeks. The other two residents were artists, too. One painted landscapes and played Ella Fitzgerald on loop. As much as I loved hearing it, I needed Ben's heavy metal when it was time to pound out my anger. The other neighbor was quiet and brooding. I caught glimpses of his black leather jacket and long black hair as he slipped in and out of his studio and nodded when our eyes met across the parking lot. He never talked much. Ben said he was a photographer, but I never saw him with a camera or any kind of equipment.

I put my phone down when the train slowed for Thursday's stop. I looked up when she walked by me, hoping we'd make eye contact again, but she clutched her white box with both hands and strolled by me as if I weren't even there. I leaned back and watched her step off the train and disappear into the rush-hour crowd.

Where was she going? This stop was an older neighborhood that had been upscale decades ago, but once the suburbs of Chicago spread out, it was quickly forgotten. It lacked modern conveniences like Starbucks and fast-food joints but boasted Italian bakeries and diners that were open twenty-four hours. I had no idea where she was going, but I decided that, one day, I was going to find out.

CHAPTER TWO

Where do you think she goes? I mean, she must be visiting someone because that neighborhood is mostly rows and rows of greystones."

"Maybe she lives there?"

"And takes the train home only one day a week?" I asked. Trish and I were having coffee in her office, discussing the meeting I'd skipped out on and everything I didn't do on the train but should have.

"You know, all you have to do is strike up a conversation and find out. I really need to discover why this woman is your kryptonite." Trish topped off her cup and added a splash of heavy cream and sugar.

"Maybe I'm just fixated on her because she's completely untouchable. Remember when I crushed on Dominique in high school?"

"Remember when you dated Dominique in high school? Yeah, you always get the girl. Let's figure out why this mysterious woman has you all flummoxed." Trish leaned forward and put her elbows on her desk. We both had the same color eyes, but I was blessed with my mother's long lashes, and Trish's heavily applied mascara couldn't compare. She rested her chin on her linked fingers and stared at me. "She's beautiful, but she's not friendly."

"We don't know that she's not friendly."

"She didn't smile at you when you smiled at her, and you have the best smile in the world. And you are the epitome of cool. I mean, I know your confidence is tender right now, but trust me, people are drawn to you. Always have been."

"Then she's not gay."

"My straight friends all want to fuck you."

I smiled. She wasn't the first person to tell me that. "Maybe she's into femme women, not tender butches who weld."

"Everyone's into artists. And you are barely butch."

I snorted at her generalization. I had on slacks, a button-down shirt, sensible wingtips, and I wore makeup only when I was sick or had a party to go to. And even then it was very minimal. My dark hair brushed my collar and swooped across my forehead. I was constantly running my fingers through it to push it away from my eyes. Trish thought it looked adorable. I gave her the that's-not-the-look-I'm-going-for scowl. "Your straight friends are into me?" I was deflecting because I didn't want to continue this conversation. I wouldn't put it past Trish to follow me to the train station and strike up a conversation with Thursday.

"Put it this way. I will never leave you and Kimberly in a room alone together."

I waved her off. "Oh, please. She's so married, it's ridiculous."

"Oh, she's married, but she's not dead. And she always talks about you like you're the cat's meow." Trish held up her finger to stop me as she anticipated my crude retort about pussy.

I laughed. "Well, you don't have to worry about me and Kimberly. She's cute and all, but I'm not about to be her experiment. Those never end well." I cringed when I remembered my first mistake with a straight woman. And my second. It seemed to be a lesbian curse. Inevitably, we fell for a straight woman. I now avoided them like the proverbial plague. "Let's talk more about business. When does Anna plan to take maternity leave?"

"I think she's planning on taking half a year, starting in three months. I have a feeling she's going to want to become a hands-off partner after the babies are born. It's smart for us to plan ahead. You need to sit in on the interviews though. She's very emotional right now, and I need a levelheaded person to help make this decision."

"That's fine, but in the meantime, I need to figure out how we're going to do a generic box set for randomly sized toys." I held up two figurines from a video game, Alien Alliance, that were different sizes. This was going to be hard since the company was going to just randomly fill the twenty-compartment box with a selection from three hundred character figurines.

"You might just have to make all the sizes the same." Trish shrugged. She was the consultant who made every person feel like their project was the most important thing to our company.

I was responsible for sitting in the meetings, taking notes, and designing the product. "That's too boring and too easy. Besides, you don't want the figurines to rattle around."

"It's not like they're going to break. They're plastic. You've got this. I'm not worried." Trish always said that.

"I'll head to my office and get started." I was already planning a cardboard design with sliding compartments. These projects were fun. Plus, the clients were young and excited about the success they were experiencing, so their thrill was infectious.

"Don't think I've forgotten about Thursday," Trish yelled as I was almost in my office.

I waved her off even though she couldn't see me. I needed to focus on this project, but mentioning Thursday threw me. What was it about her that made me so nervous? I used to smile and laugh with strangers, whether I was attracted to them or not. Now I couldn't even find the confidence to talk to a beautiful woman. My last relationship had truly destroyed me. I don't know how I'd allowed myself to get that low, but I vowed never to do it again.

My work phone rang. Clearly Trish wasn't done with our conversation. "I know, I know. Thursday. Next Thursday. I'll make my move."

"You know I love you, right?" she asked.

"I know. I love you, too."

"I only want you to meet her because…" She let the unspoken words rest between us.

"Because my track record sucks."

"Samantha was a bad relationship. And I can't even talk about Mandy yet."

"Samantha was a really bad relationship," I said. She was my college sweetheart and the reason for my inability to hold down a relationship. I had never known anyone more determined to settle down with somebody financially secure. At first, I thought it was just youth and how we all wanted to make money when we were done earning our degrees. We had big plans for the exorbitant salaries we dreamed of making. Samantha and I were going to travel Europe together after graduation, but then she realized that artists didn't make the kind of money doctors, lawyers, and business graduates did. She strongly encouraged me to take a few business classes, which I did, but dumped me the minute a woman with a trust fund and a membership to a country club showed up in her life.

I considered the poor college life charming and the quintessential American experience: the mountain of debt when I graduated, ramen noodles and peanut-butter sandwiches as a daily staple, and a degree that would serve me no purpose other than to say I went to college for four years. Trish was there when Samantha broke up with me. I thought she was going to knock her lights out. It took all my strength to hold her back. I was heartbroken, with substantial debt that I racked up trying to buy Samantha nice things to keep her happy.

"And don't worry. I'm not going to fall in love with someone who has such different goals from me. I won't do that again. My true love will love me for me."

I thought that comment would get me a heavy sigh, but Trish surprised me. "I would give anything for Samantha to see you now, baby sis. Successful business and a famous artist."

"Oh, stop. I'm sure she's forgotten about me by now."

"Good riddance." I heard the bite in Trish's voice.

"It won't happen again." The Samantha Incident had really hardened me. Once Tuft & Finley was up and running, I had a few hours here and there for myself, so I hit the gay bars and blew through a lot of women. My reputation five years ago was questionable. Trish had to stage an intervention and get me back on track. Breaking hearts around Chicago wasn't good for me or the business. I took a step back from my life, and that's when I met Mandy. God, what a fucking manipulator. She made Samantha seem tame.

"Don't worry. I won't make that mistake either. As a matter of fact, I'm going to hang on to your debit and credit cards the next time you date somebody. I'll dole out cash when you go on dates."

"I almost want this to happen. Almost." I couldn't think about how many tens of thousands of dollars Mandy stole from me over the course of our joke of a marriage without wanting to throw something or cry.

"You're too nice and generous. This would be so much easier if you liked men. They are so easy to read."

"No, thanks. You and Rob are wonderful, but I'll find somebody after I'm done with my show. Right now, that has to be my main focus."

"And your video-gaming clients."

"Let me get to work. Hey, thanks for looking out for me."

"That's what family does. We look out for one another. Go to work. You have a deadline."

I hung up, smiling. Even though my love life was shit, my home life was strong. Our parents were only about thirty minutes from work, and my mother baked cookies or muffins for the company every Friday. It was nice to see her during the day because my nights were for welding. Even though she tried hard not to play favorites, she had a soft spot for me because I wore my heart on my sleeve like she did. Trish took after our father: headstrong and all business. I looked at the clock. Only a few more hours of design work, and then I could head to my studio and lock myself in it for the weekend.

Sometimes I slept in Lucy, and sometimes I crashed on the couch in the communal area. Ben cared only when he wanted to do the same. A sofa sleeper for my studio was probably a good idea. There was plumbing for a shower in the small bathroom, but I never got around to putting a showerhead on it. My life would be easier if I did and kept a change of clothes there. I worked better when I was clean. I was used to the smell of welding, but it wasn't pleasant.

I made a list of what I needed to get done this weekend and then jumped online to buy new things for my shop. My summer was going to be intense. Truthfully, I didn't have time for Thursday or any other woman until after my show. At least that was the lie I told myself.

CHAPTER THREE

"When's your show again?" Ben held the door open for me on his way out.

"September tenth. Why? Are you going to be there?"

"I told you I'd help unload your sculptures. Of course, I'm going to be there." Ben was a nice guy, but if people met him in a dark alley, they would assume he had a collection of bodies in barrels hidden somewhere on the closed-off second and third floors. He stood well over six feet, shaved his head, and sported a giant black, bushy beard that gave off a murderous lumberjack vibe.

"I don't think they'll need your help since they have a crew who does it." I couldn't tell if he was offended or sad, so I quickly added, "But I would love to have you around as a supervisor. I'll let you know when I find out. And thanks, Ben. You're the best."

He grunted and continued his trek down the stairs until he reached his white windowless van. It didn't help how people perceived him, but Ben didn't care. He was great at his job, and people waited months for him to work on their classic cars. He offered to beef up Lucy for me, but she was perfect the way she was.

I unlocked my studio door and threw my bag onto my new sofa sleeper. I was the proud owner of a matching set of furniture, a coffee table, two new lamps, and a desk. The shower finally worked. I'd also picked up a cheap refrigerator, a gas stove I would never use, and a microwave that would get plenty of use. It was nothing like my loft in the city, but I could live here comfortably for a few days if I got distracted by my art. My phone buzzed in my pocket.

I'm here. Let me in.

I took a deep breath and buzzed Trish in. I knew she was going to ask me a zillion questions about Thursday, and then I would have to confess that I'd chickened out. But when I opened the door, she kissed my cheek and flung herself onto my new couch.

"I'm glad you finally decided to make this place a little more civilized. Oh, maybe you can do a watch party here."

"What are you talking about?"

"You know, watch you sculpt."

"Shut up. I got all of this only because I'm going to spend my weekends here for the next several months."

"Well, baby sis, you've classed up the place a lot. Show me what you've been working on."

She followed me into my work area and didn't mention Thursday once, which set me on edge. "Those are going to the show." I pointed to several sculptures ranging in sizes from only a few inches to ten feet tall. "I'm supposed to have eighteen to twenty pieces. I have thirteen that I know I'm going to display, two that are maybes, and so I have about five more to create."

"Oh, I like this one. What is it?" Trish stood a few inches from an installment I was working on. I could tell she wanted to touch it but knew better.

"It's called...*Broken.*" I was hesitant to tell her the title because it was raw and summed up the last two years of my life. At first glance, it looked like a bunch of metal flaps, like birds, escaping a round hole, but it was the exact opposite. The hole was my heart, somewhat twisted and burned around the edges, and I was pulling my emotions back inside. I was nervous to see her reaction.

"Nico, it's beautiful."

"Thank you. It's the one I need the most time on."

"How did you get it to look so colorful?"

I smiled at her. "You can touch it. It won't break." Because it was already broken. "It's a technique with different types of metal and heat. Boring stuff."

She turned to me. "Mom and Dad are going to be so proud of you. This is definitely my favorite."

I toed the leg of one of my work tables. It was one thing for Trish to praise me as creative director at Tuft & Finley because we talked all projects through with clients and each other. My sculptures were all mine. They were a part of me. My pain, my success, my indignation, my defeat. I wanted a happy sculpture, but inevitably they turned sour when I allowed my emotions to show. "Thanks, sis. But as you can see, I have a lot of work to do."

"So, no weekends at the lake?"

"Fuck that. Of course, I'm going to the lake. If I stay here all the time, my sculptures will be even darker."

"Well, dark or not, they are beautiful, and I'm so excited for your show. Have you talked to Lindsay any more about what we can do for it? Decorate? Cater?"

I laughed and squeezed her shoulder. "We have a ton of time. I promise that once she gives me the go, I will put you in contact with her, and you can do your magic."

Trish clapped her hands. "Yes. I promise it will be nothing short of spectacular."

I rolled my eyes even though I was secretly touched. "I'm sure you'll go overboard, and we'll be stuck with bottles of wine and cookies and finger foods."

"Stop bursting my bubble. Now, show me the ones you aren't sure if you want to use, and I'll let you know what I think."

I showed her three smaller sculptures that I liked, but they were just practice pieces. The welds were sloppy, and since I was putting my artwork on display for the world to see, everything had to be perfect.

"Just call this one *Mistake*. Art critics will eat that shit up," Trish said. She picked up the smaller piece I didn't point out and carefully turned it over and over. "What's wrong with this one?"

"It's kind of small and too childish." I gently took the giant ladybug and flipped her over. "The welds are clean, but it's too perfect. I didn't do anything special. I mean, a kid in Vo-Tech could make this."

"Shut up. The details are great. I mean, you made eyelashes. Out of metal. You really should put this in the show. And low, for the kids to see."

"Kids aren't going to be there, are they?" I panicked when visions of small children racing around my sculptures filled my head.

"I doubt it, but you never know." Trish shrugged.

"I just don't want critics to say 'oh, this isn't art' and ding me because I have something cutesy out," I said.

"Listen to me. You have a lot of incredible shit here. Very deep, very emotional, very raw sculptures. I think this is a nice breather." Trish picked up the ladybug again and nodded. "Yes, add this to it. I'm sure Lindsay isn't going to complain. The more you have, the better everyone does."

I pointed to the other one I was working on. "This is almost done. I'll probably start something new this weekend."

"Do you need anything? Do I need to stock your refrigerator? Order a pizza? Help me help you."

"Thank you, but I'll get it done. I just need time."

"Well, I'll try not to overload you at work." Her smile was strained, and even though I nodded in agreement, we both knew that was an impossible promise to keep.

❖

"I can't go in there," I hissed low to Trish, nodding my head in the direction of the windows surrounding the conference room. I fisted my hands to keep them from shaking. She had paged me in the warehouse because I'd lost track of time and forgot about a meeting with a new client. In my defense, Trish had told me about the meeting only that morning. I normally had more time to prepare. I had enough time to splash water on my face, run my fingers through my hair that was plastered from a hard hat, and shed the safety vest.

"Yeah, you look a little rough, but she's hot as hell. You'll thank me after."

"Trish."

She stopped and threw her hands up. "What?"

"She's Thursday." I waited for that fact to sink in. When Trish's eyes widened, I nodded. "Yeah, out of all the people in Chicago, Thursday's here."

Trish grabbed my elbow and ushered me to a more private corner. "Are you shitting me? That's Thursday? This is perfect then."

"No. I just yelled at her to move her car. She was parked in a loading zone. I couldn't see inside of her car because of the sun's glare and barked for her to move. And used hand gestures. Honestly, I thought she was a vendor."

Trish slowly shook her head. "I told you not to work in the warehouse today. I told you to stay clean because we had a client coming in, but no. You had to go and play on the forklift."

"With the shipping guys at OSHA training today, who else was going to help load the trucks?" I looked at my jeans and sweaty T-shirt. Even though I had a fresh set of clothes somewhere in my office, no way could I go into that meeting. Not with Thursday. Not after being a jerk to her.

"Come on. You can do this. Just change your clothes, freshen up, and I'll stall." Trish uncurled my fists and shook my arms. "We always talk about opportunities and regret the missed ones. Don't let this one get away."

I took a deep shaky breath. "I can't. I'm sorry. I'll do the job, so take really good notes."

"You're making a mistake."

"I'll be in the next meeting with her. I promise."

Trish sighed. "Do you want me to conference you in? I don't want to fuck this up and forget to ask important questions."

"That would be great. Call my cell. I'll be in my office."

"Okay." Her features softened. "I'll try to get all the info I can. And let you know how pretty she really is. And find out if she's single and gay."

"Stop. I'm nervous enough. Give me two minutes," I said.

I turned and headed to my corner office. I closed the door and put my office phone on Do Not Disturb. I sat and stared at my cell phone until Trish's name appeared. I almost yelped. I took another deep breath and answered.

"Nicole Marshall."

I knew Trish was rolling her eyes at me. And why was I making my voice deep?

"Nicole. I'm sorry you couldn't make the meeting today. I'm here with Sophia Sweet, whose company, Sweet Stuff, is branching out to start a line of upscale chocolates. She is looking for a design that is modern, attractive, and clean."

"Hello, Sophia. I apologize for not being there. Tell us a little bit about your company." Now what was I doing with my voice? I turned my head and cleared my throat.

"Well, we've been around for about fifty years. My grandparents started the business, passed it down to my parents, and now my brother and I are running it. I want to try something different, so I'm launching a division of handcrafted chocolates called Sophia's Collection. It's going to be a mix of truffles and chocolates with different flavors."

Her voice was quiet with a slight rasp, like someone who doesn't talk a lot. I shivered, wondering what it would be like for her to whisper in my ear. I shook my head and focused on the discussion.

"Sophia was kind enough to bring in samples. You're missing out." Trish was teasing me. "What flavor is this? It's delicious."

"That's a piece of blueberry lavender dark chocolate. I will have bars, boxes of assorted bonbons, and different confections like chocolate drinks and sauces. I want a design that is classy and eye-catching. The design we have now for Sweet Stuff could use a little polishing, but my main concern is this new line."

While Trish was gathering information on what Sophia wanted, I googled Sweet Stuff. I would have done it before the meeting, but I'd gotten distracted in the warehouse. The artwork was dated but still somewhat charming. I waited for Sophia to finish answering Trish's question before I spoke up.

"Are you going for simple lines or something more involved? Do you have a particular color scheme in mind? Do you have a logo yet?" I knew I was throwing a lot at her, but a logo was the best way to identify a brand.

"Not for this, no. The company has one, but I want this to look completely different."

I didn't blame her. Their existing company logo looked like a squashed red Christmas ornament with the company name drawn by hand. It had an art-deco vibe, which, even though it was making a comeback, was still too dated to ride the resurgent wave. I was sure her grandparents were proud of it, but art and technology had grown tremendously since the seventies. "I understand. I have a few ideas already." I was going to give this project all my attention. I stayed on the phone another half an hour until it was time for me to go and for Trish to get her signed. I paced my office to expel the excess energy that had been building inside and looked out the window until I saw Sophia Sweet walk out to her car. I wanted ten seconds of uninterrupted time just to stare at her, but Trish burst in my office without even knocking.

"You startled me." I turned and blushed, knowing I was completely busted.

"Oh, baby sis, you will have your hands full with this ice queen." The smile on Trish's face was a mixture of sass and snark. "Why did you bail? It would have been fine with you there."

"Yeah. I don't know what in the hell is wrong with me." I rubbed the back of my neck and shook my head at Trish.

"She's really pretty. No jewelry, and the only personal information she let slip was that her brother is running the business into the ground, and this is her last-ditch effort to save it. It's just the two of them and their grandmother."

"I wonder what happened to their parents?" It always made me sad when families were fractured. We were so close that it was hard to imagine a family of just three. I was close to my two uncles and aunt and all my cousins. Family affairs were a hair shy of complete chaos.

"She didn't say, and I wasn't going to ask."

"I wouldn't have asked either."

"Now you have a name. Sophia. While it's a beautiful name, I liked the mystery of the name Thursday." Trish put her arm around my shoulders. "Now you can talk to her on the train."

I groaned. "I was so rude to her. I'm surprised she didn't say anything to you."

"She did. She told me this asshat yelled at her not once, but twice for parking in the wrong spot."

My mouth dropped open, and I stared at her in complete disbelief. "She did not."

Trish held a straight face before she burst out laughing. "No, she didn't, but let that be a lesson to you. Don't make assumptions about people, because it could come back to bite you in the end."

CHAPTER FOUR

You look so strong." Kelsey, Tuft & Finley's receptionist, wasn't afraid to let me know she was interested. Cute, perky, and femme, she was so very young but so very off-limits. Fraternizing was against company policy. Kelsey was the first employee who piqued my interest, but I avoided her. A lawsuit wasn't something I needed.

"I just didn't feel like lugging everything to the studio. Wearing it seemed like the better idea." I looked down at my new flame-resistant pants and new safety welding boots. They weighed a ton. My long-sleeved T-shirt was tight, as a safety precaution, and showed off curves I didn't want. I adjusted my new welding helmet under my arm and nodded to her on my way out.

I'd spent all day designing Sophia's logo and boxes and was eager to show Trish, but she had a meeting across town, so I'd decided to skip out early and get some serious welding time in. I was excited to try out my new equipment. Ben had signed for a new plasma cutter this morning, and I was keen to test it.

While I was shopping for upgrades, I'd decided to add to my wardrobe. My old welding shoes weighed a ton, and I was working in coveralls that were a size too large. I'd learned the hard way that the clothes you wear could either protect you or hurt you. The burn mark on my inner thigh that I got ten years ago when I was young and stupid was still angry and red. "Kelsey, please call me if something important comes up."

She gave me a doe-eye look and slowly blinked. "I will. Have a great afternoon, Boss." Her voice was slightly breathless when she said the word "boss."

I ignored her blatant flirting and hurried out the door. It was a few minutes after three on a Wednesday afternoon, so finding a spot on the train for me and my new welder's helmet would be easy. The weight of the steel-protected boots and the hot sun added to my discomfort as I made my way to the platform. The slightly cool air on the train was a relief. I found an open seat near my normal seat and plopped down, brushed my hair out of my face with my fingers, and pushed the helmet under my seat with my foot. I closed my eyes and leaned back. The sun felt good on my face. Trish was having a barbecue at the lake house this weekend, and I was seriously considering going. I missed my family. With the pressure of my upcoming show, I'd decided to hole up and missed all of spring and the first of summer. A weekend away from my life sounded fabulous.

When the train slowed down to Thursday's—no, Sophia's stop—my mind darted to last week and conjured up the image of her walking back to her car from Tuft & Finley, the smooth skin of her thigh peeking out from her skirt as she slipped into her sedan. I loved watching her. She walked like a model, but not with fast purpose. The slower taps of her heels caused a different sound than most people were used to and caught their attention. It worked on me.

I would see her tomorrow, and it was going to be awkward as hell. She thought she knew me, and I for sure knew her. I was going to have to say something to her. I scooted my long legs closer to the seat as people jumped on the train. What I wasn't expecting was the slow tap of heels I'd come to recognize immediately. I looked up and stared right into Sophia's eyes. She looked at me, hesitated for a moment, and kept walking. I glanced at my phone just to be sure. Wednesday. What was she doing on the train? Once the train started moving, I stood and made my way to the back of the car.

"Hi." Trish would be so proud that I was standing right in front of Sophia, trying to strike up a conversation.

Annoyance flashed across her face, but coldness immediately replaced it. This wasn't going well. "Hello."

I sat down without asking for permission. "I wanted to apologize for last week. I didn't mean to yell at you. We were waiting on a late truck and were short-handed." Silence. I nodded. Okay. I was going to have to try harder. "I hope you don't take my rudeness out on Tuft & Finley. They are a great company, and whatever you are asking them to do, they will do a stellar job."

She turned toward me. Her nearness made me swallow hard. Trish said she was beautiful and had amazing eyes, but I wasn't prepared to have the wind knocked out of me. I held my breath to keep her from stealing it again. "I like the company." She broke eye contact and looked down at her phone.

"Where's your box?" I asked.

"Excuse me?"

I shook my head at the awful question. "Every time I've seen you on the train, you always have a little white box with a red ribbon. Today you don't have one." I didn't mention that I knew she was on the train every Thursday. I took a moment to appreciate her scent. Today she smelled like cotton candy and something else. Lavender maybe?

"First you yell at me and now you stalk me? Should I be worried?"

I snapped back to the conversation and froze when her words sank in. I would have scurried away in complete embarrassment had she not given me a soft smile. Instead, I held my hands up and leaned back. I flipped into charmer mode even though my stomach fluttered and sweat gathered at the back of my neck.

"It's not every day a beautiful woman rides the train. I'm going to notice."

She was quiet for a moment. Maybe I'd gone too far.

"Nice shoes. Perfect for summer."

I laughed. "Yeah. They're not the most practical, but I didn't want to carry them, so I decided to wear them. My welder's helmet is just as heavy." I pointed to the helmet under the seat where someone else now sat.

"You're a welder." I detected no judgment in her voice. Just a matter-of-fact observation.

"It's one of the things I do." I shrugged.

"And you drive a forklift."

"Sometimes, when they need me to, I step up. What do you do?"

"I own a candy shop." She ran her fingertips back and forth across the top of her phone. Did I make her nervous?

"That sounds yummy. And probably the best job in the world."

"How long have you worked at Tuft & Finley?"

"Since the beginning. About twelve years. I'm Nico, by the way. It's nice to meet you. And thank you for forgiving me."

She cocked her head. "I never said I forgave you."

"You're still talking to me, so even if you haven't, I'd say you're close."

"Hmm." She quirked her eyebrow.

I put my hand over my heart. "What? I'm not forgiven?" I leaned forward and whispered to her, "I really am sorry. It was a stressful day because we were so shorthanded."

She abruptly stood. "This is my stop."

I looked around in surprise. "That was quick." I stood with her, and she gazed at me in alarm. I pointed to my helmet. "Don't worry, Sophia. I am not stalking you. I need to be with my helmet."

She started to exit the train but turned back to me before the doors closed. "Nico."

I nodded at her and smiled. Maybe I'd read her wrong and made a good impression after all.

"I wouldn't say you are stalking me..." She paused and tilted her head. As the doors were closing, her voice picked up. "But then again, I never told you my name."

Chapter Five

O kay, to be fair, I talked to Ms. Anderson about what happened at the warehouse, and she told me your name. Do you mind if I sit down?"

It had been twenty-four hours since Sophia had surprised me by being on the L on a Wednesday. Today I had actively sought her out. She was hidden between two men when she boarded the car, and we couldn't make eye contact. In a bold move, I followed her back to the section where she was sitting.

Sophia looked up at me and nodded when I pointed to the seat next to her. I raked my fingers through my hair. "Thanks." It was hard not to lean toward her because today she smelled like chocolate and sugar. "What's in the box? It smells delicious." Realizing I was entirely too close for comfort, I leaned back in the seat and crossed my ankles, trying to look relaxed.

"A new recipe."

"Dark chocolate?"

Sophia nodded. "With a little bit of lavender and blueberries." Her voice was low, as if her ingredients were a secret.

"Really? That's very interesting." I knew she was marketing more upscale chocolates, but I wasn't prepared for such diversity of tastes and smells, even though she and Trish had discussed the flavors when she conferenced me in during the initial meeting. I wanted to pull the red ribbon that perfectly cradled the white box and see what blueberries, lavender, and dark chocolate smelled and tasted like. I was sad when she didn't offer. "So, what's Tuft & Finley doing for you?"

"They are designing a new logo and different styles and sizes of boxes."

She wasn't much of a talker, but at least the conversation was progressing. "What do you have now? That?" I pointed to the plain box but made sure I had no judgment in my voice.

"This?" She carefully held up the box. "No. This is just a white box. It's kind of a family thing."

"Oh?"

Her shoulders sagged a bit, and I didn't know if I'd struck a nerve or pushed the conversation too much. She surprised me by relaxing against the back of the seat. "My grandparents used white boxes with red ribbon when they first started the business, and since I am taking these to my grandma, I like to give her a reminder of her history. She smiles when she sees the box."

I noted the simplicity of it and decided to offer a second logo suggestion the next time she met with Trish, based on the history of the business. I could already see it in my head. "Oh, that's so sweet. Does your grandmother give you advice on your new flavors?"

Sophia nodded. I liked the way she ran her fingertip slowly back and forth along the tiny ridges of the ribbon. "She's excited about the new project."

It was hard not to jump in and ask everything on my mind. I had to play like I didn't know her story, even though I had at least a dozen questions that balanced on the tip of my tongue, ready to fall out the second she opened up the conversation. "So, you take the L to see your grandmother? Where is your shop? I mean, I don't mean to pry or anything, but you aren't on the train every day."

"But you're not a stalker," she said playfully.

I groaned and playfully hung my head in mock shame. "It sounds bad, but it's not every day I see somebody like you on the

L. I'm assuming that your shop is back there?" I thumbed in the opposite direction we were headed.

"Yes. It's quicker than driving. I visit for a few hours and head back to the office."

"Why Thursdays?"

Sophia shrugged. "It's the one day my grandma has free."

"Except for yesterday."

Sophia nodded. "Except for yesterday."

"She's a busy woman, huh?" I sat up and straightened my shirt. Today I wore a cream-colored linen shirt French-tucked into skinny jeans. A pair of black leather classic loafers completed the casual, simple look. Trish had given me a raised eyebrow when I got to work and she saw what I was wearing. She wanted us to always dress for success, and even though I looked good, my outfit wasn't professional enough for her taste.

"She stays pretty busy, and Thursdays are good for both of us."

"That's really sweet." I waited for her to ask me a question, hoping she would show some interest in me, my life, anything. She wasn't on the train for very long. The window of opportunity was closing.

"No welding today?" She pointed at my loafers.

"Not until later tonight."

She nodded. "Interesting."

Was it? What made it interesting? Interesting like I want to know more? Or interesting like I really don't want to know, and I'm just filling the void? And just like that, our conversation was over. She stood as the train coasted to a quick stop. "Have fun with your grandma. I'm sure she will love the new recipe." I whispered loud enough for her to hear me.

"Thanks."

"See you next Thursday."

She waved at me without turning around, but I knew she was smiling. At least I hoped she was.

❖

"Don't you think you should come clean with her?" Trish was setting up the conference room for our two o'clock meeting with Sophia, which I was absolutely not participating in. "And what are you wearing? This is an office."

"What's wrong with this?" I looked at my Wonder Woman T-shirt and steel-toe boots, then back at Trish. I held my hands up. "I look great."

"What's your goal? I mean, why can't you just be yourself with her?"

I sat in one of the chairs and leaned back. "There's just something about her. I mean, how wild is it that she's Thursday? Out of all the women in Chicago? Blows my mind. And I just want her to like me for me, not because of who I am."

Trish sat across from me after she finished lining up the water bottles, labels out, like soldiers in perfect rows. "You're making a mistake."

I looked at my watch. We had over an hour before Sophia arrived. Earlier, I had waved off Trish's lunch invitation claiming I had to clean up the presentation, but I was too nervous to eat. It wasn't as if I was going to be in the room, but it was my work, and I wanted Sophia to like it. "Trust me. I have a plan."

"Whatever it is, it's ridiculous."

"You're the one who wants me to be cautious."

Trish smacked her palm on the table to get my attention, and it worked. I stared at her in surprise. "Do not put this on me. Plus, we don't know anything about this woman. You're jeopardizing a client all for what? You can barely talk to her."

I tamped down my anger at Trish's truth and sighed. "I promise this won't get in the way of our business. It's unfortunate, or fortunate, that my crush happens to be a new client. I mean, what are the odds?"

She took my hand. "Okay, fine. Tell me your plan."

"It's simple, really. I want her to like me. Not my success or my money, but me. I'm going to try to get to know her as Nico. Not Nicole Briar Marshall."

Trish leaned forward. "She doesn't strike me as somebody like your thief of an ex-wife Mandy. You're taking a big risk. And you're assuming a lot. Is she even attracted to you? Is she single? Do you have anything in common? Is she interested in dating? I get the feeling she's more focused on her family business right now."

"I don't know, but I'd like to find out. I just don't want money to cloud her perception of me."

"You're assuming she's attracted to money."

"Judging by her shoes and purses, money means something to her. Maybe it's her own, or maybe she's in a relationship and somebody spoils her, but she likes it. I want her to know me. The real me."

Trish pointed at me. "This is the real you. Owner of a successful company. Artist. Family-oriented. Mentor to kids at the local YMCA. That's who she needs to know. You. Not some fake 'oh-I'm-so-poor-but-love-me-anyway' crap. It's a stupid idea. She's going to be angry when she finds out you lied to her."

"I promise you I'll come clean if there is the chance at a relationship, okay?" I squeezed her hand and stood. "In the meantime, call me if you have any questions. I'll be in my office. At least I will be when the meeting starts."

Trish rolled her eyes at me. "Do I even want to know where you're going now?"

I shook my head and grabbed a water on the way out, purposely knocking others over to ruin her perfectly lined bottles.

"You suck." She jumped up to realign them.

"That's what she said." I could hear her laughing all the way down the hall. Instead of turning right to go to my office, I turned left and headed for the warehouse. I planned to grab a golf cart and coincidentally pull up next to Sophia when she arrived for the appointment. I found a charged cart and made a quick drive around the property. Our production facility was working on the video-game packaging, and it was a good idea to check in with them to see if there were any issues. It was a test run, so we were only printing a few for customer approval.

"How's it going?" I slid out from behind the wheel and met Rian, our production manager, at the door. A stickler for rules, she handed me a safety vest and a hard hat, which I promptly put on, even though I risked messing up my perfectly mussed hair.

"Hey, it's going great. I was just going to call you. Take a look at this." She held up printed EcoBoost cardboard with the bright graphics and smiled. "The customer is going to love it."

"It's perfect." EcoBoost cardboard was the centerpiece of our line, but all our products were a hundred percent recyclable. A lot of younger customers were willing to pay more for a product that made them environmentally responsible. "Let me know when you have a few assembled, and I'll run them over to the customer." I looked at my watch. Sophia was due in fifteen minutes. Last week she was ten minutes early. I shrugged out of the vest and carefully removed my hat.

"Customer coming in?" she asked.

"Yeah." I handed her back the warehouse garb and patted down my hair. "I better get going. Thanks for the good news."

"Your hair looks great." Rian winked.

I bit my cheeks to keep from smiling. I didn't need everyone to know my business. It was bad enough Trish gave me a hard time about it. "I'll be back after the meeting."

"I'll have something by then."

I carefully put the cart in reverse and headed to the office. My heart skipped a beat when I turned the corner and saw Sophia driving into the parking lot. I pulled up beside her and waited until she exited her car. I gazed from her black heels to her above-the-knee gray skirt and mauve sleeveless blouse, glimpsing her suit jacket folded on the passenger seat and the cleanest interior of a car I'd ever seen that wasn't brand-new.

She removed her sunglasses and raised an eyebrow. "Nice ride."

I shrugged. "It's great in the summertime."

"Nothing says summer like a convertible."

She wasn't moving. "Want a quick ride around the facility?" I patted the empty seat beside me.

She glanced at her watch. "I can't. I'm meeting Trish in less than ten minutes. I'm sure she's already waiting."

I held up a finger and reached for my cell phone. "Hey, Ms. Anderson. Your client is here, but I'm going to take her on a quick tour around the place."

Trish kept her voice low. "You owe me big-time."

"Ten-four, Boss. We'll see you soon." I hung up and waited for Sophia to climb into the cart. "I'm a safe driver. You can trust me."

"You're Wonder Woman after all."

I burst out laughing. Sophia didn't talk much, but everything she said packed a punch. "And I haven't scared you off by now." She turned her head to look the other way, but not before I saw her smile. I drove slowly around our property, pointing out things I thought she would be interested in. I kept my voice steady, even though my chest was threatening to burst with pride. I really loved my business. "And I'm not sure what kind of packaging you're looking at, but if you can afford it, I recommend the EcoBoost. It's great for the environment, and it will make you sleep better at night to know that you're saving Mother Earth."

Sophia's full red lips pinched together in a tight smile. I had obviously hit a nerve either about money or recycling and had to do some careful backpedaling. "I mean, all the packaging here is very environmentally friendly, but the EcoBoost is a newer product that leaves no footprint. Once your chocolates are gone, the packaging isn't far behind."

"I'll ask Trish about it. Isn't it hard to recycle anymore? Aren't there so many restrictions about what can be recycled and what can't?"

"You know your recycling. Yes, there are restrictions. That's why the EcoBoost is so good. It's a hundred percent recyclable and biodegradable, so it doesn't have to be sent to paper mills or overseas for recycling. It costs more, but in the long run, it's worth it." I slowed down when we reached the sorting facility. Because the equipment was so loud, I had to lean into her so she could hear me. She smelled like vanilla. "We keep this away from the main building because there are so many nicer smells than this. Like vanilla beans or heavy sweet cream."

Sophia turned to me. Her lips parted to reveal straight white teeth. "Today was vanilla truffle day." She tucked a piece of hair behind her ear and bit her bottom lip before turning away.

I almost whooped with delight. That was a sign, at least in my book. Encouraged, I winked at her. "I'd better get you back to the office before Ms. Anderson calls for my head."

Sophia shielded her eyes with her hand. "Thanks for the quick tour. It's good to get outside when the weather is this nice."

"You're welcome. Hopefully one day you can return the favor." I pulled up next to the door. "Safe and sound. Have a great meeting."

"Thank you, Nico."

I smiled at the familiarity of the slow click of her heels on the sidewalk as she disappeared behind the front door. Damn, she was sexy in a quiet, calming way. She was curvy in all the places I liked and carried herself with confidence. I sighed with longing and returned the cart to the lot. Then I quickly walked back to the office, checking my phone to see if Trish needed me for any reason. My heart sank when I didn't see any messages. I couldn't help myself. I had to know if Sophia had any questions. Did she like the designs?

How's it going?

Nothing. Not even bubbles. I put the phone down on my desk and stared at it. She'd been in there only a few minutes. That barely gave them time for pleasantries, maybe a cup of coffee and only the start of the presentation. I was going to have to wait this one out, too.

Chapter Six

The handle was a lollipop. I stopped myself from shaking my head at the juvenile prop and pushed my way inside. I couldn't decide if the shop was purposely decorated in retro color schemes or if they'd never updated. Either way, it was cool. For now. The display case housed several boxes of chocolates with a few of them propped open to reveal different types. Some were wrapped in colorful foil and held mysterious appeal, and others were dyed different colors. Candy tins lined one wall where customers could bag and weigh their own licorice bites, gumdrops, and malt balls. It was no different than anything one would find at a chain candy store, but it did have old-fashioned charm. I understood Sophia's desire to start an upscale division.

"Hi there. Can I help you?" a pleasant-looking blonde who stood behind the counter asked. I could hear low voices from behind the swinging door and wondered if one was Sophia's.

She looked so expectant that I felt obligated to buy something. "Yes. I'd like one of those boxes." I pointed at a long box of thirty-six assorted dark and milk chocolates. She carefully picked a box and rang up the sale. I handed her my credit card and rocked slowly on the balls of my feet.

"Will there be anything else?" She handed me a bag with the box and my receipt and tilted her head at me expectantly.

"Is Sophia working today?" Even though I had walked in wanting only to meet her, my heart still kicked up a few notches when the words left my mouth.

"Yes. Is she expecting you?"

I stared at her. Did Sophia get a lot of visitors? "No. I'm a friend. Can you please tell her the welder is here?" I smiled at her look of confusion.

I'd headed here today despite how hard I tried to talk myself out of it. Trish said the meeting had gone well and Sophia loved the logo and the box design. She needed to narrow down the different-sized boxes so we could finalize everything and begin production. I wanted to get a better feel for her vision, and the best way was an impromptu visit to her store.

"Ah...sure. One moment." The door swayed as she pushed through until it slowed and rested a half inch from the frame. I saw movement in the crack and relaxed as somebody made their way to the front of the store. I averted my eyes and looked at some fudge slices I wished I had purchased instead of chocolates that I would leave in the break room at Tuft & Finley.

"Nico. What a surprise. What are you doing here?" She ripped off the plastic hairnet and smoothed down her apron. A cute flush splotched on her cheeks and neck when we made eye contact.

"I was near the neighborhood and wanted to see if I could get a tour of your place. I mean, it's Thursday, so I'm sure you're working on something sweet for your grandmother." It was noon. If Sophia was open to a tour, then I planned to follow it with an invitation to lunch. "Plus, I wanted to get some treats for the warehouse crew." I held up the bag and smiled.

"You didn't have to do that, but thank you." Her blue eyes held mine for several seconds before she nodded. "Okay. Let me show you around."

"Do I have to wear a hairnet and an apron? Because I will. I mean, I'm used to messing up my hair with hard hats."

Sophia immediately smoothed her hair. "Only if you want to get up close and personal with my chocolate."

My eyes widened. That remark sounded suggestive even though I knew she meant it innocently. "I definitely want that to happen." And my response sounded just as bad. I quickly added, "I mean, how many times does one get a private tour of a chocolate factory?"

She held the door open. "It's a small factory. We have only seven employees."

"Does your brother work here, too?" I looked around. All the employees were women.

Sophia put her hands on her hips and shook her head. "He's supposed to, but he's too busy being lazy. His interest in the company is financial only. And not in the good way."

I nodded. "That's a bummer. I'm sure your grandmother appreciates your work though. What flavor are you presenting her today?"

"We're done with flavors and have narrowed it to eight bonbons, four different ganache, malted dark-chocolate peanut-butter balls, dark-chocolate pralines, and six flavors of macarons. Now we are focusing on a new look and heavy marketing."

"That's why you're working with Tuft & Finley." I took the hairnet and tried to put it on without messing up my hair.

"Here. Let me help you before you end up looking like a porcupine." Sophia moved closer and carefully pulled the net over my hair, tucking it behind my ears. She was so gentle. I had an overwhelming desire to touch her, put my hands on her waist or brush my fingertips over the bare skin of her wrists. She dropped her hands after she seemed satisfied with the results. Her gaze darted to my lips and back up to my eyes. She took a step back. "Okay. You're good to go."

I groaned playfully as I felt the cap crush my carefully coiffed hair. "No pictures, please. My reputation will be shot."

Sophia turned to me. "The hairnet will ruin your reputation?"

I laughed. "You're right. This is the least of my worries."

I followed her as she took me around the factory. Most of the information was overwhelming, but I focused hard. When she led me into a room that housed air brushes and tools I was familiar with, I perked up.

"Oh, tell me about this room." After she nodded her approval when I pointed at an air brush, I picked it up and gently flipped it over. "Is this for the new line?" The tools looked relatively new and very clean. I was a messy artist and bad about cleaning up after I was done.

"You've seen Sweet Stuff's chocolates. I've decided to do a classier version of them." She opened a small refrigerator and pulled out a tray of the most beautifully decorated chocolates I'd ever seen.

"No way." I took a step closer and stared at the rows of bonbons that were shiny metallic green with lime-splattered domes. "That is not chocolate. It can't be. How did you do this? Is it even edible?"

Her smile was breathtaking. "It's definitely edible. It's a rich caramel infused with rosemary, all in a decorated chocolate shell." She crooked her finger at me to follow her into a side room, where trays of geometric and heart-shaped chocolate shells were ready to be filled.

"These are handmade?"

Sophia nodded. "I pick colors and spray or splatter the molds first. Then I pour a thin layer of chocolate that takes twenty-four hours to cure. After that, the flavored caramel or ganache cures for another twenty-four hours. And, finally, the last layer of chocolate." She shrugged like it was no big deal.

"So, it takes three days to make one of those fancy chocolates?"

"Want to try one?"

"Yes. All the yesses." It wasn't that I loved chocolate, but I was enjoying our conversation so much that chocolate suddenly became my favorite thing.

"Follow me."

I followed her to an area where miscellaneous chocolates were piled in two bins.

"Is this your distressed pile?" Hundreds of beautiful artisan chocolates with minor flaws lay there. I picked up a yellow dome that Sophia identified as salted banana and inspected it. "What's wrong with this?"

Her fingertips brushed my palm as she took the confection and turned it over. "See this tiny circle? It's an air bubble. A flaw. I can't sell this."

"Are you kidding me? Nobody's going to see the underside. They're going to pick it up and pop it in their mouth right away."

She shook her head. "With something this pretty, you have to take your time."

I openly stared at her as she inspected the piece again. Even though her hair was pulled back in a twist and covered by a hairnet, I could still see the dark-honey highlights. Trish was right. She was even prettier up close. Her makeup was light. A touch of mascara on her eyelashes made her eyes pop. Her lips were either naturally red, or the lip color she applied was so perfect that the only way I was going to be able to tell was to kiss her. I smiled at the thought.

"What?"

"What?" I leaned back because I was completely in her personal space.

"You just had a really big smile."

I tried to play it off. "I'm just so surprised you have so many pieces left over. I'd eat them all and either have really high blood sugar or have to run marathons to dump the calories."

"All things in moderation." She handed me a purple bonbon with a beautiful swirl design on top. "Try this one. It's lavender."

I was glad she gave me the heads-up because I was thinking grape. I moaned when I bit down. I swallowed and cleared my throat. "I would have never thought lavender would pair well with chocolate and caramel. But, oh my God, this is delicious."

She laughed at my theatrics. "So, I want to market this to different clientele. Upscale hotels, caterers, companies who have large events or corporate outings. There's a market there. I just need to tap into it."

"Your ideas are great, and these chocolates will be a big hit."

"Not too many chocolatiers in the area are doing artisan chocolates, so maybe I can get a head start and save this company." She clamped her mouth shut, and I knew that wasn't something she wanted me to know. The desire to help her grew inside me, but I didn't want to make any promises I couldn't keep, so I changed the subject.

"I'm sure you will. And I'm not just saying that."

"Thank you. If the line takes off, then we'll make more space and set up for bigger production." She motioned for me to follow her out of the factory and back to the offices.

I whipped off the hairnet and touched my hair to ensure it was still styled the way I wanted. "If you aren't busy, do you want to grab lunch somewhere?"

Sophia looked at me for a few moments before answering. I tried to keep my face as innocent and casual as I could.

"There's a good sandwich shop a few doors down."

I swallowed hard to extinguish the fireworks that exploded in my chest. "Great."

She removed her apron, grabbed her purse, and looked at me expectantly.

I didn't move out of her way but smiled slyly at her. "So, you look great, and maybe it's your thing, but I think you would look ten times better if you took off your hairnet so I could see your beautiful hair."

"Gah." She quickly pulled off the cap. The adorable flush was back, splotching her cheeks and her neck.

I bit my lip and tried hard not to smile. I liked that she was nervous around me. New friends weren't nervous. Not like this.

The walk took five minutes. We talked about the nice weather and upcoming plans for summer. We were both workaholics but had some fun planned later in the month. I was going to a big party at my parents' lake house over the Fourth of July, and she planned to take her grandmother to visit her best friend in Detroit. With the show fast approaching, I needed most of the weekends to get ready. I was struggling with my creative process. I wasn't ready to admit it was because Sophia was on my mind a lot, because she was, but something stirred inside me that I hadn't felt in a long time. Hope. It was hard to go down the road of darkness and finish my latest sculpture when that positive emotion was bouncing around inside me. I wanted to abandon what I was working on and make something that had life and light to it.

"You can order anything here, and I promise you it will be worth it." Sophia ordered a salad and a Diet Coke. I went with a chicken-parmesan sandwich and an iced tea. Since it was almost one in the afternoon, several tables were open. We found one near the back to stay out of the hot sun coming through the front windows, and I wasted no time digging into my lunch.

"A salad? When you can have this deliciousness?" I held up half of my sandwich as an offering. She shook her head no.

"I'm stuck in Saladville. It's bathing-suit season, and I haven't shed my winter weight yet."

"You look great." She did. Sophia was the type of woman who always caught my attention. She had nice, full curves and filled out everything she wore perfectly. She knew how to dress to accentuate her body type.

"Thank you." Her voice was low, and she looked at her salad, avoiding eye contact with me.

"Tell me more about you. Do you have any pets? Hobbies? Girlfriend? Boyfriend?" I took a drink to stop myself from talking. I knew my voice was shaky as I waited for the answer I'd wanted to hear for weeks.

She held up a finger as she swallowed. "I don't have any

pets. Most of my life is at the shop, so I don't have time for any of those things."

I was going to have to work harder to get my answer. At least I knew she was single. "There's always time to date. That's what my sister tells me. She's forever trying to set me up on blind dates, and I blow her off because I work a lot of overtime."

She shrugged and offered up no other information. Plan B. Fuck it, why not? "If you're not busy this weekend, let's go to the Navy Pier. It can be a date or just two new friends getting to know one another." I took a bite to stop myself from rambling again.

I couldn't taste the food in my mouth and had to force myself to chew as I waited for her answer. She stuttered when she brought the fork up to her mouth and completely stalled as she seemed to think about it.

"New friends sounds good."

I nodded. "I can live with that." I took the last bite and wiped my hands clean. "For now."

Her eyebrow jumped for a second, and right before she took another bite of her salad, I saw a smile form on her lips.

"My sister and I loved it when our parents took us there on the weekends. It'll be nostalgic for me, so thank you."

"My grandparents raised us, and they were always at the shop, so my brother and I didn't do much but work, too. My best friend and I would do things with her family, but when I turned sixteen, I was working full time at Sweet Stuff. I mean, I did stuff as a teenager, but it was always low key. And I read a lot."

I wanted to know about her parents but didn't want to pry. "Oh, what do you like to read? Wait. Wait. Let me guess." I put my finger to my lip and stared at her like I was in deep thought, but the pause really just gave me a reason to study her face. "Romance. Deep down, you are a softie. Like you just said, people should take their time with beautiful things, and you sell chocolates."

She wiped her hands on her napkin and pushed her salad away from her. "Couldn't be further from the truth. I like science fiction. You know, zombies, aliens, different worlds."

My mouth fell open. "Wow. Okay. I wasn't expecting that. To be fair, I don't read the genre, but I like watching sci-fi movies."

"Don't tell me you read romance?" Sophia asked.

I sat back in my chair and put my hand on my chest. "What's wrong with me reading romance? The answer is yes, by the way."

"Huh." She tilted her head and looked at me without saying anything.

"Should I be offended? I think the answer is yes. Yes, I should be offended, and I am." I playfully glared at her.

"I just don't have time to read either type of book."

"Oh, come on. Audio books. Put in your earbuds and download a nice romance and listen to it while you're on the L or mixing chocolate or boxing it up. Then eight hours later, you're done."

I nodded at my suggestion like it was the best idea. And it was, because the smile she flashed me stopped my heart.

CHAPTER SEVEN

W hat are you going to wear? Your selection here is dismal. What time are you picking her up?"

Trish looked at the small pile of clothes I'd managed to collect at the studio and frowned. "At least they're clean, right?"

I'd gotten carried away after buying furniture and ended up hiring my brother-in-law's construction company to wall in my studio space. The studs and frame were already in place when I moved in, but I'd never finished the walls or put up a ceiling. It took them less than a week. My workspace was now hidden behind a door, and the metal smells from my welding weren't as strong. A few strategically placed scented candles and it was as if I had a real four-hundred-square-foot studio apartment. Tiny, but fully functional.

"Oh, I'm going home to change." I looked at my watch. Trish was right. I had to hustle to get back to my place, shower, and get dressed. "Yeah. Let's get out of here."

Trish gathered up her things and followed me out. "I want all of the information when you get home, or I will call you incessantly, ruining your date."

I pushed her through the door so I could lock it. "I'll turn off my phone during my so-called date and will turn it back on when I'm done."

"You want a ride to your apartment?" Trish pointed to her car that was parked on the far side of the street on the other side of the warehouse. She wasn't taking any chances on blowing out a tire, and I didn't have the time to change it if she did.

I shook my head. "Nah. I'm taking Lucy."

She put her hands on her hips and stared at me. "You can't be serious."

I shrugged and unlocked Lucy, tossing my stuff onto the passenger seat. "Don't worry. I'll take the Audi on the date. I need Lucy for other things." I was donating my old dining-room set to one of the halfway houses Tuft & Finley sponsored and told the manager I would be by tomorrow.

"That's what I want to hear. I like this girl, and I think she could be good for you. Plus, you designed the artwork for her new line and a new logo, which she loves."

"I'm glad she likes it, but I'm not putting too much into this maybe date." I casually leaned against Lucy and crossed my arms while Trish continued to give me the disbelief eye roll. "Besides, she wants to just be friends." I told Trish a little about the impromptu lunch date. I left out the part about Sophia's tiny smile that gave me hope.

"Friends will understand if you come clean now. But if this turns into a more serious relationship and she doesn't know who you really are, she's going to be pissed, and I won't blame her."

I thought Trish was being a bit overdramatic. I knew Sophia would be surprised, but I also knew that, deep down, she would understand. At least that's how it played out in my mind. "Look, I get where you're coming from and appreciate your concern for us. I'll come clean." I climbed into Lucy while Trish glared at me. I shot her a smile and blew her a kiss. "Thanks for loving me as much as you do. I'll call you later."

I watched her shake her head at me and cross the street to her car. Once she slipped inside, I put Lucy in reverse and dodged potholes in the parking lot. I whipped her out onto the asphalt and followed Trish until we parted ways. I parked in visitor parking at my building and told Tommy I'd move it tonight. I had very little time to get ready. Sweet Stuff was at least a twenty-minute drive in normal traffic. I took a quick shower and put on shorts, a button-down short-sleeved shirt with tiny pineapples, and Sperry boat shoes. I spent the most time on my hair. It was a warm day, but there would be a breeze, so product was necessary. With no time to spare, I headed to the garage to switch cars when I found my Audi was not in my spot. I called Tommy immediately. "Where's my car?" I kept the panic out of my voice. I wasn't worried that somebody stole it; I was worried I was going to be late. Sophia didn't strike me as the kind of person who tolerated tardiness.

"Hi, Nico. Let me check." I waited for ten incredibly long seconds. "I'm sorry, but the dealership hasn't returned it yet. Do you want me to call them and find out when you can expect it?"

Shit. Double shit. I'd forgotten that McKellan Automotive had picked up my car to do the suggested maintenance. "Yes, please."

I looked at my motorcycles parked next to the Audi's empty spot. They weren't an option. Not for a first date. I took the elevator to the main level. I waved to Tommy and walked to Lucy. I put my hands on my hips and sighed. I had no choice. I hopped in and headed to Sweet Stuff. The air conditioner worked when it wanted to, and today I was blessed with coldish air. I turned on a coffee-shop station and pointed Lucy into the direction of Sweet Stuff. I parked with one minute to spare. Sophia was waiting for me just inside the door with her purse and a small cropped jacket in hand.

"Hi. How are you?" I gave her an appreciative up and down, admiring her sundress. It was light blue and clung to her curves nicely. With her makeup faint, and her hair styled up and away from her face, she was breathtaking. To me, she looked like she was definitely on a date. My other friends didn't care about their appearance this much.

"I'm good. Looking forward to an afternoon out in the sunshine."

"I'm stalling only because it smells so good in here." I

inhaled deeply and made a sound when I exhaled. It wasn't quite a moan, but I made sure she knew I appreciated the smell.

"We have a lot of orders for the Fourth of July and some family reunions, but summers are kind of slow, so we're baking cookies."

"Any distressed ones we need to take with us? I mean, if they're just going to be thrown away, I could probably find a good place for them." I pointed to my stomach and gave her a cheesy smile.

"I could probably find one or two. What's your favorite?"

"That's like picking a favorite child."

"Narrow it down for me." She walked behind the counter and disappeared behind the swinging door.

I yelled out. "Peanut butter is my favorite. But chocolate chip is an American favorite for a reason." I listened to the noises behind the door and raised my voice. "Sugar cookies are simply delightful as well. And don't even get me started on chocolate with chocolate chips."

She returned with a white box and a red ribbon. I felt my insides go soft at the care she took to wrap up cookies for me.

"All for me?" I took the box from her.

"Well, I might help you with one or two."

"That's very sweet. Thank you. Come on. Let's get out of here before I ask for a sample of everything." I led her outside, where Lucy sat gassed up and polished. Or as polished as Lucy could get. I opened the door for her and tried not to smile at her horrified expression. "She might be old, but she purrs like a kitten." I was going to tell her about the Audi, but her reaction was priceless. I couldn't resist keeping up the illusion that Lucy was my only car.

Sophia turned around. "We can take my car. I mean, parking is probably difficult in this size truck." Her voice tapered off as she looked around the cab.

"It's okay. I drive Lucy all the time. She's always been reliable." She looked like she didn't believe me, but she climbed in anyway. I went around the front and hauled myself into the driver's seat. I tapped the dashboard with affection and turned the key. She roared to life. I winked at Sophia. "Buckle up. She's pretty peppy, too."

She gingerly snapped the old seat belt into place. "She's lived a long life, huh?"

"Older than I am, but in better shape."

Sophia turned around and looked at the truck bed. "That looks pretty beat up."

"I haul a lot of stuff in her. I have a dining-room set that I need to deliver tomorrow." She didn't seem to care about the story so I changed the topic. "Tell me more about you. You work a lot, and you read science fiction. Do you have any nieces or nephews? Aunts? Uncles?" Traffic was thickening the closer we got to the pier. Most of the time traffic pissed me off, but we were all there with the same goal. Fun on a perfect summer afternoon. And I had a beautiful woman sitting two feet from me. I loved how she held the white box on her lap.

"My brother can't seem to settle down, so no nieces or nephews yet. I have an aunt and uncle in Oregon and a cousin who I communicate with only on social-media platforms."

"That sounds sad. If you don't mind me asking, what happened to your parents?" I assumed it was a car crash, because how could both be dead already?

"My mom died of cancer when I was eleven, and my dad died of a broken heart."

I turned and stared at her. "What?"

She pointed to the traffic in front of us to get me to focus on the road.

"I'm sorry about that. Your mom and your dad. That must have been hard at such a young age." I was floored and sat in silence as I digested this awful news.

"My mom died of breast cancer. My dad was stuck with two kids he barely knew, and the love of his life gone. He turned to the bottle to help him cope. One night he decided to go swimming and forgot he didn't know how to swim." She said it so matter-of-factly.

"That's awful. I'm so sorry." I wanted to say a thousand things to her, but I didn't know what to say since our relationship was so new. I couldn't imagine what life was like for Sophia without her parents. I had the best relationship with my entire family, and to lose any of them would be devastating. "Even though your brother really isn't about the business, are you close to him at all? Does he visit your grandma or you?"

Sophia stared out of the windshield at the crawling traffic ahead. "Once my parents died, he kind of did his own thing, so we aren't close. And it's always awkward when he comes into the store and takes money. He waits until I'm not around. And the employees don't feel comfortable stopping him. It's not their job anyway."

"Well, that sucks. I'm sure your grandmother isn't happy either. I'm sorry. Let's talk about other things. When was the last time you were down at the Navy Pier? It's been a few years, and so much has changed." I pulled into the Lake Shore Drive parking garage and wondered how I was going to maneuver Lucy into a spot. It was already busy down at the Pier, but after a nice conversation and a fat tip, the attendant allowed me to park in one of their utility-vehicle spots right up front. "See? No problem." I patted the tailgate and smiled at Sophia, who only shook her head at me.

"So fucking charming," she said.

I put my hand over my heart. "What language! I'm offended." I smiled at her to let her know I really wasn't.

"Somehow I don't think so."

"If my mother was with us and I said that, she would either swat me or make me rinse my mouth out with soap."

"Even as an adult? I think I'd like your mother."

"Again, I'm offended." I liked the way she smiled at me. Butterflies fluttered in my stomach, and I squelched the extra energy they generated. "Come on. Let's go have fun." I slipped on my sunglasses and followed her out into the crowd. It was always packed on nice summer weekends. The breeze off the water made the afternoon bearable.

"You don't read romance, you love chocolate, and you hate my truck. What else should I know about you?"

"I don't hate your truck. It's just big and bulky. Probably killing the ozone every time you drive it."

"Lucy's been good to me over the years. And she's passed every inspection, so I think I'll keep her until she's had enough. I'll let her decide. Enough about the true love of my life. Tell me something else about Sophia, the chocolatier." I had committed to the Lucy joke because I didn't want it to slip that I had an Audi too. I also had a Ducati and a Yamaha two-seater for special dates. I needed to take the Ducati out soon because I was starting to feel cooped up working so hard. I needed a break. Operation Make Sophia Like Me was a very nice distraction, but I was getting antsy. I needed to expel energy. That meant one of two things: sex or riding. On a great day, that meant both.

"Sophia the chocolatier is very boring. Trust me." Sophia shielded her face with her hand and looked ahead through the throngs of weekenders. "But I'm kind of excited to ride the Centennial Wheel."

"We can grab lunch and get a private car." Sophia eyed me warily. I held my hands up. "Or semi-private. Or we can be stuck in a car with a family of six who have screaming infants. And don't even get me started on the diaper changes in a small, confined space. The choice is yours."

She crinkled her nose. "You're right. No dirty diapers. At least if we happen to get stuck, then you'll entertain me with stories."

It was the perfect afternoon. The sun didn't sting my skin, and the breeze prevented me from sweating. People were friendly and Sophia seemed relaxed. There was something so peaceful about water. I loved it. I should have bought a condo closer to the water, but I wanted to be near my family. Not so close that they could just pop in unannounced, but close enough that I had time to quickly pick up the place. Not that I was messy or even home most of the time. We got sandwiches and chips, bought our tickets, and made our way to the line.

"Nico. Nico!"

I turned to find the brother of one of our warehouse employees waving us to the front of the VIP line. I'd forgotten that he worked here.

"Do you know him? What does he want?" Sophia asked. "I don't want to cut the line in front of all these people."

"That's exactly what he wants. Hang on. Let me go talk to him." I jogged up to him and shook his hand.

"Come on through this way," he said.

I was so tempted, but Sophia seemed uncomfortable with the idea. I didn't want that.

"Thank you, but I think we'll stand in line. This is somebody I want to impress, but in a different way."

"Okay. You'll be waiting at least thirty minutes."

"Thanks, but no thanks. I'll spend that thirty minutes learning all about her." I winked at him and walked back to Sophia.

"What was that all about?"

"He wanted to move us to the front of the line. I told him no because this way you would be forced to talk to me longer."

Sophia blushed. Even under the bright sun and dark shadows, I saw her red face. "Thank you. I don't think I could have cut the line anyway. I would have been too embarrassed."

She was lovelier than I imagined. Every one of my exes would have wanted to take advantage of that perk. If it was anybody other than Sophia, I would have done it.

"How do you know him?"

"His brother works in the warehouse. Both guys are cool. I know their family pretty well. Tuft & Finley is pretty close-knit." When their mother passed away three years ago, Tuft & Finley paid for the funeral and set up a college fund for the two siblings still in high school.

"I'm glad I'm working with Tuft & Finley. The more I hear about what your company does for the environment and for the employees, the more I feel it was the right choice," Sophia said.

"I can't think of a better place to work. Family-oriented, great benefits, and our repeat business is astounding." I needed to tone it down because I didn't want her to feel bad. I knew Sweet Stuff was almost out of business. She mentioned a few things to me that indicated there might be some struggle, but I'd gotten most of her story from Trish.

"I should work there. The perks sound great, and you're obviously very happy."

"What you do makes people happy. Who doesn't love chocolate? If you offered a delivery service, I'd be the first to sign up to drive. Watching people's faces when they get chocolates or flowers. That's it, right there. That's what makes a job exciting. You should do that for your new line."

"That's a great idea. Maybe I can get a small delivery company car," she said.

"Wait, are you saying I can't deliver if I'm going to drive Lucy?"

She crinkled her forehead and winced as if in pain. "Well, first impressions are everything."

"Look at us. I knew you were a classy, beautiful woman the moment I saw you, but you probably thought I was mean, gruff, and rough around the edges." I held my hands out and shrugged like she had everything wrong about me. "And now we're sitting here like old friends."

She laughed and held her forefinger and thumb about an inch apart. "Only a tiny bit mean, but mostly sweet. Truth be told, I like that you noticed me. It's kind of nice."

I puffed out my chest a bit and winked. "Truth be told, you're kind of easy to notice."

CHAPTER EIGHT

Thank you for agreeing to go out. As friends." We were next in line for a car on the Centennial, and I was antsy. I'd been on it several times but didn't want to go into details that would make both of us blush. "The view is incredible. I think you'll really enjoy it." The time flew by, but I was tired of standing. Welding was a stationary art for the most part, so I compensated by running on the treadmill. I was sorely lacking any physical activity today. "As a workaholic, how do you stay in shape?"

"Have you seen my hips? I'm a far cry from being in shape. And every waking minute I work on new flavors and recipes and taste everything. I don't have the time to exercise, even though I need to. It sounds lame, but time is so important right now," Sophia said.

"You look fine. No, you look great." Her summer dress showed off the flare of her hips. I thought she was perfect. "And thank you for taking time out of your busy day to spend it with me."

Once we were seated in an enclosed gondola, she put her hand on my forearm and gave it a squeeze. "I needed to get out, so thank you for inviting me. Really. It's very much appreciated." Sophia smiled at me. "Look at the view from up here. I really love Chicago," she said when we got to the top. She pulled out her phone and snapped a few photos. We were sharing the car with two other couples, and it was funny to watch everyone adjust for either selfies or to get out of the way of somebody taking a picture of the view. As much as I wanted to whip out my phone and take a picture of us, I decided to play it cool and act as if I could care less.

"Do you Instagram or Twitter?"

When did social media become verbs? "No, not really." That was true. Trish was forever telling me to use social media as a selling tool to get more recognition as an artist, especially on Instagram. Ride the wave, she said. I put her in charge of my artist page, which already had over ten thousand followers. When she'd stopped by the other night, she took a close-up of one of my sculptures with the date of my exhibition, and the photo got over two thousand likes. I barely knew how to text. And I never talked on the phone unless it was business. My iPhone wasn't something I enjoyed; it was something I needed. How people got lost on them for hours was beyond me. I was a millennial who didn't care about social media. Probably the only one.

"Too bad. I was going to tag you."

I watched as Sophia clicked and tapped away at her phone. "I take it you do?"

She shrugged. "I do, but mostly for business. The key is to show the world that you are a person and that it's not just about chocolates or sales."

"I'm sure your Instagram has awesome photos. Can I see?"

She handed me her phone and leaned forward to tell me about each photo. It was hard not to stare at her cleavage, especially since her phone was low between us.

"Oh, there's the banana bonbon." I pointed to the familiar dome-shaped yellow shell with a spackling of brown. "It's so perfect and pretty." Sophia leaned closer. Don't look, don't look, I repeated to myself. It was hard. She had beautiful breasts. Her skin was lovely: unblemished and not a freckle or mole in sight. Her voice was smooth with a hint of a smile as she explained picture after picture. I was fascinated with her business, but more fascinated with her. I finally had permission to be in her space and stare at her like I secretly had for months. She was beautiful. Blue eyes, long lashes, and a crooked bottom tooth, which made her human and less goddess-like.

"I'm hoping to generate private business this way. As soon as Tuft & Finley gets the boxes ready, I'll send out samples."

I jumped. "Are you happy with the design? I mean, how they've handled you as a client?"

She looked at me curiously. "I'm happy. I like how the artist used clean lines to represent what the product is."

"What do you mean?" I seemed entirely too invested in what she was saying, so I exhaled and relaxed.

"Our store colors are red and white. My own line has a different logo that's black and white, and the artist has these cool lines depicting what the product is. Like lines around the edges of the chocolate bar, swirly round things in the corner of the boxes for the bonbons, and the best design for malt balls."

It was so hard not to beam with pride. She was genuinely happy. In front of Trish, she was professionally pleased with the design. Not once did Trish see or tell me that Sophia was bubbling with excitement about the artwork. "That's great. I'm sure we'll have the sample boxes ready in no time." I was going to have to check with Rian on the schedule.

"I've already reached out to different businesses and hotels. Hit or miss with them, but I'm still excited," she said.

I couldn't tell her this was the reason I loved my job. I got to be creative and see the reaction of satisfied customers. "Seriously, if you need my help, just let me know."

"Thank you, but you have your own job to do."

"I'm excited for you. I really am."

We didn't talk about work after that. We talked about family, our angsty teenage years, foods we liked, and the things we hated. Sophia was an introvert. I had my moments, but mostly I was an extrovert. Sometimes life got to be too much, and that was when I lost myself in my art. It was nice to get away from people and noises. But I loved days like today, and Sophia seemed to be enjoying herself, too. She slipped her cropped jacket around her shoulders as the breeze picked up.

"Do you want to go? We can grab a cup of coffee or hot tea somewhere."

"That sounds good. As nice as it is out here, I'm ready for some quiet time. There's a coffee shop not too far from Sweet Stuff if you want to go there."

Made sense. Close to her work and she could make a quick getaway, although something told me she wasn't in a hurry to get away. I tipped the attendant again and slowly merged Lucy into traffic. I stole a glance at Sophia and noticed she wasn't as offended by Lucy's deep rumble or how she vibrated when idling. It took only twenty minutes to reach the coffee shop. Even though I was hungry and wanted to suggest dinner, I didn't want to push Sophia. I wanted her to like me, not run away because I was trying too hard.

"Can you drink coffee this late?" she asked.

"I'm pretty sure coffee runs through my veins, so it's not a problem." During my downward spiral after my divorce from Mandy, vodka had kept me alive, or was slowly killing me, but Trish got me on the right track.

I ordered a coffee and added a splash of skim milk and a teaspoon of sugar that I couldn't taste, but it took the bitterness bite out of the coffee. Sophia ordered a chai tea. We found an open table in the back of the shop and settled in. Sophia was adorably shy, but I could tell she was getting comfortable with me. She leaned in when I told her stories of my childhood and getting into trouble with my cousins.

"It sounds like you had a perfect childhood," she said. I tried to keep the sadness off my face when I thought about her childhood but failed. "It's okay. It's nice to hear fun stories. I have fond memories, too. When we were a complete family, we had fun, too. It took a bit to adjust to life after both my parents died, but my grandparents tried."

"I'm just glad you had a place to go, and you obviously have a close relationship with your grandma. And come on, candy? Chocolate? Best job ever."

"What was your first job?"

"My parents owned a pharmacy, so I was cashier, stockroom lackey, and anything they told us to do."

"How on earth did you get into welding?" Her expression wasn't one of distaste or judgment. She seemed genuinely interested.

"My dad and I rebuilt a little vintage sports car, and we had to weld the frame a lot, so he showed me how. I loved it. I loved how you could manipulate something so strong and hard into whatever you wanted. It was fun." I shrugged because my explanation didn't sound exciting, even to me. It was something somebody needed to experience and have interest in to appreciate.

"So, you've built cars before?"

"Only one. And a motorcycle. Now that was fun."

"Do you still ride?"

"I do. I was just thinking it was time to go for another ride. Do you like motorcycles?" If she said yes, I was going to book the next date.

"I've never been on one. They seem dangerous. Tell me you wear a helmet?"

"Always. I can't mess with this perfection." I made a circle motion in front of my face.

She laughed. "It would be sad if it got all banged and bruised up."

"Oh, so you agree. Interesting." I rested my chin on my forefinger and thumb as if I was in deep thought. The cute blush splashed on her neck and cheeks. This woman was not going to be able to hide anything from me.

"I didn't say that. I mean, your parents would be devastated. Plus, I'm sure you would be a terrible patient."

I nodded. "I really am. Let's hope I never catch a cold and call you. You'll end up hating me, and I can't have that." The blush again. Or maybe it had never left during the entire conversation. I leaned closer. "As much as I've enjoyed today, I need to go."

She covered her look of surprise quickly, but I saw it. "Oh, yeah. I have things to do, too. It was nice to take a break and get away from all things chocolate."

I turned our cups in and walked her out. "Thank you for today. I had fun."

She had a hard time making eye contact. I didn't want to make her uncomfortable, so I held my arms open and gave her a shy smile. She could either embarrass me by ignoring it or make my entire day by walking into it. I almost melted when I felt her press against me. I ended the hug quickly for fear that I was pushing too hard. "Let's do it again soon. Maybe a ride on my motorcycle?"

She shook her head. "Next time, let me plan."

I couldn't help myself. "So, you're saying it's a date." I winked and walked away.

"Friend date. Just friends," she yelled after me.

I waved at her without turning around.

❖

"How many did she order?"

Rian held up the assortment pack. "One hundred of these sample packs. I'm glad you all talked her into the EcoBoost line. It looks so much better than the ones from the other companies that have the dark-plastic trays."

Rian had come to the company later, after the business had already taken off. She was a consultant in the beginning but ended up being too valuable with her knowledge and skill. Because of her recommendations, we were able to purchase the right equipment to cover several different types of projects. We weren't set up or rated to package food, but we could supply the end product, and since Sophia's Collection was small, it was cheaper to give her the packaging so she and her staff could fill it.

"When do you think they'll be done?" I asked.

"By the end of the day. We can deliver them in the morning."

That gave me a reason to see Sophia again. "Perfect. I'll deliver them. I have to go that way anyway."

Rian lifted her eyebrow at me.

"What? I have some business in her neighborhood," I said.

"You expect me to believe that?"

"She isn't far from my studio."

"I don't care if you want to take them yourself. She's cute. And you've sulked long enough."

"Sulked? I don't sulk. I'm a Marshall. We don't sulk."

Rian pointed to my sleeve. "See that?"

I looked and saw nothing but brushed it just in case it was dirt or a bug. "I don't see anything."

"It's your heart. Be careful, Nico. Make sure you're being careful."

I gave her the nod. "It's all good. If something happens, great. If not, no biggie."

"Yeah, no biggie. Just be careful."

"Noted. Okay. I'll bring the van by at eight tomorrow. See you later."

Sometimes I hated that I worked at a place where everyone knew everything about me. Just once I wanted anonymity. Rian was very close to Trish, and I was sure I came up in discussions.

It had been only two days, and I was trying to find a valid reason to text Sophia. I was hoping time apart would make her miss me a little.

You up for breakfast tomorrow?

Bubbles right away. *Tempting but I have a lot of chocolate to make.* Sad-face emoji.

The sad face made me smile. That meant she wanted to spend time with me but couldn't. *Too bad. I guess I can just drop off the boxes and leave.*

Oh, they're ready?!

Just about. They'll box them up tonight, and I plan to run them by in the morning. I thought we could maybe have breakfast and pick up where we left off on Saturday.

We can go to the coffee shop. They have yummy pastries.

Sigh. I guess it's better than nothing. I followed up with a wink and put my phone down.

This flirtation had evolved into a social experiment that I needed to put a stop to. I genuinely liked Sophia. The misunderstanding squeezed my heart. Only a few of the butterflies I was feeling could flutter through.

Chapter Nine

I opened the van and grabbed one of delivery bags. "Tell me where you want it." I bit the inside of my cheeks to keep from smiling at Sophia's shocked look. "The boxes? Where do you want me to put them?"

"Oh. Yeah. In the back. We have a sterile room for them."

I followed Sophia to a back room, where she asked me to leave the bag in front of the door. I returned with the other two bags and gently placed them beside the other one. "We recycle the delivery bags, so whenever you're done with them, just let me know, and I'll collect them."

Sophia poked one. "These are really great."

"We seal them so the product doesn't get crushed. And then, of course, deliver them by hand with love and care."

She blushed and smiled. "Thank you for taking time away from your job."

I waved her off. "It's a great excuse to get out of work. Plus, I get to spend time with you, and that's always fun."

A few employees shuffled by, but not before smiling knowingly at us. Sophia's cheeks reddened even more. I found that response interesting. Maybe she'd talked about me to her employees, or maybe they saw us and just assumed something was up between us.

"Let me grab my purse. Today is my treat," she said.

I nodded and waited. When she joined me, her lips had a touch of color on them, and her hair was freshly brushed. "You look nice today."

She glanced down. "Thank you." She looked up at me, but this time her gaze didn't falter. "So do you."

I tingled, not at her words, but at her look. I detected interest there. I just needed to draw it out of her, slowly and carefully. To be honest, I did look good today. We had to wear a Tuft & Finley shirt when we delivered product, but since I was the boss, I'd decided to wear what I wanted. A black shirt, jeans, and wingtips. My hair was the perfect length, and I even wore a little bit of makeup. "Thanks."

The coffee shop wasn't crowded. I ordered a black coffee and a slice of lemon pound cake. Sophia ordered a hot tea and a blueberry muffin. We waited for the barista to fill our order and looked at all the delicious treats behind the counter.

"It's not healthy, but I can't say no to a freshly baked muffin. Working so close to the coffee shop is dangerous," Sophia said. She picked a piece of the muffin top and popped it into her mouth when we sat down at a small bistro table near the window. I liked it because it was small and I could be in her personal space. Even with all the delicious pastry smells and strong coffee in the shop, I could still smell Sophia. Today she smelled like dark chocolate and marzipan. I was going to recommend that she offer her different scents in oils and candles, maybe in a different store or online. The sweet smell could drop me to my knees, and I knew I wasn't alone. A lot of people liked sweet smells.

Sophia wore skirts and dresses a lot. I hadn't seen her in jeans or pants ever. Today she was wearing a taupe skirt and a turquoise blouse. I was sure a matching suit jacket was somewhere in her office. It was a matter of days before the sun would be too hot to be out in it longer than to just stroll to a coffee shop three blocks away from Sweet Stuff. "Do you wear heels all the time? Even when you work with chocolate?" I pointed to her cute taupe heels that couldn't have been comfortable, but then again, I never understood how women could outwalk me in three-inch heels while showing no signs of pain. It was baffling.

"I change into different shoes when I'm making chocolate. A small drop of warm chocolate will instantly turn the floor into a Slip 'N Slide," she said.

"Well, that's probably a sexy look. This, plus black restaurant-style shoes." I pointed up and down at her outfit.

"It's a good thing I'm not trying to impress anyone."

I put my hand over my heart and grimaced. "Ouch." I smiled and sat forward. "But you're not wearing them now, so maybe you're trying to impress me."

"I don't have time to date. I told you that."

"I know, I know. Friends. I'm in the friends category." I air-quoted "friends" with my fingers. But even I didn't believe it. "There's a cute little brunette I hang out with some weekends. She keeps me pretty happy."

Sophia turned red. Not the cute blush I'd seen on her pale skin before, but red as if she was angry. I quickly pulled out my phone and showed her the picture of my parents' chocolate Labrador retriever. "Look? I don't get to see her very often, but she really has my heart."

Her shoulders visibly sank, and she leaned back in her chair. "I love dogs. We had one when I was a kid. I'd love to have one as an adult, but as you pointed out, we're workaholics. Maybe if this line of chocolates takes off, I can hire people and relax and get a small dog."

"I really would love to help fill those boxes. I mean, if you need the help. I promise to eat only one or two pieces," I said. I finished off my lemon pound cake. "Or I can help you deliver them."

She folded her arms in front of her and stared at me. "Why are you so interested in my business? I don't mean that in a rude way. I genuinely want to know."

I put my elbows on the table and rested my chin on my linked fingers. "I'm interested in you. I want to get to know you better. Your life is your business, so that means I'm interested in why it's everything to you." I gave her my look, the one I used to let people know not to doubt me.

"But there's nothing remotely exciting about me. Why me? Out of all the people in Chicago, why me?"

Because I can't stop thinking about you. Because I love your legs and how the clicking of your heels on the train or on the sidewalk gives me shivers, and how you can see right through me and my bullshit. Because I want to touch your soft skin and bite your bottom lip and kiss you until neither of us has a concept of time.

"Months ago, I noticed a beautiful woman getting on the L on my way to my studio, but only on Thursdays. It became my mission to know her. Why on Thursdays? Only Thursdays? And then when you walked into our business, I was floored."

"You yelled at me," she said.

"Come on. You blocked the dock. Truthfully, I couldn't see you in the car. The glare was too bright."

She smiled. "It was kind of surreal seeing you on the L and then at Tuft & Finley."

"The true definition of a small world." I squeezed her hand. She didn't pull away. "So, please. Let me help you. Let me be a part of your world for just a little bit."

"That means hairnet, white jacket, and better shoes."

I looked down. "What's wrong with my shoes?" I really loved my wingtips. Smooth, Italian leather that was more comfortable and more fashionable than high-end running shoes.

"You would fall."

"I guess I could wear boots."

"Not your welding boots. Those would be too heavy."

"So bossy. Are you doing it today? I can go change." It was ridiculous how many changes of clothes I had at the office, the studio, and my own place.

Sophia looked at the clock. "Can you come by after two? Wait. Can you even get the afternoon off?"

That was going to be the tricky part—convincing her that I had flexibility at my job. "Oh, sure. I was doing deliveries today, so I just need to dump the van and come back."

"How many more deliveries do you have?" she asked.

I was already knee-deep in one lie; I couldn't afford to be in another. "You were the only one." Her stern look did nothing to deter me. "It's all good. Trust me." Sensing her anxiety, I stood. "Come on. Let's get you back. Thank you for breakfast."

❖

"Wait up. How'd it go?"

I slowed so Trish could catch up. I was headed into my office to get started on another in-house project, but it was futile. I was too excited to see Sophia again. "It went well. I'm going to head over there at two to collect the bags." Something told me not to inform Trish that I was going back to help. I leaned against the door frame. "What's going on?"

"Nothing. You just haven't said much about her lately. I barely heard anything about the date on Saturday."

I shrugged. Did I really forget to tell her anything about it? "It was fun. We're still just friends. We talked a lot about family and what life was like growing up."

"That makes me happy. Do you think there's a chance there?"

"Meh. It's still too early to say either way."

"Okay. I'll let you get to work. Don't forget about the big party this weekend. I know you're swamped getting ready for your show and have other things on your mind." She looked at me pointedly.

I looked Trish up and down. "I haven't forgotten. It's a major holiday. Wait a minute. This isn't some sort of weird intervention, is it?" It had happened before.

"Not at all. Just keeping you in the loop. Everyone knows you have a lot on your plate right now. How's sculpting going?"

"I'll get my pieces done. I started planning a new one that I hope to have ready by the exhibition." It was laid out in my mind, and I was excited to start it.

"How are things here at the office? Are you keeping up? Do you need help with anything?"

"I'm good, I think. I'm going to work on Jet Pen's box design and then pick up the bags and head to the studio to work. Long day." I left out the four hours I planned to spend with Sophia boxing product and maybe having a quick drink somewhere.

"Keep it up. We're rooting for you." Trish gave me a quick hug and walked to her office.

I sat down and frowned at the weirdness of the entire exchange. Did I look tired or overwhelmed? Did a client complain about something? I knew Sophia was happy, and I knew our young gamer clients were happy with their Alien Alliance containers with the sliding walls. I checked the timeline for Jet Pen, and I was good on that. The customer had a specific design in mind so I just had to create it. Sometimes I offered a second suggestion, but this time I was going to do exactly what they wanted. I didn't have the time.

"Hey, Mom. What's up?"

"Hi, honey. How are you? Did Trish remind you about the party?"

"She did. Any special reason? Do I need to bring anything?" I was already thinking of texting Sophia and asking her if she would be interested in making something for the gathering. When my parents threw a party, a lot of people came, and some of them could use Sophia's business. I could grab her business cards and place them by the chocolates. And the cookies. How could I forget her delicious cookies?

"No. We're fine. Just yourself. Plan on staying Saturday night, if you can afford the time."

"We have a new client who is selling artisan chocolates. Maybe I'll grab a few boxes to get her started."

"I heard about her."

We were both silent for about three seconds. "Oh?" I asked.

"She's the one who has you all tied up in knots. Of course, I know about her. I'm your mother."

Damn Trish and her mouth. Telling Rian was one thing, but our parents? "I wouldn't say that. She's a nice woman I met on the L, who happens to now be one of our clients."

"You do what you want to. It would be nice to meet some of the ladies you date. I'm worried about you," she said.

I rubbed my hand over my face and cracked my neck. I was frustrated but took a deep breath and held the phone away while I exhaled. "Don't worry about me, Mom. I'm good. Sophia is nice, but we're just friends." I silently added "for now" for my own ego.

"Bring some chocolates, but remember it's July in Chicago. I'm practically melting. I can't imagine how long the chocolates will last."

When my parents threw a party, it was basically a step below black tie. It wasn't a barbecue, like most families in America hosted, but the kind where waiters walked around with trays of food and champagne. My parents knew a lot of doctors and pharmaceutical reps, and for some reason, the Marshall party was the event of the summer. Too bad this was the weekend Sophia was taking her grandma to Detroit. "We'll keep the chocolates inside or on chilled trays." My parents weren't wealthy, but they were comfortable and had influential friends. I normally hated the Fourth of July barbecue because the people who attended weren't fun. It was a networking weekend for me.

"You know, maybe you should bring a few of your sculptures, and we can display them on the deck."

"Mom, that's a great idea." A little taste of my exhibition to people who could afford them was genius. I knew my mom would pimp the show, too. I was going to have to show her how to send the information to people using the QR code on her phone instead of handing them a flyer, which was her preferred method.

"Do you have any display pedestals?"

"I could probably get Lindsay from the gallery to loan me

a few. I know she'll want most of the pieces to be unveiled at the show, but a peek of what's going to be there will drum up interest." I said bye to my mom and texted Lindsay, who thought it was a great idea and asked if I could pick them up before Thursday. I promised to be there in the morning.

With only a few hours before I had to be at Sweet Stuff, I closed my door, put my phone on Do Not Disturb, and focused all my attention on Jet Pen. The only person allowed to interrupt was Shelby, the intern, and that was only because I'd given her a new client, much to her and Trish's surprise. I sat in the meeting with them but let Shelby ask the questions. Sometimes I piped up, but for the most part, I took notes and stayed quiet. I had to remain available in case she needed help. Not only was she all about saving Mother Earth, but she was a great artist, whether she was using an iPad Pro or just sketching. Maybe with her on board, my life would ease up in the next few years.

CHAPTER TEN

I took the L from work to Sweet Stuff. It wasn't necessary for me to have Lucy. I was there to work and convince Sophia to let me buy several chocolates, some cookies, and assorted other confections. A few kids would be at the party, and kids loved sweets. "Reporting for duty, Boss." I mock-saluted Sophia when she pushed through the swinging door.

She looked me up and down and nodded. "I approve your boots, but you still have to wear a cap and a coat. Follow me."

I rolled my eyes playfully. "Okay, but again, no pictures." I wondered what she did with the photo she took of us at the top of the Centennial. "At least not with the hairnet on." I slipped into a jacket that was a size too large. She handed me another one that fit and adjusted my hairnet for me like she had before. I stifled a shiver as her fingers brushed behind my ears.

"Are you ready to work?"

"I was born ready." I slipped on anti-static gloves and followed her to the clean room.

"Are we the only ones?"

"For this assembly line? Yes. The other employees are working on Sweet Stuff chocolates." She opened the refrigerator and pulled out several trays of dome-shaped bonbons and put them on the stainless-steel counter. "We have five slots for bonbons, four for ganache squares, and one for the tiny baby lavender chocolate bars."

"This is amazing. Listen, I know you have only a hundred boxes to hand out, but I want to buy a dozen and some other things. My parents are having a party this weekend, and I thought maybe this would help get your name out there." I couldn't tell if the look she gave me was one of disbelief that my parents would have a need for her artisan chocolates, or if she didn't believe I would use them for that purpose. Maybe she thought I was blowing my paycheck on her chocolates to impress her. "It's not as strange as it sounds. Just keep in mind that my parents were pharmacists and are friends with a lot of doctors, pharmaceutical reps, and others in a very large industry, who do the same things as the clients you're reaching out to."

"Wow. That's really nice of you."

"I also want to order some cookies, if your workers have the time." I turned and touched her arm. "I know it's last-minute. And I don't want any special pricing."

"Thank you so much. It's a great idea. Let's box some up and see how many are left."

I opened my mouth, about to say something, but she held up her hand.

"And no, you can't take the distressed pieces. First impressions are everything."

There it was again—the whole first-impression thing. It was clearly very important to her. "Okay, okay. Those are just for me to eat. Got it."

To say I was proud of our boxes was an understatement. Rian had done a fantastic job of punching the trays to fit the box perfectly. I don't even want to know how many she had to recycle to get it right. It didn't take us long at all to fill them. After she reviewed her list of potential drop-offs, she offered me a dozen.

"I'll buy the dozen and take any loose pieces you want to sell. We can put them on chilled serving trays." Another weird look. "What? I know what they are."

She looked at me as if I were delusional. The very thing I

was trying to make her believe about me, which she was, was starting to piss me off a bit.

"My parents' parties are pretty amazing affairs. Your chocolate will fit right in. I believe in your product, and I believe in you."

Her features softened when she realized that she'd offended me. "I trust you. I didn't mean to make you feel bad. Thank you for wanting to help me. I'd be more than happy to give you extras for your party."

I held up my finger. "Sell."

"Fine. Sell."

"How many can you spare from all of your lines?" I knew she had some flavors that weren't in the sample box.

She checked her refrigerator and did a quick count. "I can give you four dozen," she said. "But don't forget about the quantity discount I'd offer anyone."

After it was all said and done, I was going to pick up twelve sample boxes, peanut-butter dark-chocolate malt balls, and three dozen bonbons of Fleur de Sel caramel, salted hazelnut praline, and vanilla bean. I put in an order of two dozen chocolate-chip cookies and a dozen snickerdoodles for the cookie munchers in the crowd. "Now that we're done here, how about grabbing a quick drink to celebrate boxing samples on the eve of your new line going live?"

"I didn't think of it like that, but yes, that sounds perfect. I know a place." She removed her hairnet and gloves. "And I'm driving."

"Sounds perfect." I knew it took a lot for her to come to an agreement on the price of everything, so I had to give a little. I handed her my jacket and gloves and tossed the hairnet. It was almost happy hour. She returned wearing her blazer and the black heels I loved.

"Ready?"

I nodded and followed her to their tiny private parking lot

beside the building. Her practical sedan was extremely clean. I leaned over to check her odometer, completely in her space.

"What are you doing?"

I shifted and stared into her light-blue eyes. "I wanted to see how many miles you had on this car, because in the history of automobiles, never has anyone had a car so clean."

She broke eye contact to look around as if seeing the interior of her car for the first time. "I guess I don't use it other than to get to and from work."

"Am I the first person in your car?"

She laughed. "I'm not that lonely. My grandmother's been in it, and Becca, my best friend."

"You have a best friend."

"Why do you sound so surprised?"

"We've hung out a few times, and you've never mentioned her before."

Sophia shrugged. "Becca's busy with a husband and three kids. I don't expect to hang out with her for at least ten years—until after the kids are grown."

"Isn't that the truth? All my friends who are in relationships are hard to spend time with. Impossible, if they have kids."

"Will you see all of your family this weekend?"

"I'm sure. At some point this event turned into a local family reunion with cousins, aunts, uncles, and the misfits," I said.

"Misfits?"

"You know. The black sheep of the family. Me, my cousin Ethan, and his wife Starr." I lifted an eyebrow at her and nodded. "Yep. Starr. With two r's. She's exactly how you're picturing her right now."

"She's got orange and pink hair, fishnet stockings, and a Bostonian accent. And she pops gum every ten seconds, annoying everyone who can hear her?"

I gasped at her. "Oh, my God. You know her?"

We both laughed until I cried. "You're not far off. Starr is from the East Coast, but she's more of a hippie than a wearer of fishnets." She was an artist, a holistic enthusiast, and a life coach. My dad and Trish talked behind her back constantly. My mother always berated them for gossiping. "I actually like Starr. She's just quirky and misunderstood." And she was a big supporter of my art. She understood how difficult welding was and how beautiful manipulating steel could be.

"If she's nice to you, then I like her," she said.

I smiled. Sophia was so guarded, but when she relaxed, she was innocently charming, and her kindness was legitimate. "It's too bad you're out of town this weekend."

Sophia didn't answer me. She pulled into a parking space outside a tiny bar that looked like it was something out of a fairy forest, with a thatched roof and round, thick windows. *My Precious Pints* was carved in a wooden sign on top of the door.

"Where the fuck are we?" I hadn't paid attention when she was driving, only noticing that we were headed in the opposite direction of where I lived, worked, and knew.

She wagged her eyebrows at me. "Remember when you asked me what books I like to read or movies I liked to watch?"

"Shut up. Really? A *Lord of the Rings* bar?" I opened the car door and gaped at the structure. "How have I never seen this before? I've lived in Chicago my entire life." Sophia started to laugh. I had a feeling she didn't laugh enough, and the sound filled my heart. I held the strange u-shaped door with the large iron knocker open and hesitantly followed her in. "Well, I'm disappointed."

She turned quickly and was only inches from my face. "Don't break my heart this soon, Nico."

I wanted to kiss her. She was so close. I looked down at her lips. "Never."

"Sophia! Where have you been?"

Our moment was broken by a burly man dressed as a hobbit. "Walter. How are you?"

I watched as they hugged. Her smile was genuine, and I could detect real affection between the two.

"Nico, come meet Walter. The man who was always there for me when I needed help."

I shook his hand and smiled at him. He was gruff, and honestly, I couldn't tell if he was in costume or not. "It's nice to meet you, Walter."

It was hard to keep up with their conversation, but it appeared that Walter, their grandmother's neighbor, had been a father figure for Sophia and her brother after her father died.

"So, you helped keep Sophia in line when she was a teenager?" After his nod, I pushed. "She must have been a handful. I mean, she's barely containable now."

He threw his head back and roared. "Believe it or not, she *was* quite a handful. She used to sneak out at night with that boy, Andrew. I can't remember how many times I busted them."

"Andrew?" I gave her a look.

She shrugged. "Andrew."

"Interesting." Panic flooded my stomach as I thought that maybe I had everything wrong about her.

"Turns out, they were sneaking out to talk to girls. The older girls in the neighborhood who drank and smoked and stole things."

Sophia playfully pushed Walter's shoulder. "My only role model was a grown man who dressed like Frodo. I needed more."

I quietly exhaled the breath I'd been holding. Girls. They were chasing girls. "It could have been worse."

"Worse? How?"

"They could've been chasing boys."

Another howl of laughter.

"I like this one, Sophia. How about an ale?"

He was so damn likable. "I'd love one. In a wooden cup or whatever you call it."

"Tankard," Sophia and Walter said simultaneously.

I nodded. "Tankard."

We sat on stools and watched Walter fill two tankards. I turned to Sophia. "I can't believe you're such a *Lord of the Rings* nerd."

"I got into it because of Walter. One day I was in the backyard throwing a ball at the fence, and he barked at me. He asked me what I was doing, and I said, 'Nothing.' Then he asked if I was bored. I did the typical teenage shrug so he handed me a copy of *Lord of the Rings.*"

"The size of that book probably scared you."

"I handed it back to him and said no way."

"So, what did he do?" I asked.

We toasted our mugs filled to the brim with God only knew what, and I motioned for her to continue.

"He started reading it to me. At first I pretended not to listen, but I stayed in the yard, close enough to hear. He read a chapter a day, every day. I loved the attention. I couldn't wait to hear more."

Her story completely intrigued me. "Did he have the bar already, or did it come from that experience?"

"Oh, he's had the bar forever. I spent my twenty-first birthday at this very place, drinking with Walter and my grandmother."

I loved hearing her open up. It was like watching a flower bloom right in front of me. This was her comfortable space. We both nursed our ales and ice water, also served in tankards, for two hours. It was like a different Sophia was sitting in front of me. I held up my tankard, which held maybe one final swig of lukewarm ale, and toasted her. "Here's to the success of Sophia's Collection, and here's to learning who you are day by day, chocolate by chocolate."

"Thank you for your support, Nico. I mean it. You've made the transition so much easier, and I feel confident because of you."

"Are you kidding? I'm excited to be on the ground floor of

your new endeavor. I couldn't support another idea more than I do yours." I drained the wooden mug and slammed it down on the bar. "And now, with much regret, I must depart."

"That's more Shakespeare language."

"Really? I feel like it could be Middle Earth English."

"I can teach you Adunaic or Westron. And there are so many Elvish languages." Her entire face lit up with excitement.

I groaned and covered my ears. "No, please. Modern-day English only. Although I have to say, seeing this side of you is very cute."

She touched her cheeks. "Stop. You're making me blush."

I moved closer. "This isn't the first time." I so wanted to kiss her. Instead, I leaned back. "It's getting late, and we both have a busy day tomorrow." I had to weld tonight for a bit. My desire to be with Sophia was seriously starting to cramp my desire to finish at least three more pieces before the show.

"Oh, okay. I understand."

Squaring up with Walter took another twenty minutes. By the time we got out of there, it was already dark.

"Why don't you let me drive you home?"

"Oh, no. Just drop me off at the station." The last thing I wanted was for Sophia to see either of my places.

"We're friends now, right? I should know where you live."

"Seriously, just drop me off at the closest station. It'll be quicker."

She turned to me. "What's wrong?"

I shook my head. "It's nothing."

She touched my arm. "Wait a minute. Are you embarrassed to show me where you live? Because I don't care. I'm not that kind of person."

"I'm in the opposite direction of My Precious Pints."

"So am I."

She wasn't going to let up. I gave her the studio address and strapped in. "My studio isn't much. Don't expect a lot." I had to think how I'd left it yesterday. Was it messy? Was the sink full of dirty dishes? Oh, God. Let there not be dirty clothes everywhere.

"I'm not even worried, so don't fret."

"Is fret another Middle Earth word?" I was good at teasing.

It took us twenty-five minutes to reach the building. I told her to park on the street, not in the lot. The last thing I wanted was for her to get a flat tire on the way home. When we pulled up, I glanced at her. I had to give her credit. Her expression revealed nothing. "You don't have to come up if you don't want to."

"Oh, I've come this far. I might as well go all the way."

I shot her a look.

"I mean, all the way to your studio."

I looked at my part-time neighborhood through her eyes. Some graffiti, litter pressed up against chain-link fences, and the parked cars looked a bit rough, but there was charm, too. A lot of starving artists lived down here and displayed their art in their windows, doors, balconies, and even on the sides of buildings.

"There's a lot of character in your neighborhood." At least she wasn't scared.

"And we've had only a few murders down here." She stumbled. I took her hand to steady her and pull her closer. "I'm just kidding." Honestly, I had no idea. I'd been in the studio for only two years. I kept talking because she didn't shake my hand loose. I told her how long I'd lived there, all about my neighbors, and how it was dangerous to park in the lot because of the metal, which, for the record, wasn't because of me. I dropped her hand to open the door at the exact same moment Ben was headed out. Sophia smacked against his chest, and he steadied her with his strong arms.

"I'm so sorry," she said.

I couldn't help but giggle as Sophia practically bounced off him. "Hey, Ben. How's it going?" I asked.

"Good. Looks like you're good, too." He nodded at us and kept walking.

Sophia waited until he got to his van. "He's your landlord? He's a giant."

"He's a giant teddy bear, you mean," I whispered, motioning for her to enter.

"He looks like a killer."

"He looks like he should work at My Precious Pints." I laughed at my own joke. I sobered up when we got to my door. "Again, don't expect much." I said a quick prayer that the place looked decent, flipped on the light, and sighed with relief. My studio was clean. A glass was in the sink, but my tiny selection of clothes was put away, and the sofa bed was folded up.

"It's cute. You do need more things on the walls though," Sophia said.

The only thing hanging was a painting I'd bought from my neighbor because it reminded me of a warm, safe place.

"Yeah. I don't spend a lot of time here."

She looked at me. "Where do you spend most of your time? Your parents'? Work? The apartments of the millions of women you've charmed across Chicago?"

I snorted. "I'm either working or trying to win you over. I don't have time for other people."

She sighed. "You know now isn't the best time for either of us to date."

I took a step closer. "Why not? Because we work a lot? I mean, we went out tonight and last weekend. If we want to find time, we will." My heartbeat ramped up as I waited for her to agree. It took so much effort not to run to her and literally charm the pants off her. Instead, I sat on the chair and gave her the entire couch. I crossed my legs and leaned forward.

"With the new line launching tomorrow, I just don't know how much time I can devote to a relationship right now."

"I understand that. Would I even be somebody you'd date?"

She looked down and played with the fabric on the couch. I waited patiently because everything I had done to get to this point hinged on her answer. Sophia was worth the wait. When she looked at me, her eyes narrowed, and a hundred butterflies spread their wings in my stomach. It was a look of hunger, and I was falling. I gripped the armrests and waited for her words.

"Why else would I be here?"

That was the moment I knew I was all in.

CHAPTER ELEVEN

I'm so excited for you!" Trish squeezed my hands. Hard.

"Ouch." I freed my hands and shook them for circulation. "Thanks. I'm pretty happy, too." After Sophia and I talked the other night at my studio, we decided to go out on a date. Next week sometime because we were both busy over the holiday weekend. It almost felt like a business proposition, and I'd half expected her to shake my hand after we agreed on parameters. Instead we hugged. I walked her out to her car and kissed her cheek. Now that I had the green light, I was much more comfortable going slow.

"Okay, Romeo. Let's go. Mom and Dad are expecting us." She closed the back of the SUV that housed all of the Sophia's Collection chocolates and Sweet Stuff cookies. Trish had opted to pick me up because she wanted me to take a break and to ensure I didn't skip out. That wasn't even possible because I had three sculptures already at their house and needed to see reactions.

"I don't know why you want to get there so early. We don't have to set up anything. Mom's handled it all," I said.

"It's called day-drinking. Humor me, okay?"

"I guess I can day-drink with you." It had been a stressful week at Tuft & Finley. We were breaking in new hires and trying to keep up with demands. It was tough right before a holiday. The employees were happy to have the extra day off, but work still piled up, and that meant next week was going to be hell. We both deserved a day or two of day-drinking.

"How's sculpting?"

"It's going well. I've blocked off enough time to finish what I need to." I didn't want to get her excited, even though I was brimming with energy. I was inspired again. When Sophia agreed to go on a date with me, something inside me grew. My confidence sprouted, and I didn't see the world in cold, gray metal anymore. Sophia, as quiet as she was, had given me hope, and with hope came color.

"Will you be able to relax at the party?"

"Of course. I'm here, right?"

"And I don't want you to spend all your time worrying about Sophia's chocolates. They are beautiful and tasty, so don't feel like you have to push them, okay? They'll sell themselves." We stopped at a light and she turned to face me. "You need to take time for yourself. Just look at you." She gently touched my face. I thought she was being nice. "You're starting to wrinkle."

"Jerk." I punched her gently in her arm.

"Do not impair the driver!" Trish rubbed her arm and threatened to tell our parents.

I laughed. "Never tell a woman she's wrinkling. Not even your sister." We both laughed because we shared everything. Rob would die if he knew the things Trish told me. She knew things about me that no one else did. When Mandy nearly cleared out my bank account, we didn't let my parents know. To sue her would have brought a lot of attention, and I'd begged Trish to just let it go.

The credit-card charges were my fault. I'd approved all the purchases because I knew I was working a lot and she liked nice things. She maxed out one of my cards before I realized I was redecorating her secret apartment and filling both her and her girlfriend's wardrobes. When I saw the statement and checked my bank account, I blew up. She had wiped out five years of hard work. I thought Trish was going to kill her. The divorce was swift and extremely painful. The only thing I got out of it was a fresh start. It didn't sound great at the time, but now I was starting to appreciate its significance. I reminded myself that was in the past, and I had no reason to give her or our brief marriage another thought.

"It'll be good to see everyone again. Did you bring your bikini?"

"Ha-ha. When was the last time I wore a bikini? When I was ten? You know I wear trunks and a tank."

"Okay. Did you bring your swimsuit?"

I loved Trish. She was so fierce about me, but she still treated me like a kid sister even though we were both adults. "No. I don't plan on swimming. Not this time. Maybe when it's just us."

"Worried about your reputation?"

"Shit. I gave up on that a long time ago."

She squeezed my hand again, but this time with affection. "You're still wonderful. Don't worry about the past. Your future looks pretty damn good. Especially when you have your exhibition coming up. I'm so proud of you!"

Lindsay had priced the sculptures that were completed, and if I sold even half of them, I would be doing quite well. I still had to complete and price four sculptures: the ladybug that Trish begged me to enter; *Broken*; the unnamed one I was working on; and the one I was excited to start. "Thanks. It will be stressful, but I'm looking forward to it."

The rest of the drive we gossiped about family and our parents' friends who would be at the party. My parents didn't shoot off fireworks, but the neighborhood association had an entertaining display. By then we were usually all relaxed and having a good time. It was my favorite holiday besides Christmas.

Mom met us in the driveway to direct us up the path. "Don't park there. Park behind the third slot."

"Are you going to do this all night?"

She leaned in and kissed me on the cheek. "I want to make sure one of us can get out if there's a problem."

"If there's a problem, we're calling 9-1-1," Trish said. She parked the SUV and hopped out to give Mom a hug. "We could use a little help carrying things up."

Mom looked around. "Where's Rob?"

"He'll be here later. He had some work to do."

Summertime was Rob's busy season. It was hard to turn down a job in summer because construction in winter was miserable. He tried to get enough work in the summers to maintain his crew through the winter months, when working in twenty-degree temperatures was dangerous. I was lucky he was able to spare the workers to finish my studio.

"Are these the chocolates?" Mom asked.

I was proud of the bonbons even though I had nothing to do with them. "Aren't they gorgeous?"

"Let's get them out of this heat."

We grabbed boxes and trays and found room for them in one of the refrigerators. I insisted Mom eat a Fleur de Sel caramel. The look on her face after she popped it into her mouth was exactly what I was hoping for. Pure satisfaction.

"Oh, my God. This is delicious."

"See? And maybe your friends will love them and want to order them for their private events or holiday parties."

"Are these your boxes?" She opened the sample box and read the flavors that were stamped below each bonbon. "Such a gorgeous design."

"Nico did that. Very simple and exactly what the customer wanted. Oh, and speaking of the customer." Trish's voice drifted off and caught my mom's attention.

"Oh, yes. This is the girl, right?" My mom suddenly gave me all her attention.

Heat pressed against my cheeks, and I couldn't help but smile. "Yes, this is the girl."

"Go ahead and tell Mom everything," Trish said coyly.

"Nicole? What's going on?"

I held my hands up and shrugged. "She agreed to go out on a date with me."

"Is she a good person, Patricia?"

Trish nodded. "Somewhat of an ice queen, so I'm excited to see how Nico does with her."

"I'm right here. I can hear you both."

"I'm sure she'll do just fine. If you approve, then I know she's right for Nicole."

"I think she might be too good for Nico."

My jaw dropped. "What?"

Trish nudged me. "I'm playing. I think she's finally found her match. Sophia is very business driven and seems nice. Not to mention she's very attractive."

"My children." My father entered the room and stood there with his arms open.

"Don't be weird, Dad," I said and walked into his hug. Trish said something similar, but honestly, his hugs were the best.

"Are you ready for this shindig?" My dad draped his arms over our shoulders and led us to the window overlooking the deck. "Look at all of this. Why do we do this every year?" Dad had three grills and a smoker on the large deck that ran the length of the house. Rob was going to help grill, and my dad's best friend would carve the meat in the smoker. Mom had most of the sides catered.

"You do this because you and Mom are extroverts, and everyone loves your parties."

"You girls love them, too, right?"

"We're here for the wine," Trish said.

He looked at me. I nodded. "She's not wrong."

"What's this I hear about a date?"

I groaned. "It's nothing. I have a date next week with a nice woman. Trish knows her so, of course, the whole family must know."

"Did your sister set you up?"

Trish and Mom giggled.

"Not really," I said. He folded his arms and looked at me expectantly. "Okay, she's a client, but before you get all righteous, I knew her before she was a client."

"Knew is a strong word. More like obsessed," Trish said.

"I saw her on the L." I turned to Trish. "Really?"

She smiled at me. "Okay, not obsessed. But it has been delightful to see my baby sister completely derailed by a nice, attractive woman."

"You know the rules. Don't mix business with pleasure," Dad said.

"I know, I know. I'm completely avoiding all women at Tuft & Finley. But, in my defense, Sophia doesn't work there, and now that we have all the designs, I can excuse myself from the project. Shelby can make any changes if necessary." This wasn't going in the direction I wanted it to. "Can we talk about something else? When are the guests showing up?"

My dad looked at his watch. "Not for another hour."

"Since we are here, let the day drinking commence," Trish said. She grabbed a bottle of Moscato and grabbed an opener from the drawer. "Who wants a glass?"

I raised my hand and moved closer to the kitchen island, where Trish was expertly opening the bottle. "Can we move on to a different topic?" I whispered, low enough for only Trish to hear.

She reached over and pinched my cheek. "You got it." She passed out glasses of wine. My dad grabbed a beer instead. "I'd like to make a toast. Here's to our successes in life and in love. We are lucky to have a family that has an abundance of both. Happy Fourth."

We clinked glasses and sipped to Trish's toast. Any other day I would have rolled my eyes at the love part, but it didn't sound too bad this time. Plus, I had a wonderful family, and once all my cousins showed up, we were bound to have fun.

When the caterers arrived, we scattered. I intended to put

the chocolates out when the guests arrived. I didn't trust my dad around sweet things. Trish and I refilled our glasses and found chairs in the shade across the yard. That way we could see who arrived and gossip in private without anyone overhearing us.

By the time Ethan and Starr showed up, we were really relaxed. I hugged them and told them how much I missed them over and over. Even I heard how ridiculous I sounded.

"We have news," Ethan said. He waved off the wine bottle and dragged over a bench for them to sit on.

"Oh, I love news," I said. I grabbed Starr's hand. Something made me think it was the best kind of news.

"We're pregnant," Starr said.

I stood, whooped, and threw my hands in the air. "I love babies." I really didn't, but I was deliriously happy for my cousin. They were so cute sitting so close and so much in love. They'd been married five years, and every time I saw them, they acted like a fresh couple. Ten years ago, Ethan got arrested for assault and spent a month in jail. He was eighteen, restless, entitled, and fell in with the wrong crowd. After he was released from jail, we offered him a job at Tuft & Finley. He was still an angry young man, but also thankful. He started off in the warehouse and worked his way up to shipping manager. When he met Starr, they decided to move closer to her parents and to start a natural-soap business. Ethan was such a whiz at sales that they were up and running successfully after a year.

"Shh. We haven't told anyone yet. We thought we would wait until the whole family was here," he said.

Trish and I took turns hugging them. I was ready to spoil the shit out of a tiny baby. Most of my cousins' kids were around ten years old. They were fun now, but I missed the baby and toddler stages, when their personalities were developing.

"Congratulations, both of you. You're going to be awesome parents." I truly meant that. Starr was super gentle and Ethan was so relaxed now.

"Thanks, Nico. And thanks for always being so supportive," Starr said.

"Are you kidding me? We're family. That's what we do," I said. I was starting to feel all mushy inside and blamed the wine. I put my glass down. I needed food. "I'm going up to the house and get something to eat." People were starting to show up, and I wanted to get the chocolates out and grab a handful of chips.

"Nico. How are you?" Uncle Ken, my dad's younger brother, gave me a quick hug. He was a dermatologist with a practice just outside the city. His second wife, Marcia, had two sons who were already in the pool playing water basketball. His first wife had moved to Seattle years ago. I liked her more than Marcia, but they had divorced so long ago that my memories of wife number one were fuzzy.

"Uncle Ken. Hi. I'm good. How are you?"

"Great. It's summer, life is good. Business is good. How's the paper business?"

It drove me crazy that he called it a paper business, but I got tired of correcting him years ago.

"Can't complain. We're staying busy." My other uncle, who wasn't here yet, was a big supporter of recycling and of our company. He referred us to several of his customers. It was hard to believe the three of them came from the same womb. "Hey, I brought over some artisan chocolates. Make sure you taste them. I think you might be able to use them in the future for gifts or whatever. We did their packaging." I didn't want to appear too eager.

"Will do. Marcia's inside with your mom if you want to say hi."

I pasted on a smile and nodded. I was headed to the kitchen anyway. The grills were heating up, and my dad was already instructing Rob on how to do the job, even though Rob knew exactly what he was supposed to do. He humored my dad, so I sent him a sympathetic smile on my way inside.

"Nico, it's so good to see you. I love the sculptures you have out in the yard." Marcia hadn't been outside yet, but at least she was trying, which was more than I was doing.

"Thank you. I'm excited about the exhibition."

"That's next month, right?"

"In a few. September tenth. Are you going to be there?" I could almost see her eyes roll into the back of her head. My mom gave me the look. I backed down. "I mean, if you're coming to the city. I know it's hard with kids."

"I'll talk to Ken."

I nodded and escaped, only to drop right into another conversation I didn't want to be in the second I turned around. A plastic surgeon and his trophy wife were talking to one of my parents' neighbors about the health benefits of Botox. I made a quick excuse and darted to the dining room. Trays of food were out. My mother shooed me off, but I doubled back and grabbed some crackers and a handful of cheese cut into cubes and stars from the kids' table. I stole a glance at my phone and saw a message from Sophia. My heart flipped.

Traveling with my grandmother is proving to be harder than originally planned.

I wasn't expecting to hear from her until Sunday night. *I'm actively avoiding so many people here. I just want food.*

"I've come to rescue you and find some food, too," Ethan said.

I looked up at Ethan guiltily and slowly lowered my phone. "Nothing."

Had I just kept quiet, he would have moved on as though everything was cool. But no, I had to be weird and answer the question I thought he was asking instead. He grabbed my phone out of my hand and held it high over our heads so quickly that I didn't have time to react. I was tall, but he was six inches taller.

He taunted me with it. "It's like we're kids again. Are you texting with a girl?"

"Duh. Now give me back my phone." I rolled my eyes and pretended it didn't bother me that he had the one thing that could destroy me with all ill-timed text to a woman I was desperate to please.

"Let's send her a pic of us. Come on. We're beautiful people." He put his arm around me and held the phone out. "Ready?"

I smiled and stared at my phone. He took a pic of us from a bird's eye view. Cue Starr, my mom, Rob, and a waiter who photo-bombed on the second one. It was a great picture, and I couldn't wait to send both photos to Sophia, but I just took my phone when he handed it to me and slipped it into my back pocket.

"Who's the girl? And why don't I know about her yet?"

I sat at the table with Ethan and Starr and told them I was moving slowly with Sophia.

"Do you have a picture of her?" Ethan asked.

"No. She took one of us but didn't share it with me."

"Just send her one of us and ask her to return the favor."

Ethan's suggestion had merit. I found the pic of just me and Ethan and sent it to her. I set my phone on the table as if her response didn't matter, but I glanced at my phone more than I should have. Sophia was starting to get under my skin more than I was willing to admit. When I saw bubbles, my stomach dropped, and every second felt like a minute. I stopped breathing when she sent me the photo of us from the Centennial Wheel. It was a great one. She looked perfect, and I looked pretty damn good, too.

"Give it here, cheeseball," Ethan said.

He motioned for my phone, and I gladly handed it to him.

He let out a low whistle. "She's into you?"

I threw a grape at him. "Totally. Look at me. I'm the whole package."

"She looks like she's the whole package."

"True. She really is everything I've ever wanted." I took

the phone from him, shot off a quick text to her, and put my phone back in my pocket. "We met on the train." I wanted to talk to somebody about Sophia who didn't know my predicament and who could just appreciate my fairy-tale beginning with a beautiful woman.

CHAPTER TWELVE

Come on. Where's your sense of adventure?" I handed Sophia a helmet, which she immediately waved off. She threw her hands into the air in disbelief.

"First of all, I'm wearing a dress. Secondly, you should've asked me. You can't just show up on a crotch rocket and expect me to jump on the back."

She looked beautiful. Her pale skin turned pink across her neck and shoulders, and her light-blue eyes flashed with anger. I cringed at my lack of sensitivity. I'd thought it would be cool and impressive to show up on a motorcycle.

"This is hardly a crotch rocket, but you're absolutely right. I should have checked. I just figured because you had a hard time with Lucy, this might be more exciting." I patted the seat of the Yamaha FJR1300. It wasn't a glamorous bike, but it was the most comfortable for two riders. She would have died had I shown up on the Ducati. I pulled out my phone.

"What are you doing?"

"I'm ordering an Uber."

She covered my phone. "I can drive. You can leave the bike here."

I held her hand softly. "I'm really sorry. Next time I'll ask." I pulled her gently toward me. "Is this strike one?" I tried my best to look chagrined.

"This is strike two," she said.

I couldn't tell if she was joking. "Wait a minute. What was strike one?"

"Stalking me."

I laughed. "I thought we agreed I wasn't stalking you. I was merely interested."

"Very."

I gave her a single nod. "Very interested in finding out who you were, and I believe you said it was somewhat flattering."

She shrugged and touched the handle on Gerty, my Yamaha. "A tiny bit, yes."

"Maybe one day you'll take a ride with me?"

"With like a two-week notice and just around the neighborhood." She smiled at me for the first time tonight. "And I'm going to need a copy of your driving record. You know, just in case you're too dangerous." She quickly added. "On a bike. I'm too pretty to die or mess this up." She pointed to her face and winked.

A joke. Sophia Sweet had humor. It made me want to be around her even more. "I promise I'm the best driver of all things." I held up my fingers and counted. "Forklifts, golf carts, old pickup trucks, motorcycles, even cars." I put both helmets in the saddle bags and pushed my bike to the side of Sophia's cute small Tudor house. I was dying for a tour, but we would have time for that later. Maybe later tonight.

"Okay. You win. You're right. You've kept me safe, and I've seen you do a couple of three-sixties on the forklift."

I straightened my clothes and tried hard not to run my hand through my hair. "Oh, you saw that, huh?"

"I'm surprised your boss didn't reprimand you."

"To be fair, nobody was around, and I was testing the steering." It was new and I was breaking it in. I wasn't showboating either. Learning new equipment was an important part of any business, and I took great pride in knowing how to run all the equipment at Tuft & Finley.

"It looked like you were enjoying yourself." She put her hands on her waist and lifted her eyebrow challengingly.

I winked. "Come on. Let's go. I don't want to miss our reservation."

"Do you want to drive since you know where we're going?"

"If you trust me, that would be great."

She handed me the fob. I unlocked the car and held the passenger door open for her. Her thank you was more of a whisper, and my confidence grew. I could tell my nearness was affecting her.

"The restaurant isn't too far away. Have you been to Moreno's?" I'd given Sophia several options, and when she picked Mexican, I knew the perfect place.

Sophia shook her head. "But I made dessert for us based on dinner."

"Whatever it is, I'm sure it's delicious." Sophia's Collection had been such a hit at the party last weekend. All her business cards had disappeared, and several people commented on how tasty and beautiful the chocolates were. "Tell me how a person becomes an official chocolatier?"

"Besides my entire upbringing? I went to culinary school and became a pastry chef. I studied chocolate with some of the best chocolatiers across the country. My grandparents had a system of making chocolate that was more or less candy, but real chocolate takes time and finesse. I had to learn it. That's why I want to push these artisan chocolates, because they are so different."

"Does that mean you'll tell me what's for dessert?"

She shook her head. "That's a surprise."

"Oh, I like surprises."

By the time we reached Moreno's, Sophia was leaning back in her seat smiling faintly. She was relaxed. The anger from the misunderstanding earlier had dissipated. That could have gone much worse. I felt like a jerk. "Here we are."

"I can't remember the last time I had Mexican food."

I held the door and followed her into the dimly lit restaurant that smelled like chicken and salsa. "This is my favorite place. Who doesn't love Mexican?" We were seated immediately. After ordering margaritas on the rocks and guacamole, I leaned forward to get to know the beautiful woman sitting three feet away a lot better. "How do you feel about art?"

"What kind of art?"

"Any kind of art. Painting, sculpting, music. Do you like museums? Theater? Movies? Who's your favorite band?"

She waved her hands at me. "Hold up. One question at a time. Please."

She had the greatest smile. I could feel myself melting right there at the table. "Okay. Do you like paintings?"

"Yes." She nodded firmly.

"Do you like sculptures?"

"Yes."

"Pottery? Origami?"

"Yes, and yes. I'm sorry I'm not better at dropping names. My world has been candy and chocolate forever. Tell me about you. What's your favorite kind of art?"

I admired how easily she turned it on me. "I love all of it. Sculpting, welding, pottery, even graphic design."

"But you have only one painting in your apartment."

"It's a work in progress."

The waiter delivered our drinks, and I paused my explanation of my lack of decor to toast Sophia. "Here's to the first date of many. Thank you for tonight, even though I know you're super busy with Sophia's Collection, which I predict will be a smashing hit."

With her glass still tilted toward mine, she flashed me a smile that made me weak-kneed. "Here's to chances. For both of us."

Her toast didn't give me the warm fuzzies, but I took it. I clinked my glass to hers and sipped the smooth lime and tequila. I kept eye contact with her until she looked away. "Okay, since you aren't a sculpture or painting aficionado, tell me about music. What kind of music do you like?"

"Don't laugh, but I love eighties music. Give me Madonna, Bon Jovi, Whitney Houston, Cher, Salt-N-Pepa, and so many more."

I laughed. "Seriously? That's so awful and good at the same time."

"Oh, and I love Bob Marley."

"Now that I can get behind."

It took the waiter only one minute to prepare our guacamole tableside. I waved off the cilantro and served Sophia a scoop after he left. "I love everything about this place, but the guacamole is my weakness."

"I forget how much I miss restaurants," Sophia said.

"You don't eat out a lot?"

"I usually grab takeout or cook. I'm the most boring person on earth."

"I don't think so at all. I think you are brave and beautiful, and I'm excited to really get to know you. The side that you haven't shown anybody in a long time," I said.

Our dinner seemed lightning fast as we darted in and out of conversations. I hoped once she got comfortable with me again, like she did the night we had drinks, our chemistry would bubble up, and I wasn't wrong. There was some flirting, albeit reserved, and I respected her boundaries. I knew she was delicate, even though she pretended she wasn't. I paid for dinner and suggested we free up a table by going back to her place for whatever dessert she had waiting for us.

"Thank you for trusting me with your car." I pulled into her driveway and handed her back her fob. "And I have to say, I adore your house from the outside. I'm sure the inside is just as wonderful." I followed her up the path and waited for her to unlock the door.

"I love the neighborhood. I feel like I really belong to something here," she said.

I wasn't prepared for the splash of warm colors inside.

Sophia struck me as a person who liked different shades of gray with a drop of color. I was greeted with the exact opposite. Reds, oranges, yellows, and taupe made up the sitting room, with a library of books that made my jaw drop.

"I'm not even three feet inside, and I already love it. I thought you didn't like to read much?"

She turned, and I almost bumped into her. "I don't read romance, but I read a lot of other things."

I looked at her full mouth, then back up to her eyes. "Do you care if I take a look?" Her mouth was slightly open and her pupils dilated. She wanted me to kiss her. I was going to, but not until neither of us could stand it anymore. She nodded and I slipped into the room. "This wingback chair is gorgeous. Everything about this room is my favorite." I ran my fingertips along the shelf of murder and mystery books and shook my head at her. She smiled and leaned against the door frame, waiting for me to finish my own tour of the room. "You have a shelf for geography?" I could probably name twenty countries on a map. Sophia could probably name them all. I looked at her again. "Political autobiographies? Do you like politics?"

She shrugged. "There's a lot more to the house that I would love to show you when you get a minute," she said.

For a split second, I forgot she was there. I found an old Mark Twain book that I opened and regretted immediately. "Oh. This is an old book. Why don't you have a cover on it?" I carefully closed it and turned it over to inspect the spine.

"It's not in the greatest shape. Plus, what good is having a book if you can't read it?"

"Good point." I slipped the historical gem back in line with the rest of her American classics. "Show me the rest of your house." The tour lasted about fifteen minutes. It would have been only five, but I had several questions about how and why she did certain things. I was curious by nature, and even more intrigued because it was her.

"Are you a coffee-at-night kind of person?"

Sophia pulled a beautiful cake from the refrigerator. I leaned over her shoulder to admire her work.

"That's gorgeous. How do you even expect us to eat that?" I couldn't tell if the sweetness I was smelling was her or the cake. For a brief moment, she leaned into me. Her shoulder pressed into mine, and her ear was a few inches from my mouth. If she had turned to face me, our lips would have brushed. I took a step back to give myself a break. The old me would have kissed her, but the new me wanted to take my time. I wasn't big on first kisses, but I knew to be gentle with her, so our first kiss was going to be memorable.

"It's Tres Leche Pastel. Since we were going to a Mexican restaurant, I wanted to keep the theme going."

"It looks delicious, and yes, I would love a cup of coffee." I liked that she was still wearing heels, even in her own home. The clip-clip of them on the tile floor was sexy. Too bad she was on the other side of the island so I couldn't admire her legs. She slid sugar and creamer over to me, followed by a dark, rich cup of coffee that smelled heavenly. I took a sip and sighed happily.

"No sugar?"

I shook my head. "I'll get the sweetness from the cake." I watched her expertly cut into it. It looked moist. I waited to take a bite until she sat across from me at the island. I couldn't help but moan at the perfection in my mouth. It was creamy, soft, sweet, and I wanted to shovel the entire piece into it. "Soph, this is fantastic. Maybe you should add cakes to your menu, because this is the best thing I've ever tasted."

"Thank you. I'm glad you like it."

"It's perfect. Really."

She offered me a second piece, but I declined. I had eaten too much tonight, which was mistake number one on a date. Although I knew nothing was going to happen, I didn't want to be miserable while we made small talk.

"Let's relax in the living room. Unless you want to go outside?"

"No. There are too many bugs, and it's still pretty warm out." Honestly, I didn't want to be dripping sweat. I still looked good, but that was only because of the massive amount of hair product and the air-conditioning.

"Agreed. Can I get you anything to drink before we get comfortable?"

At the look she sent me, chills raced down the back of my neck and arms. "Maybe just ice water." She poured herself a glass of Vengeance Red Zinfandel and followed me into the living room. "The library is probably more comfortable, but I don't want to lose you to the books."

I smiled. "I'll see the library another time. Tonight is about relaxing."

She sat on the opposite side on the couch and crossed her legs. Of course, I looked. Everything about her screamed "look at me," from her curled hair, to her peep-toe heels and pedicured toes. I sat on the couch and draped my arm casually on the back cushion. She leaned slightly closer to me, holding her glass of wine with the tips of her fingers. We talked for a solid two hours before I finally stood and announced it was probably a good idea to leave. "Tomorrow is an early day for both of us. Walk me out?"

"Are you too tired to ride?" She had genuine concern on her face.

"Not at all. One day when you trust me, we will go for a ride, and you will see how invigorating it is."

"I'll need to change my wardrobe. I can't imagine wearing a dress on a motorcycle," she said.

I fingered the fabric of her dress. "It's not tight on you, and it might ride up a bit, but the person who's most interested is going to be in front of you."

"Good point, but will it be a distraction?" Was she flirting?

"It will definitely be a distraction. A nice one." We were close but not close enough. I pulled my helmet from my saddlebag and straddled my bike. "Thank you, Sophia, for having dinner with me and baking a delicious cake. I hope we can do it again very soon." She bit her bottom lip as if she had something to say to me but didn't know how to open up. I let her squirm uncomfortably for about two seconds before I crooked my finger at her. "Come here." I playfully pulled her closer and slipped my hand behind her neck.

She leaned over, and when our lips finally touched, everything happened in slow motion. I lost track of time. I almost melted at how soft and warm her lips were. Our lips moved perfectly together, as if we'd been kissing forever. I sucked in her bottom lip and ran my tongue along her top one. Her hand pressed on the back of my neck and the other below my collarbone. I could feel her passion under the restraint of our first kiss. Her body shook ever so slightly, and a small sigh escaped when I finally ended it. "A perfect kiss to finish a perfect evening."

I really wanted to march her back inside, kick the door shut behind us, and make love to her on that couch. I winked at her and slipped on my helmet. I rolled my bike quietly down the driveway, waiting to start it until I hit the asphalt. The kiss shook me. I wasn't prepared for such passion from her. She was very guarded, so to feel the heat she was capable of gave me chills the rest of the ride home.

CHAPTER THIRTEEN

W hat a gorgeous day," I said.

I knocked on Kelsey's desk to get her attention. She was nose deep in her phone and didn't hear or see me come through the front door. She looked up guiltily and put her phone in her desk drawer. I lifted my eyebrow at her and nodded. I didn't mind if employees were on their phones, but I didn't like them, especially the receptionist, to completely miss somebody walking into the business.

"Good morning, Nico," Kelsey said.

I waved behind me, refusing to let her bring me down. I practically skipped to my office, dumped my bag, and headed for the kitchen. I needed coffee immediately. Last night was a late night with Sophia, and I'd been so full of positive energy I couldn't sleep. I worked on my latest sculpture, sketching changes and adding more emotion. Finally, I dropped off around four in the morning. When the alarm shrilled at seven, I popped up like I'd slept a solid eight hours.

Trish bumped her hip against mine while she poured herself a cup of coffee. "I already know you had your date last night with Sophia. Thanks for telling me."

I grabbed a doughnut and motioned for her to follow me to my office. Too many ears were nearby, and I didn't want my social life splashed around the office. "So, you talked to Mom, huh? I'm sorry. I should've told you. It happened so fast."

I wanted to do something without her helicoptering me and offering suggestions. I loved her, but sometimes she went too far. "I showed up on Gerty, and she flat-out refused."

"Are you serious? You didn't ask her first?"

I smiled sheepishly. "Yeah. That was a shot in the dark."

Trish flopped down onto my couch. "Had you told me first, I would have helped you make better decisions." She crossed her arms and stared at me. "Okay. Tell me everything."

I sat across from her, sipped my coffee, and described the evening. "It always takes Sophia a few minutes to warm up to me, but once she does, our conversation is great."

"Is she just super guarded or wary of you? I mean, she can't possibly know about your past already."

I tossed a crumb of the doughnut at her and scowled. "Ouch."

She sat up. "I mean, I wonder how big your world is and if you know some of the same people or have even dated the same people."

I shoved the rest of the doughnut into my mouth and held up my finger for her to wait for my answer. "She's an introvert. And a workaholic. Her best friend is married with kids, and she doesn't get to see her very often. She said she doesn't have time to date."

"Maybe that's true, and she doesn't date but has relations to satisfy her lustful cravings." Trish delivered the line with dramatic flair. "I mean, come on. Everyone has time to date. She's beautiful. Why hasn't anyone nabbed her? Is she really an ice queen?"

There was the opening I needed. I leaned back and smirked. "I felt her melt when we kissed."

"Shut up." Trish's eyes flared, and she squeezed my knee. "Tell me now." Even as hard as Trish was about business things, she was a die-hard romantic inside. "Who initiated? Who ended it? Just one kiss or like throughout the night?"

"Even after the whole screwup with the bike, she still wanted to go on the date with me. I ended up driving her car to Moreno's. We had a nightcap back at her place."

"Oh?"

Trish's grin made me smile. I shook my head. "Nothing happened other than the amazing kiss. And it was only one, but a long one. A nice one. The kind that made me want to go back inside, but I respectfully left," I said.

She clinked her coffee cup against mine. "Atta girl. Respect."

"I really like her. I know something good can happen, so I don't want to screw it up."

"Well, you've already screwed yourself. You know you're going to have to tell her who you really are."

Kelsey interrupted to announce our eight-thirty appointment in the conference room.

I stood. "I'll tell her in good time." A mixture of a growl and a groan followed me into the conference room. We had narrowed down Anna's outside sales-rep position to two candidates: Neville Johnson, a business major from Northwestern who had worked at Boise Cascade for five years, and Julia Newport, a communications major with a similar background. Both had a lot of outside sales experience and were impressive in person. It was going to be a tough decision. "Good to see you again, Neville." I shook his hand and sat across from him. Trish did the same and took the seat next to me.

"What's your favorite packaging that we've done?" I wanted to find out if he knew our product like he claimed to, and where to put him so he could start strong and continue from there.

"I like Chicago's own Dugan's Dairy. The packaging and artwork are very creative, and I can't help but smile when I see it in the dairy aisles."

He had a comfortable smile and a trusting face. His use of hair product rivaled mine, and his wardrobe was impeccable. He was my favorite. Plus, he'd picked one of my favorite clients. It was a paper milk carton that resembled a cow. It was amusing and purposely childish, designed for toddlers who drank whole milk with vitamin D and other essential vitamins. It was a hit with families of small children. Their two percent and skim-milk products weren't designed as whimsically but still had a similar design on a regular-shaped carton.

"Nico designed that line."

"I love it. That's the kind of milk we use in our family," Neville said. He showed us a photo of his two young sons, blond like their mother, with dimples like their dad. Both Trish and I nodded at the picture, confirming their adorableness in unison.

"You have such a beautiful family," Trish said. She asked several questions about his likes and dislikes regarding his present job, asked again why he was looking, and where he saw himself in five years and ten years.

I hated interviewing, but I sprinkled in a few questions. "Do you feel that working for a smaller company will stifle you?" We were a medium-sized company with about seventy employees.

"No. The opposite, actually. I love sales and developing relationships with people. But my kids are young, and I want to be able to go home to them every night and tuck them in."

That answer worked for me. Neville had had only two jobs after college. He wanted to put down roots in the area. His family lived north of the city, so his support group was close. "Well, we should be near a decision by Friday, and we'll give you a call either way." That was Trish's job. She called all the candidates, either extending offers or turning them down. We shook hands again and walked him out.

"Oh, I just transferred Ms. Sweet to your voice mail, Trish," Kelsey said.

That remark got my attention. I turned to Trish, who shrugged. Then I followed her back to her office. She teased me at first by not putting the phone on speaker, but finally she hit the button after listening to the message first.

"Sounds like she's ready to expand."

"She said she got some business from Mom and Dad's party.

I'm sure she's heard from some of the hotels and stores if she's placing another order." I tried to keep the excitement out of my voice. It was a sizable order that included two different-size boxes for just the bonbons, and more samples boxes. It took all my effort to not text Sophia about it. That would have blown my cover wide open.

"I'll call her back after we're done discussing Neville," Trish said.

I almost pouted. "Okay. I really like him. I mean, I like Julia, too. Ack! This is so hard."

"They're equally matched." She checked the time. "Okay. We have an hour before Julia's second interview. Is there something you don't like about Neville?"

"I can't think of anything. He's tight with his family, he knows something about our business, and everyone gave him a glowing recommendation. He's young, hungry, and loyal." He was only looking for a new job because his company was relocating, and he wanted to stay in the Chicago area.

"I agree. He seems perfect, but let's not jump to a decision until after we meet with Julia again."

"What does Anna think?" I asked. We saw less and less of her as she adjusted to pregnant life.

"She's left it up to us."

I groaned. "I hate responsibility."

Trish shooed me out of her office. "That reminds me. I need to go call a certain person, and you need to do something artsy."

I groaned again. "Okay. Let me know when Julia gets here. You know how lost I get in my projects." I lost track of time so easily when I was working. Even early this morning I felt like the time flew while I was sketching. I wanted to weld, but welding was a loud process, and I was warned on several occasions that quiet time started at midnight and lasted until eight in the morning. I slipped into my office, eager to text Sophia for so many different reasons.

Thanks again for last night. I had a good time.

When she didn't respond right away, I put my phone down. She was probably talking to Trish. I opened my project files and reviewed the work that Shelby had done. It was good. She was thorough, careful, and a tad slow, but only because she was just learning the business. I already knew I was going to hire her full-time.

Sophia wrote back. *It was a nice evening. I still can't believe you showed up on a motorcycle and expected me to get on the back.*

Gerty. She has a name. And you've already told me that you would. I'm holding you to it. I added a motorcycle and smiley-face emoji.

Busy morning. I need to get moving. Lots of chocolates to make. I pulled three chocolatiers from Sweet Stuff just to help me fill orders!

Great problem to have. Good luck. Call me later?

Will do. Bye.

I wanted to offer to help, but honestly, I knew I wouldn't be able to do much other than fill the samples boxes. I jumped online and was impressed with her updated website. I didn't know who was taking the photos, but they were doing an excellent job. Her logo really popped, and whoever had designed the website did an amazing job.

"Julia Newport is here."

Kelsey's announcement surprised me. Where had the last hour gone? "We'll be right there." I stood and slipped my jacket on. Trish and I met in the hallway on our way to the conference room.

Julia was energetic, bubbly, and even though she interviewed well, Neville was the clear candidate for the job. When Julia left, Trish agreed.

"She's great, but I think we would be a stepping-stone for her. We need somebody who wants to be here."

Trish and I rarely argued, especially at work. We squabbled at family functions, but work was a different animal for us. Anna left most business decisions to us unless it involved money for new equipment or a major purchase. She was the financial backing Tuft—the original name of our fledgling business and an old family name. We gladly accepted her money and threw her last name on the business.

"Go make the call." I nodded at her and returned to my office. The weight of the day and lack of sleep were starting to sink in. I told Kelsey to hold my calls. I locked my door and fell onto my small couch. I was anxious to get back to my art, but I was too exhausted to even think about Jet Pen or any other little project going on.

My cell phone started ringing, but the sound was muffled. I blinked and realized I'd fallen asleep facedown on my couch. My phone, in my front pocket, vibrated, along with blaring out the most annoying ringtone Trish could find. We knew each other's passwords, so what had started out as fun secret photos when we were away from our phones had turned into changing ringtones and contact photos. "Baby Shark" continued to annoy the shit out of me until I pulled it out of my pocket. "Lindsay. Hey. What's up at the gallery?" I cleared my throat a few times.

"Did I wake you?"

"It was a long night."

"I wanted to get together with you and Trish and talk about your exhibition."

I rubbed my eyes and looked at the time. I'd been asleep for over an hour. My schedule was all screwed up. I needed to focus and get those pieces done, but I couldn't let my company suffer either. Now I was behind. "Yeah, sure. When are you thinking?" We came up with a time to meet after hours at the gallery.

❖

"I think we'll be at full capacity," Lindsay said.

"No way," I replied.

"It's true. There's a lot of interest for your show. And the teasers you have on your Instagram account are brilliant." She made an okay sign with her forefinger and thumb.

Trish jumped in. "She won't let me post her gorgeous face, so I've been settling for welding pics, close-ups of what's going to be at the show, and tools of the trade."

"I think it's great. Intriguing, mysterious, and talented artist. Everyone is going to want to meet the elusive Nicole Briar. Plus, this entire look will sell."

When I sold my first sculpture to my friends who own the coffee shop, we didn't include a nameplate or anything. I wasn't expecting anyone to notice it. Then a reporter from the *Sun-Times* called and asked for my name. I didn't want to say Nico Marshall. Too many people knew Nico Marshall. So I gave them my first and middle names.

"I'll be ready. I think you'll be pleased with my final two pieces."

"I have no doubt. Now, let's talk about food and drink. Champagne? Finger foods? Here's a list of what the caterer has available."

Trish and I put our heads together and perused the menu. We picked trays of eight different cheeses, two white wines, one red, and one champagne. I told her I wanted to use Sophia's Collection for the sweet menu. I handed her Sophia's business card and told her to order whatever. Lindsay would get a hefty commission if even half of my sculptures sold.

When we got out of there, I was pumped. "Trish, if my art sells, I don't know what I'm going to do."

She put her arm around me. "You're going to be famous, baby sis. I can feel it."

CHAPTER FOURTEEN

Iwasn't sure what kind of beer you like, but based on the ale we had last week, I decided on one of Chicago's finest." I held up a six pack of Fist City Pale Ale in my left hand. "And if I was wrong, then I have this." I held up a six pack of Berghoff local artisanal root beer in my right hand.

"Both are perfect. Come on in."

Sophia stepped aside and patted down her hair. "I just got home two minutes ago. I haven't had a chance to change or get ready."

I immediately put the beverages down and held both her hands out away from her body to playfully give her a look-over. I smiled when I saw bare feet and rose-pink toenails. My favorite heels were kicked haphazardly in a pile by the front door. "You look great, but I get that you want to change." I pulled her just a tiny bit closer and softly kissed her cheek. "You smell delicious though. Today was caramel and chocolate day."

She leaned back in surprise. "How do you know that?"

"I've come to learn all the different flavors you use. But caramel is one of my favorites." I gently let her go. She looked away shyly, as though she wasn't comfortable getting compliments.

She nodded. "I spent all day making Fleur de Sel chocolates. I got a rather large order that I need to fill by next week."

"That's great. I'm so happy things are picking up for you.

Did you get a lot of business from your samples?" I followed her into the kitchen, eager to find out who placed the order. Trish and I had decided to place an order for fifty sample boxes to hand-deliver to customers when we introduced our existing customers to Neville, but I didn't think she'd placed the order yet.

"I did. Let me go change into something more comfortable, and then I'll tell you all about it. Give me five minutes."

I watched her walk slowly out of the room and up the stairs, excited to see what "more comfortable" was to Sophia. I was wearing jeans, a button-down shirt with the sleeves rolled up, and loafers. My outfit was a little bit nicer than I would've worn to hang with Trish or my parents. She left a menu on the kitchen island for me to peruse. True to her word, she was back in five minutes.

"Wow." That was all I could say. The suit had been replaced with black yoga pants that showed off her curves and a long-sleeved, light-blue T-shirt with the name of a 5k run she did last year.

"What?" She touched the back of her neck and tugged a few hairs that had escaped her ponytail.

"Adorable doesn't even begin to explain." I couldn't stop my cheesy smile. She was a combination of cute, sexy, and something else. When she smiled, it came to me. She was warm. Gone was the emotionless shell of a struggling businesswoman, replaced by somebody I really wanted to get to know. "What a nice change." I didn't want to push it. After such a busy week, Sophia probably needed the night to rest, but I'd asked for another date anyway. She'd surprised me by agreeing to it.

"A nice change?" She smirked.

I smiled harder because she wasn't offended. She wanted me to say the words. "As much as I admire the classy, sexy look in a crisp, clean suit, this casual thing you have going on does funny things to my stomach." I moved closer and slid my hand over hers. "I know you had a rough week, so thank you for agreeing to pizza night."

She linked my fingers with hers. "I decided I needed to make time for myself, too. As much as I want the collection to take off, I need to step away from it." She looked at my mouth. "Plus, I need food and beer."

I slid the menu in front of her and walked around the island so we were on the same side. "Then let's find a pie. For the record, I'll eat anything but onions."

"You don't like onions?"

"Not on date night."

"Oh. Do you have a lot of date nights?"

I looked up at the ceiling as though silently counting. "Including tonight?"

She playfully nodded along.

"In the last eighteen months, I've had two date nights, and they were both with you."

Her jaw dropped open, but she quickly closed it and stammered. "Um. Okay. Because you've been working so hard?"

"I was in desperate need of a break from relationships. My ex was quite the trip and pretty much shredded me, so I needed time to heal." I didn't want sympathy. It was a fact of life. I had healed and was ready to move on. "What about you?"

"My last date was at the beginning of the year. It didn't go well."

My cheesy grin was back. "I'd say I'm sorry, but I'd be lying. Because of your last bad date, I'm here now."

"Let's order dinner and drink beer so we can toast our horrible pasts and celebrate that we're both here today." She handed me a glass for my beer.

I was comfortable drinking it from the can, but Sophia was a bit more polished. I waited until the froth on mine threatened to overflow and tapped against hers. "Here's to date night." I opted for generic rather than emotional because I knew I could push her away by opening up too quickly.

"That's the best you can do?" She shook her head.

"Okay. Then you make the toast."

She rested her hip against the counter and held her glass close to mine. "How about to new beginnings? For both of us."

"Or to just us?"

She tilted her head as if contemplating the phrase and nodded. "To us."

Her eyes never left mine when we sipped our beers. My stomach fluttered when her eyes narrowed. I don't know what she was thinking, but I was tingling at the look she gave me. She put her beer down long enough to order a pizza.

"It'll be here in thirty minutes. Let's go relax in the living room."

"I know I've told you this already, but I really like your house. It's the true definition of charming." I followed her and sat on the couch next to her, but with enough distance between us to not make her uncomfortable. "How long have you lived here?"

"About seven years. I plugged my inheritance into this house. I love everything about it."

"It's so warm and cozy, unlike my place." I was talking about my studio. My condo in the city was full of color and was spacious, but it lacked life. I didn't have any plants or pets. Sophia had a plant on every windowsill in the kitchen and larger plants tucked in corners of the living room, where I imagined they received light during certain parts of the day.

"You just need some art on the walls. I mean, the one landscape you have is beautiful, so you're on your way."

"Apparently, it's not a high priority for me." For the first time, I felt guilty for lying to Sophia about my life. She would probably love my condo. "But I'll try harder. I mean, I live in the art district. I should be able to bargain with my neighbors, right?"

"If you need help picking things out, I'd love to go on a shopping spree with you."

She looked so confident and comfortable sitting there, it was hard not to want to scoot over and kiss those full lips again. Our first kiss had been perfect—under the stars in the heat of the night, her hands on my shoulders and my hand on the back of her neck keeping her close. The way she looked at me now was the same as when we'd said good-bye the other night. Hungry and determined. Tonight was going to be interesting. Our small talk was fun and flirty, but I wanted more. Just as I was about to slide closer to her, the doorbell rang.

"Pizza's here. Surprisingly early."

I sighed and waited for her in the kitchen. "I'm not going to lie. That smells delicious." When she opened the box, I leaned over her shoulder and put my hands on either side of her on the counter. Only a fraction of space was between us. Her movements stopped when she realized she was trapped. I placed a whisper of a kiss on her neck. She tilted her head to the side, affording me more skin. Encouraged, I applied more pressure and worked my way up to her cheek. When she turned, I released the counter and put my hands on her waist. She kissed me slowly. Her hands looped around the back of my neck, and I sank against her. Both of us moaned. She was soft, and her mouth was demanding. Her tongue pressed against mine, circling it, sucking it into her mouth. I was surprised at how assertive she was and took control of the moment. When we finally broke apart, I stumbled back a step. My knees were weak and I felt light-headed. "What are you doing to me, Sophia Sweet?" I cupped her face. She was so beautiful, vulnerable yet strong.

She put her hand on my chest right below my collarbone again. "The question is, what are we doing to one another?"

I kissed her swiftly and pulled back. It would have been so easy to press on and make love to her on the kitchen floor, but I didn't want to do that to our tender relationship. This wasn't one of my one-night stands. She wasn't a woman I met at a bar and followed home, knowing that I could easily score. This was Sophia, the woman who had helped me feel again and made me nervous with just a single look. Nobody in my history had ever had that much power. I hadn't realized it until this moment, and

I wasn't ready for those feelings. "Let's eat before it gets cold." When I pulled away, she looked shocked. I took her hands and kissed the back of them. "I'm sorry. I just want to take my time with you because you mean so much to me, and I always manage to fuck things up."

She squeezed my hands but didn't let me go. "I understand."

I took a deep breath. "It took so long for me to get here, in front of you." I wanted to kiss her again, but it would send me down another spiral. I dropped her hands and excused myself to her bathroom. I needed space. I closed the door and leaned against it. I was expecting light flirting and some soft kisses, but not that powerful explosion. I washed my hands and looked at my reflection. My face and my neck were red from the warmth I was radiating. I wasn't splotchy but flushed. My eyes sparkled and my lips felt swollen. I took another deep breath before I opened the door and returned to the kitchen.

"I fixed you a plate," Sophia said. She wouldn't meet my eyes, so I knew our moment had affected her, too.

"Thank you." I accepted the plate and glass of root beer. "I can't tell you when the last time I had a root beer was."

"Did you want another beer instead?"

I noticed she had a root beer, too. "No. Sweet and savory is perfect. And the pizza looks yummy."

The Chicago Cubs was the only team we both supported, so we put on the game and sat on the couch to cheer them on.

"This new pitcher is on fire," I said.

"I mean, sure, baseball is a pitcher's game, but if you don't have a great defense, you can't win games."

"What?"

"The Cubs won the World Series because of the dynamics of the first and third basemen."

I burst out laughing. "Never in a million years would I have pegged you for a baseball fan."

She looked at me, a tiny crumb on her cheek. I pointed to my own cheek until she got the hint and wiped it off. "If you live in Chicago, you have to be a Cubs fan. I mean, right? We're a baseball city."

"And football, and hockey, and basketball."

"Only baseball counts." She smiled.

My heart fluttered. "Well, then we should go to a game. I have box seats. Let's pick a night or a weekend."

"You can afford box seats?"

I stopped for a moment as I processed what she asked. "Well, Tuft & Finley has box seats and a suite, and they always give tickets to their employees."

"Aren't the games usually packed?"

"Don't worry about it. Here. Let me pull up the schedule, and we can plan our next outing." Trish and Anna let me handle employee relations. Most of the time, we gave away our tickets to boost morale, but usually we waited the week before in case we had to entertain customers. Since we were smack-dab in the middle of summer, it was probably a good idea to get the suite. "How about a week from tomorrow? We're playing the Cardinals. The suite is available."

"Are you serious? That sounds amazing. Yes."

I blacked out the calendar for the entire suite so we would have it to ourselves. I was sure Trish would have something to say about it if she checked. "Done."

"Thank you. That's exciting. I haven't been to a game in years."

I threw up my hands. "How do you even call yourself a fan if you don't go to the games?"

"Nobody ever wants to go with me."

She sounded so sad I took her hand. "I want to go with you. Most of my friends aren't into baseball like they are football or basketball."

"Baseball is so easy. It's easy to learn, easy to follow, and it's the only time when you can eat and drink and not feel guilty."

"Sounds like another dream date for us."

She was still holding my hand. We were a bit too far apart on the couch for it to be comfortable, so I scooted over. She smiled. We watched the entire game holding hands. After she went to get us beers and pretzels, she sat down a little closer than before and reached for my hand once more. The gesture was sweet, but her nearness was driving me crazy. When the game ended, I stood. I was suffocating at being so close to her, and the desire to touch her had finally become too much.

"Are you okay?"

"Do you want to go for a walk? It's a nice night."

She stood in front of me. "Wait. Nico Marshall, are you nervous about being around me?"

"Totally."

"I wish you weren't. I wish you weren't scared of me."

She was in my space, willingly. I held my breath while she ran her fingertip down my cheek and my neck, and then along the vee of my shirt. Being touched was the single biggest turn-on for me. I cleared my throat. "It's not you I'm scared of."

"We can set boundaries, right? Kissing is acceptable, but we won't let it get too far." I discreetly wiped my sweaty palms on my jeans. She was seducing me and I liked it. Her mouth was very close to mine. "I can control myself."

"That's the problem. I don't know that I can." I captured her lips in a kiss that turned passionate very quickly. My body was rigid against her soft, supple one. She wrapped her arms around my back, and I crushed myself against her. I kissed her with an intensity that had been building for hours, weeks, months. She pulled me down to the couch, and I landed between her legs. She wrapped her legs around my waist and dug her fingers into my back. If this was only kissing, I was never going to survive making love to her. She rocked her hips into me, and I pushed into her. It had been a long time for both of us, and I didn't want to embarrass myself by coming like a teenager with the green light. "Wait. Wait."

"What? What?" she whispered over and over before kissing

me again and again. She was driving me crazy. How was my ice queen, who almost didn't give me a chance, holding me flush against her on her couch? She was so passionate.

Resisting her was futile, but I had to try. I didn't want to fall into the same trap I'd been in for the last five years of my life. I either didn't care at all or cared too much. Sophia was going to break my cycle. That was the plan in my head. I scooted her down on the sofa so we weren't on an incline with what felt like seven thousand pillows and kissed her passionately. I only touched her face, and she only touched my back and my neck. Once I realized we weren't taking off clothes or having sex right here, right now, I was able to relax and enjoy the moment. Sophia was so soft, and hearing her moans released adrenaline straight to my heart. It beat furiously, causing me to take deep breaths between kisses.

"Are you okay?" Sophia asked.

My laugh was shaky and more of a small bark. "I'm just overwhelmed. My heart isn't used to this much emotion."

She touched my face and scratched the back of my head with her manicured nails. "This is the best date I've had in a long time, too."

It wasn't an emotional confession, but it still filled my heart. I kissed her smooth neck softly, nipping at her earlobe and finding her mouth again. We continued making out until the time came to either start undressing or leave. I untangled myself from her limber body and leaned up. "I need to go." She touched my lips with her fingertips. "And you need to stop touching me so I can."

She sat up and adjusted her T-shirt. "I know. It's been a while since I've had a fun, stay-at-home night."

I locked my fingers with her. "It was fun. And the Cubbies won. It couldn't have been better."

She raised an eyebrow at me.

"I'm serious. I miss actual dating. Too many people rush into things and forget about the small, important things like soft touches, holding hands, and respect." I sounded so hypocritical. I couldn't remember the last time it had happened for me. I pulled her up so she was in my arms. "Have a good night. Sleep well. I know you have a lot to do this weekend."

"You have a good weekend, too. I'll text you in the morning."

I kissed her softly before I left her house. Her last words to me made me smile. She was already thinking about tomorrow.

CHAPTER FIFTEEN

It took about ten minutes of begging and a few stolen kisses at Sophia's work to get her to commit, but I got her to agree to take Gerty to the game. It was going to be a hot day but cloudy, so we wouldn't feel the sting of the sun. I pulled into her driveway, grabbed my extra helmet, and jogged up to the front door.

"Hi." She was wearing shorts, a Cubs T-shirt, and sandals. It was the perfect baseball-game attire. It was not the perfect motorcycle-riding attire.

"I have a cap, too, but I didn't want to put that on since I have to wear a helmet." She screeched playfully when I handed it to her.

"It'll be fine. I'm an excellent driver, and Gerty is reliable and safe." I kissed her softly. "You look beautiful and like a true Cubbies fan." She was the quintessential girl next door with her long hair pulled back in a ponytail, very little makeup, and a body I couldn't wait to feel again.

"I'm wearing shorts only because I could use a little bit of color." She looked down at her pale legs. "And I'm bringing sunscreen because I don't want to burn."

I didn't have the heart to tell her that suite seats were inside and the twelve that were outside were in the shade. The only sun she would get was from the ride to the stadium or if we walked around the ballpark. "I don't recommend wearing shorts on a motorcycle. It's safer to wear jeans and shoes. Just put your shorts and sandals in a bag. And go ahead and rub some sunscreen on. Even though the sun isn't shining, you can still fry to a crisp."

"That makes sense. I didn't realize motorcycles had so many rules."

"I'm a good rider, but I can't account for everyone else out on the road," I said.

She looked me up and down. "Are you changing into shorts too? And how are you so tan when you work long hours?"

I pulled her into my arms. "I spend a day here and there at the lake. Personally, I love your pale skin, so protect it." Our kiss was perfect, with just enough heat to make me want more, but cool enough to make me stop. "Are you ready to trust me with your life?"

She playfully tapped my shoulder. "Yes. I trust you." She repeated herself. "Let me change real quick."

"We can put some other clothes in the saddlebag." I watched as she jogged up the steps. "You're going to love riding and insist we take Gerty on every date, even during the winter."

Sophia laughed. "I doubt that will happen." She returned in less than a minute, wearing jeans and athletic shoes. She held up the bag with her shorts and sandals. "Let's get this over with before I talk myself out of it."

I strapped the helmet to her head and gently tapped the top twice. "Let's go." I grabbed her hand and gave her a few quick rules. "Follow my body. If I lean, lean with me. Hold on to my waist or shoulders. Your seat is a bit higher than mine, so whatever you're comfortable with, okay? I promise to drive slow." I was so excited I could barely stand still. I got on first and held the bike steady while Sophia climbed on, then pointed to where her feet should go and started Gerty. The sound was so powerful yet relaxing. I turned on the microphone so Sophia could hear me. "Are you ready?" She tapped my shoulder and gave me a thumbs-up. "You can talk. I can hear you."

"Oh."

Her laughter gave me tingles. She was excited about our

adventure. I pulled slowly into traffic, letting her get used to cars around us. Sophia lived close to Wrigley Field, so I stayed off the highway and took Broadway to Addison, which was about a thirty-minute ride. Sophia pointed to things she loved about the city and all the places along the way that she liked to visit. She held me tighter when we got into baseball traffic. Once we reached the gate, I flashed them my parking pass, and they waved us down to the front of the parking lot.

"Wow. Tuft & Finley must really love baseball to have such a nice setup," Sophia said. I parked and shut down the bike, then waited for her to climb off before I put the kickstand in place.

"Come here." I unsnapped her helmet strap and gently pulled it from her head. "How was it?" She threw her arms around my neck and kissed me passionately. I could hear people off in the distance clapping and whooping. I didn't care who saw us. This reaction was better than I'd imagined. "So, you liked it?"

"It was great. I loved it." She melted into me out of embarrassment once she realized the cheering was for us.

"Nico, where have you been?"

My suite neighbor came over to say hello. I'd known him since I was a little girl. With his suite next door, we visited quite frequently. I'd completely forgotten about the regulars here. They could blow my cover by asking a simple question about my life.

"Hey, how are you?" I introduced Sophia and prayed nobody gave anything away.

"I'm great. Want a hot dog or a beer before you go in?" He pointed back at his tailgating setup that was quite impressive, even though he was going to a suite that had barbecue and beer as well. "And where's Patricia? Are she and Rob coming?"

"They won't be here tonight."

"What? The biggest rival in our division, and they aren't here?"

I shrugged and locked up the motorcycle after taking out Sophia's bag. "I think they have a party or something. Okay, we're going. See you up there."

"Nice to meet you, Sophia."

We walked toward the stadium entrance. I looked back over my shoulder, and he gave me a thumbs-up. I waved him off and followed Sophia through the gate.

"So, everyone knows everyone here?"

I nodded. "Most of these people have had season tickets for decades." We got lucky with our suite. My parents owned it and sold it to Tuft & Finley about five years ago. They gave it to us for a steal, but they got to attend whenever they wanted. Thankfully, tonight they were committed elsewhere.

Sophia was too excited to go straight to the suite. She found a bathroom and changed into her shorts and sandals. I shook my head at her and smiled.

"What?" She held my hand as we walked down the corridor of fans buying food, beer, lemonade, and souvenirs.

"I love seeing you so excited. The fact that it's about baseball makes my heart swell."

She nudged me with her shoulder. "It's all about getting to know one another, right?"

"What do you mean?"

"This. Dating. Right?"

I squeezed her hand. "Agreed. And for the record, I really like dating you."

She leaned up and kissed my cheek. "I really like dating you."

I was practically floating. "Do you want to get any junk food before we go up to the suite? I don't think they have cotton candy or slushies."

"I've had enough sugar today. I'm ready for savory."

"Let's go." I ushered Sophia up the escalator and unlocked the suite.

"Oh, my. This is gorgeous."

I stood back and watched Sophia appreciate the suite. She looked over the food. "This is great. Your company goes all out."

"Nico, it's good to see you again."

Our suite host, Sergio, walked in carrying a plate of sliced pineapple, watermelon, cantaloupe, and grapes.

"This is quite a spread here." I high-fived him and offered him a beer, which he declined immediately.

"You ordered all this," he said. He winked. The rule was simple. Whatever we ordered and didn't eat, Sergio and his wait staff got to take home. "Who else will be here?" He had a pen in his hand.

I turned to Sophia. "You should look at the seats outside. Find us spots." I waited until the glass door closed. "It's just us. Nobody else is coming."

"What? Nobody?"

"This is a very important date with a very important girl."

"I see that. What do you need from me?"

I put my hand on his shoulder. "Privacy. Take a break. Take lots of them. As a matter of fact, give me your phone number, and I'll text you if I need anything."

He laughed. "I'm all about finding love. I won't be far away. Have a wonderful afternoon." He nodded and smiled before leaving.

"Where's he going?" Sophia asked as she walked back into the air-conditioned suite.

"I sent him away. Looks like it's just the two of us for now."

"Will more employees show up? If not, this is a lot of food."

I handed her a plate. "Let's get some and head out there. First pitch is in a few minutes."

"I don't know where to start. Everything looks wonderful."

"Nothing says baseball like hot dogs." I fixed a hot dog, added chips to my plate and a few pieces of fruit, and waited for Sophia to pick through the food.

"Or chicken fingers and french fries and a cupcake. That says baseball, too," she said.

I kissed her because she was entirely too adorable right now dressed as an uber Cubs fan. "Agreed. Come on. Let's watch some baseball."

By three, it was hot even in the shade. We sat outside only when Chicago was up to bat.

"I can't believe nobody else is here. What's going to happen to all this food?" She picked a grape off the plate and popped it into her mouth.

"Sergio will take it home to his family."

"Does he have a big family?"

"Six kids and twelve grandkids. This spread won't last the night."

"Aw. That's so sweet. I'm glad it won't go to waste."

"Tuft & Finley always donates the food to either the workers or the local shelters. The entire company donates food to the Community Food Depot every quarter. It makes the employees feel like they're part of the community. They're a pretty great company."

"I'm starting to see that."

The rest of the game was exciting. The Cubs led, then trailed after the Cardinals hit a three-run homer. We sat outside and cheered them on the rest of the way. They won after a sacrifice fly out to right field in the bottom of the ninth. We high-fived the fans around us. Then we grabbed a few cookies for the road and followed the crowd out to the parking lot.

"What a fantastic game," Sophia said. She leaned into me when I put my arm around her shoulder. "Crap. I forgot to change back into my jeans. It might be too hot to ride back in shorts."

"You can change by that tree. I can stand in front of you and block some of the view." I emphasized the word "some," and she surprised me by nodding. She pulled out her jeans and marched over to the tree. I stood in front of her and watched.

"Um, aren't you supposed to turn around?"

"I'm blocking their view." I waved my hand from right to left, indicating the entire parking-lot audience.

"But you're looking right at me. Turn around." She made a circling motion with her finger and smiled at me.

I held out my hands. "Fine, fine. I'll turn around. But I'm

kind of sad that the world gets to see your panties before I do." I gave her my back and widened my stance. After a few scuffling noises, I felt her hands on my shoulders.

"Who said I was wearing panties?"

Instinct, or maybe lust, made me turn around. "Aw, you're dressed already."

She smacked my arm. "I can't believe you turned around."

I pulled her close to me and kissed her. "I knew you had your jeans on. I could see your legs behind me."

"Mm-hmm. Sure. Should I trust you?"

I shook my head. "Definitely not. I'm horrible."

She grabbed my hand. "I doubt that."

I unlocked the satchel and tucked her shorts and sandals safely inside. "Here's your helmet. Make sure it's tight across your head." I put on mine and slipped on sunglasses. The sun pushed through the clouds and started to heat my skin. I attached the sunshade visor to her helmet since she hadn't brought sunglasses.

"It wasn't sunny when we left."

I climbed onto the bike and waited for her to get comfortable. I tapped my helmet. "Are you ready?"

She nodded. "Oh, I forgot. You can hear me." She slid her hands around my waist. "I'm ready."

It didn't take long to get out of the stadium. I chose Lake Shore Drive for the view, even though traffic was more congested there. I knew Sophia was enjoying it. I stifled a shiver when she scooted closer and wrapped her arms tighter around my waist. Today was the perfect afternoon date. I slowly pulled up in her driveway and parked.

"Want to come inside for a bit?"

She bit her bottom lip as she waited for my answer. I was sweaty and sticky and in desperate need of a shower. Plus, I had about five hours of welding time ahead of me. "I wish I could, but I have plans." I inwardly groaned. It sounded like I had a date or something. "I have work."

"On a Saturday night?" She handed me the helmet.

"We have a deadline coming up. I'm sorry." I reached out for her hand and pulled her closer for a kiss. "But I'll call you later tonight?" She stroked my cheek. It broke my heart that she looked so sad, but I had to finish my sculptures. I had five weeks left, and I wasn't the fastest artist.

"Okay. I need to get a good night's sleep because I have to go in tomorrow. I can knock out a lot of chocolates by myself."

I got off the bike and pulled her into a hug. "Listen, today was great. I had so much fun with you."

"The suite was gorgeous. I can't believe nobody else showed up. Thank you for inviting me." She put her arms around my neck and kissed me gently, a hint of intimacy to come. "Be safe going home." She put her hand on my chest below my collarbone again.

I put my hand over hers. "I will. Thank you for taking a chance on the ride. You did great." I put my helmet on and jumped on the bike. I rolled it down the driveway and waved good-bye before firing it up. It had been a great day. Being inspired was a double-edged sword. I desperately wanted to stay and see where the rest of the night took us, but I was also eager to use this energy to start my final sculpture.

❖

I snapped my head up in surprise at the banging at the door. "Nico, it's late. Shut it down."

Ben's voice brought me back to reality. I flipped up my visor and glanced at the time. It was twelve thirty. Fuck. I'd forgotten to call Sophia. I untethered myself from the ladder and opened the door to a very red-faced landlord.

"Shit, Ben. I'm sorry. I've already turned off everything. I just lost my head in there."

"It's okay. I get it. Nervous about your exhibition?"

"No. Not at all. That's just it. I'm invigorated. Inspired." His expression didn't change. "Okay, maybe just a bit."

"You can start again at eight."

I saluted him. He grunted and shut my door. Was it too late to call Sophia? I shot her a text instead.

Lost track of time. I'm sorry. Are you still awake?

No.

I couldn't tell if she was mad or not. I thought that was the end of the conversation, but then I saw bubbles.

I just crawled into bed. I fell asleep on the couch. Baseball games are exhausting.

I pictured her barefoot, curled up on her couch and wearing her cute outfit from today. Maybe with a small, thin blanket she pulled off the back of the cushions.

I know. I feel like I will sleep for days. Get some rest. I'll call you tomorrow.

Good night, Nico.

Good night, Sophia.

I still had to clean up. I plugged my phone into the charger and went back into the studio to look at the piece I was working on. She was beautiful. Her angles and curves were starting to form something I could see. Tomorrow I would spend the entire day working on her. I checked the welds and marked the ones I would smooth out in the morning. By the time I was done with her, she would be over eight feet tall.

As much as I loved *Broken*, this one would be the favorite. I could feel it. I circled it one last time and stripped down before I turned out the lights and entered my living space. As I closed my eyes and felt the first wave of relaxation before I fell asleep, I thought of the perfect title for the final piece in my exhibition.

CHAPTER SIXTEEN

"Hold up. Don't move."

I froze just past Trish's office and leaned back to see what she wanted. "What's up?" I twisted around and entered.

"You went to the game Saturday, right?" Trish didn't even bother looking at me.

"Yes. Why?" I was busted.

"Who'd you invite?"

"Sophia."

"And?"

I leaned against the door frame. "And what? We had fun. And stayed the entire game. We took Gerty."

"Was anyone else at the game with you?"

"Yes. About forty thousand fans. Why?"

She gave me the look and rolled her eyes. "Did you really hog the suite for you and Sophia?"

I sat because I knew it was going to take time for her to get her frustrations out on me. It had been several days since we'd had a discussion about the Sophia Experiment, as Trish called it. Although it stung, she wasn't wrong. "Fine. Yes. I wanted to impress her."

"And she didn't question why she was in a really nice suite with nobody else except you?"

I shook my head. "She never asked a single question." I

waved my hands at her. "Look, Trish. I know you don't believe me, but it's not like it was before. She's different." This wasn't the first time I'd soloed the suite to impress a girl.

"I don't want you to go down the same path again, Nico. And I don't like that you used the company suite for one person."

"Oh, come on. I only go to a few games a year. The rest of the tickets are for the employees or customers. And technically, Sophia is a client, so if you want to call it a business outing, then call it that."

"It was so wasteful."

I threw my hands up. "What do you mean? Sophia's a paying customer, and all the food we didn't eat went to Sergio's family. It was a win-win."

"Okay, okay. Just don't make it a habit." Trish took a deep breath. "How did the date go?"

She was trying to smooth my ruffled feathers. I sighed. "It was a good day. She loved being on the bike."

"Was it a late night?"

"Nope. I dropped her off and went to the studio. I'm finally getting somewhere on my final sculpture." I pulled out my phone, scrolled to a picture, and handed it to her. "This is the last one. I'll end up with nineteen for the exhibition."

"Oh, my God. I love it." Trish zoomed in and out of the picture. "Let me come over and take pics for your Instagram. It's time to really pimp the shit out of it. Six weeks away?"

I nodded. "When are you free?"

"How about tomorrow night? I can pick up Mom, grab some Chinese food, and we can all hang out."

Trish was so proud of me. She could be pissed off by my work at Tuft & Finley or my life choices, but she stood behind my art one hundred percent.

"Isn't it kind of early for Mom to see the rest of the sculptures?"

"She'll be pissed if she has to see them first at the exhibition.

Maybe you can educate her a bit so she can work the room and sell a few for you."

Our mom had the best rapport with all types of people. She could fit into any conversation, regardless of topic. "That's a good idea. Plus, I need some family time. I'm starting to get nervous about everything and am going to need some emotional support."

"I'm texting her now on the thread."

"Boss, am I excused? I got a crap ton of work to do today," I said.

"Yes. No more single dates in the suite. We need it for customers."

I blew her a kiss as I left her office. Things were moving surprisingly well with Sophia. We were legit dating. I texted her daily, and at night we'd talk on the phone. Even through all the sweetness and perfection, my secret loomed over us. I was riding a wave of deception and had no idea how I would break the news to her. Out of guilt and because she was on my mind, I called her.

"What chocolate are we making today?" I asked.

"Hi. We are making blueberry cobbler."

"Wait. That's new. What?"

I heard her smile over the phone. "Today I'm trying different flavors. I have all the chocolatiers filling orders. Sophia's Collection is starting to pick up."

"That's great news! How's Sweet Stuff?"

"It's still doing okay. We get a lot of business on the weekends during the summers, so that carries us during the week."

Her brother hadn't been around since she started Sophia's Collection because her hours were longer and erratic, and he couldn't get away with just taking what he wanted from the cash register when Sophia was there. Whenever she used the chocolatiers for her things, they were paid from her separate account for Sophia's Collection. She wired her brother his paycheck from Sweet Stuff, which was finally starting to gain ground because he wasn't coming in and taking cash whenever he wanted. Sweet Stuff wasn't going to make them rich, but if maintained, it would keep them afloat. Sophia's Collection was a game changer, though.

"Did you look into that tempering machine?" I asked.

"I plan to place an order for it later this week. But I did order more molds and cacao beans."

I couldn't keep up with the chocolate process during the tour Sophia gave me, but I knew she needed more equipment and supplies to meet the growing demands of a new business. She would probably invest in a packaging machine somewhere down the line, but in the meantime, Tuft & Finley would continue to create simple and environmentally friendly boxes.

"Where did you get the cacao beans?" Apparently, cacao beans were as controversial as diamonds. When buying them, Sophia had to ensure they were harvested by paid workers and grown by honest farmers. That was harder said than done. And I thought packaging plants were cutthroat.

"Brazil and Madagascar. They should be here by the end of the month."

"If you need any help, let me know."

"We're good. Thank you. Now, when am I going to see you again?"

I hadn't seen her since the game, which was only three days ago. "Tomorrow I'm having dinner with my sister and my mom, but how about Thursday? Or Friday?" I wanted to see her, but I was scared, too. The guilt was starting to overwhelm me.

"How about Friday? Do you want to come over? I can grill."

"That sounds great. Just tell me what you want me to bring."

"I'll text you later. I have to get back to work."

"Thanks for picking up. It's always nice to hear your voice," I said. Our conversation was light and friendly, so different than when we first started talking. Friday was going to be a nice night. I ran through the text messages on the thread between Trish and my mom and chimed in. I wasn't in the mood to work. Not here at least. I called Shelby the intern for a quick meeting and gave her a cleanup job. I had the concept and sketch design for a natural toothpaste that I felt she could polish. She was excited to be given the opportunity. I shut off my computer and walked out to the warehouse with no purpose other than to kill time.

"What are you doing out here?" Rian yelled from her office.

I looked up and shrugged. "I'm bored. Well, not really bored, just a lot on my mind with the show around the corner. I'm nervous and can't concentrate."

She motioned for me to join her in one of the golf carts. "Well, Boss, let's go for a ride."

I smiled. Racing around on the property sounded like a great way to blow off steam. "How's production? Everything good here?"

"Smooth as silk. How are things in there?" She thumbed back to the office.

"It's great. How's Jim working out?" Jim was the new warehouse manager.

"He seems to know his shit. Nice guy. Hard worker."

"How are you? How's Sarah?" Rian and Sarah had been together a little over two years. They only fought over which Netflix shows to watch and what wine to drink at dinner. Their only problem was me. Sarah was one of my conquests when I was on my self-destructive spiral. We had been on only one date, but it was sloppy and didn't end well. When I met her months later as Rian's new girlfriend, it was extremely awkward. Rian and I limped through it, coldly, but we did it. Sarah wasn't my biggest fan but wasn't a jerk when she visited Rian at work anymore.

"Good. She finally sold her house."

"That's good news. Are you looking for a place together, or what's the plan?"

"We'll start looking this fall. I think she's the one, Nico."

I smacked her knee. "Hot damn, that's good news." I was genuinely happy for them.

"We're both going to be at your opening. Or exhibition, or whatever you call it."

"Thanks. That means a lot to me." What I really wanted to say was hey, don't worry about it, but I needed the support.

"And we've told our friends, so I think you'll have a good turnout."

"Lindsay said she thought so, too."

"Maybe now you can get to a point where you can do your art full time," Rian said.

Everyone always said that to me. I loved Tuft & Finley. I loved art. I was planning to juggle both. "Let's just see how it all plays out next month." The last thing I needed now was a panic attack. "We still have to find somebody to pick up the slack around here."

"What about Shelby?"

"Oh, she'll be full-time after college, but she's a few years from being able to take over and run with it. We'll need another artist to jump right in. I can't handle the workload."

"Didn't you start interviewing?"

"We wanted to get office help, a warehouse manager, and an outside sales rep first. Now that we have them, we'll start the interviews again." Truthfully, I was starting to burn out. So much was going on in my life, I wasn't giving work my full attention.

"I can help you, too. Don't forget that. But in the meantime, I know what will really help." Rian sneaked out of the parking lot and zoomed us to the gas station at the corner. "Sugar. Pure sugar." She sprang for two shaved ices and three packs of gum.

"Three?"

"I'm on week two of zero nicotine, and the only thing that helps is sugar and keeping my mouth busy."

"You quit smoking? Good for you." This was attempt number three.

"I know. Third time's a charm."

"Hey, whatever you need." I wasn't going to judge. "Summer is the best time. You can put that energy and anger into fun stuff like running or sailing or being in one of those Ironman competitions." I always joked that Rian looked like Xena: Warrior Princess, with her long black hair and striking blue eyes. She was tall, tan, and frighteningly built. One year she dressed like Xena at Halloween after we begged her, and I couldn't stop laughing. The resemblance was uncanny. She changed after an hour and warned us never to bring it up again. Deep down, I think she loved the attention. Who wouldn't?

"Thanks for the pep talk."

Rian pulled up next to the front door. "Anytime. Now get to work."

I nodded. "Will do, Boss. Thanks for the sugar rush."

I stopped by Trish's office so we could discuss picking up the interviews again.

"Where did you come from? I thought you were in your office."

"I was. Then went on a joyride for one of these." I held up my shaved ice. "Listen, I think we need to ask the agency for another artist. We need somebody with experience soon. I love Shelby, but I need somebody to pick up the stuff slipping now."

"Nico, we just hired four people. I know we agreed on a fifth, but I don't think we can afford an artist right now."

My shoulders slumped at the news. "Okay. I understand."

Trish walked over to me. "Listen. I'll get with Anna and see what we can do. I know things are tough for you, and you're under a lot of stress, especially with the show coming up."

"Rian offered to help. With her and Shelby I can probably limp along for a month, but we're going to have to really take this under consideration. Especially if Neville hits the ground running like I think he will."

She pulled me into a hug. "We can push out deadlines. Thankfully, a lot of our business right now is repeat."

The rule was to never turn down a job. Especially a new one. We had a team of inside representatives who took care of repeat business, but the new business was piling up. "I'm sure after the exhibition, things will slow down for me."

"If you think Shelby can handle more work, give her more."

But interns had to go back to school. She was still scheduled to work part-time during her last semester, but I would cut her projects down to one at a time. "We have her for only a few more weeks. I don't want to overwhelm her."

"Quit babying her. She's fine. And she's going to be an employee in December. She's hungry and young." She went back around her desk and sat.

"I know. I forgot when I was in my early twenties and invincible. What a different time that was."

Trish snorted. "Let's not go back there. We barely survived."

"Agreed. Okay. I'm going to approve a few things and then leave. My head's not in it today."

"Why don't you make sure you don't have anything pressing and take the rest of the day and tomorrow off? I know the exhibition is creeping up and you have this crazy idea that everything has to be perfect. I'll pick up Mom and we'll see you at six thirty. Okay?"

I leaned across her desk for a fist bump. "Sounds perfect. Call me if you need me."

"You don't mean that. I'd call you every minute of every day."

"Still my favorite sister."

"Still mine."

❖

"I love what you've done with the place, Nicole." My mom turned to admire the new walls in my studio.

"Thanks, Mom. Rob's guys came by and framed in the apartment and painted it. I even have a shower here."

"And furniture so she's not sleeping on that questionable couch in the shared space anymore," Trish said.

Mom turned to me. "Honey, really? That's just unsanitary."

I laughed. "Ben keeps the place relatively clean. Come on.

Let's eat. I'm starving." I opened the paper bag and crunched on an egg roll.

"Do you have plates?" My mom looked around as if she was back in my college dorm. She seemed afraid to touch anything and completely alarmed at the lack of amenities.

"A few. Up in the cabinet." I nodded in the direction of the single cabinet above the sink. It wasn't as if she had several cabinets to weed through to find them.

"Do you need more things for your place?"

Trish laughed. "Mom, this is her work space. Her condo's fully loaded. Let's hurry up and eat so you can see what she's been sculpting the last six months."

She was more excited to show Mom my collection than I was. I thought and overthought all the pieces behind the door until I couldn't stand them anymore. I pushed my plate away. "Okay. I'm full."

Trish put her half-empty plate down on the coffee table. "I'm full, too. Let's go look at Nico's stuff before we get caught up on life."

My heart skipped a beat when I opened the door and flipped on the studio lights. I chewed my bottom lip as I watched my mother circle the statues. Trish put her arm around my shoulders and gave me a squeeze. "Twenty bucks says she starts crying."

"She cries at everything. That's a sucker bet," I said. I was excited, surprised, nervous, and proud at the same time. Seconds felt like hours as my mom stared at each one before she stopped at *Broken*. She waved me over.

"Baby, this is wonderful." She turned to me with tears in her eyes. "And so sad." Her tears fell when she hugged me. I almost cried, too, because she got it. Over Mom's shoulder, Trish's eyes were watering, too.

"Okay, okay. Let me show you the one I'm working on. I should get this done in the next week or so. Lindsay wants to collect them the week before Labor Day and store them at the gallery. Since they're so big, they'll need more handling time."

"Nico, that gives you only four weeks. Will you get everything done? I mean, this is the biggest one you're working on, and I see the outline of her. It's a woman, right?" Trish asked.

I was a little disappointed she couldn't see it fully yet. That was okay. Maybe by the end of next week.

"I'm going to take a pic of you working and post it. Maybe over your shoulder?"

"I'm not turning on the equipment. I got into trouble the other night for welding after midnight."

"Ben's a kitten," Trish said.

"Yeah, but he likes to sleep."

Mom turned her attention back to my work in progress. "This is going to be very tall." She ran her fingers over the base that would eventually be a springboard.

"It's going to be the centerpiece of my show."

"It's amazing, sis. What are you going to call it?"

I wiped my hands on my jeans and took a deep breath. I couldn't look at Trish. "I've been thinking about that and came up with the perfect name." I squared my shoulders and looked them both in the eyes. "Her name is *Thursday*."

CHAPTER SEVENTEEN

It was too hot to take Gerty over to Sophia's, and I only had Lucy with me, so I packed a bottle of wine and a pasta salad from a deli nearby. I said a prayer of thanks when the air conditioner blasted cold air against the heat that swelled inside the truck. The twenty-minute drive wasn't bad. There was always a tipping point in Chicago when summer became too oppressive and people begged for autumn. Today was that day. I didn't mind the heat when I was swimming at the lake or inside a cold bar drinking a beer. Being in a truck with the sun blaring down was miserable. I hated sweating and wrinkling my clothes because of humidity.

I needed to look dashing tonight. I was a butch with curves and muscles and not afraid to show either off in shorts and a short-sleeve, slim-fit button-up. My sandals were comfortable, but I was eager to kick them off. Too bad Sophia didn't have a pool. My building had an outdoor pool on the roof. I didn't use it much and wasn't much of a swimmer. I preferred to hang by the side of the pool and dangle my feet in the water.

Sophia opened the door as I walked up the pathway to her house. "I heard you coming a mile away."

"Come on. Don't hate Lucy so much. She's perfect." I took a moment to look back at my truck. She really was hideous, but reliable. I turned back around and smiled at Sophia. "You look beautiful."

She blushed and stepped aside for me to enter. "Thank you. It's nice to see you again."

I handed her the wine and pasta salad and used both my hands to cup her face and kiss her. It was a soft but passionate kiss. I wanted to get closer, but now wasn't the time. I needed to cool off from the drive and from her body pressed against mine. "It's always great to see you." I looked into her eyes and saw nothing but happiness. No hesitancy, no doubt. Just a beautiful girl who gazed at me like I was her favorite person. "I'm ready to unwind with you."

"Best idea yet. Come on. I need to check on the food."

I watched the sway of her hips under a very thin, cream-colored summer dress with spaghetti straps that crossed her back. She was barefoot and braless. I wondered if she was wearing anything at all under it. Tonight, I was going to find out. "I like that you always wear dresses or skirts."

She looked down as if she'd forgotten what she had on. "Thank you. It's so hot outside that I couldn't imagine putting on pants or jeans."

"Shorts are a stretch, but I don't think you'll ever see me in a dress."

She giggled. "Yeah. I can't even picture it. When was the last time you wore one?"

"Probably my sister's wedding," I said. I did it more for shock value than anything else. I endured a mani/pedi, an updo because my hair brushed my shoulders back then, and wore makeup. A lot of makeup. I refused heels because I wobbled more than I walked and was afraid of busting an ankle.

"I definitely want to see that."

I almost whipped out my phone because I knew exactly where the picture was, but if she saw Trish, that would give my secret away. It was a good way to break the news to her, but I didn't want to ruin the night. I was a selfish asshole. "I'll dig it up. I'm sure my sister has a digital copy somewhere." I needed to change the subject fast. "Do you need help with the grill?"

"Why don't you open the bottle of wine, and we can have a glass while I finish dinner."

She'd told me the menu ahead of time. Lemon-pepper chicken kebabs and grilled squash. I needed carbs so I offered to bring a pasta salad. She'd mentioned homemade vanilla ice cream, but I wasn't going to push. I didn't want to fill up. I followed her out onto her small deck and admired her manicured lawn and garden. She was an expert on the grill and gardening. My parents were going to love her. "This is like a sliver of paradise."

She turned to me in surprise. "What do you mean?"

I waited until she closed the grill cover and pulled her over to me. "Well, your house is lovely, and you have this beautiful garden full of plants and flowers. This isn't something you see in the city."

"Technically, I'm not in the city. And while it's small, it's mine."

"It's the perfect everything." I kissed her softly. She smelled like smoke from the grill and vanilla. She felt warm when she pressed hard against me. Her meaning was clear and I was all in. I moaned when she deepened the kiss and ran my hands down her hips, giving a slight squeeze. She pressed one hand on the back of my neck and the other above the swell of my breasts. I walked her backward until her back hit the sliding-glass door. She grunted and broke the kiss.

"Wait. The food."

I was in a daze, and making love to her was my only thought. "What?"

"I can't burn the food."

I took a step back. "Okay. I'm sorry. You're right. We have all night."

She blew out a deep breath and held her hand near her throat. She looked beautiful aroused. Her cheeks were flushed bright pink and her lips swollen from kissing. I didn't even try to hide my appreciation of her erect nipples that strained against the thin dress. It took all my restraint to stop from pulling it down just to taste her. At least the mystery of what might or might not happen tonight was answered.

"Let me get back to the grill before I burn everything."

Her voice was shaky. I let her go and gave her space. I picked up my wineglass and watched as she worked. "You're very graceful. I noticed that when you were working with the chocolate. You're very comfortable with food."

"I love food. All of it. If I didn't have Sweet Stuff or Sophia's Collection, I'd own a restaurant or be a chef somewhere."

"I won the lottery with you, Sophia Sweet."

She cocked her head and smiled. "What do you mean?"

I took a step closer. "Beautiful, ambitious, and a chef."

She moved the tongs back and forth between us. "Isn't this supposed to be casual?"

I nodded. "You don't think this is more than casual? I mean, you've been to my work and my place, and I've been to yours. One day I'm going to meet Grammy, and you're going to meet my family."

She laughed. "Grammy?"

"Well, what do you call her? Grandma? Nana? Grammy? Grams? I had a Grandma and a Nana."

"She's Grandma." She turned around to the grill and transferred the food from it to a plate. "So, you think this is more than just casual?"

Nothing had happened yet. In my head and in my heart, I was more than casually dating her. I knew deep down that she was more invested than she was letting on. I wouldn't be here on a Friday night watching her cook for me if she wasn't more than a little interested in me. "I think so. I think you know this could be something really great if you're willing to give us a chance."

She handed me the plate. "Let's eat."

"Oh, my God. Are you scared of me? Would you look at that. Sophia Sweet. Scared of little old me." I made a dramatic production of putting both my hands on my heart.

She gave me a look and motioned for me to follow her.

The air-conditioning felt incredible when she opened the door. I pulled my shirt away from my sweaty body and waved it back and forth. "We should stay in the rest of the night. It's awful out there."

"Agreed." She pointed for me to sit at the table.

I couldn't decide if I wanted to pull her close and forget about dinner or play it safe and wait for her to make the first move. Sophia didn't strike me as a person who took control during sex, but so far, I wasn't always great at reading her. "I feel like I've asked you all the questions, but I don't know you as well as I should."

The wine twirled in the delicate glass that she held with her fingertips. She was different tonight. More assertive, more in control. "I would say the exact same thing about you. Tell me about your dreams."

I sat back on that one. "My dreams? I want what everybody else wants. Happiness, love, and a comfortable life."

"Happiness? Define your happiness. What would make you happy?" She leaned forward with her elbows barely resting on the table. It was as if she was baiting me.

"Happiness is finding peace in my heart. It's love. It's finding somebody to do things with, you know? Right now I'm being pulled in so many directions at work that I don't have time like this. Quality time with a woman I admire."

"Weren't they hiring somebody to help you out? Did they do that?"

For a moment I was confused. How did she know they were thinking about another artist for the production team? Then I remembered she thought I worked in the warehouse. "Oh, yeah. They told me they would have somebody mid-September." I was going to hold Trish to that promise. Neville would be able to help Trish's side of the business. Rian had a new warehouse manager for second shift, and the new office manager oversaw the inside customer-service reps and all the assistants. Everyone was getting help except me.

"So, you are going to be spread thin the rest of the summer? That sucks. You work so many hours, and that means you're missing your family gatherings."

"See? You know me. What do you feel like you're missing? You have a friend you don't see very often, and you and your brother aren't close. You deserve more than you have. Next time Rian has a party, I'm taking you to it so you can meet more people," I said.

"That's sweet. I'm alone a lot, but honestly, I'm not lonely. I promise. Some people don't need a lot of friends."

I reached for her hand. "If you got out more and met my friends and family, you would enjoy them." I wanted more from her at this moment. "Does it bother you that I work in a warehouse? Is that embarrassing for you?"

She looked genuinely offended. "Not at all. You're smart and ambitious. Maybe we want different things, but you seem so happy and carefree, and I can't help but admire that about you."

I smiled. That was exactly what I wanted to hear. She liked me for me and not my money or my name or my art. Not that I knew my art was going to take off or change the world, but I had hope. "Thank you. That means everything to me."

She filled our glasses and we finished dinner. I was ready for touching. I excused myself to hit the bathroom and check out how my hair and wardrobe were holding up after the heat and humidity. My hair wasn't as perfect as I wanted, but I still looked good. I rinsed out my mouth and popped in a mint.

Sophia was waiting for me on the couch. She stood when I returned and excused herself. Our hands brushed when she walked by. Now wasn't the time, but soon. My body was humming, and I was anxious for release, but I was going to see how long it would take for her to make the first move. I scooted over when she returned, but she stopped me by bending over and placing both hands on my shoulders.

Did I look at the creamy-white cleavage that was now in my line of vision? Yes. I moaned slightly when she lifted her dress to straddle my lap. I knew immediately that she wasn't wearing any panties. The second I realized she had just given me the green light, my instincts took over. I wasn't going to scare her by tearing off her dress, but I wasn't going to be gentle either. I held her thighs down and slowly massaged the inside of them. Her nails scratched the back of my head and across my shoulders. When she leaned to kiss me, I moved my hips into her ever so slightly. I knew what she wanted, but I needed to build her up.

"Are you okay with this?" I pulled away long enough to get a nod from her. I wanted to hold her in my arms and flip her onto the couch so I was on top, but something made me stay right where I was. Sophia had to control our pace, at least our first time. When she pressed into me, I slid my hands under her dress to pull her closer. She kissed me with hunger and need. She started unbuttoning my shirt. My hands slid behind her until the curve of her hips filled my grip. The fact that I could tear her dress off so easily and have her naked on my lap made my heart flutter. When she had the buttons completely undone and my shirt opened, she pushed my shoulders so I relaxed back on the couch.

"You're so muscular. Look at you. So beautiful and fit. I've wanted to touch you for so long."

Her fingertips brushed over my sports bra and to my abs that twitched under her touch. I was trying not to hyperventilate. My breath hitched and I let go of her. I closed my eyes while her hands roamed my body. When was the last time I let somebody touch me? I was always so quick to get off and take care of my own needs. I wasn't really a selfish lover, but it had been over a year, and I was starving. I dug my fingers into Sophia's plush gray couch and took a deep breath.

When her fingers reached the button of my shorts, I opened my eyes. She unbuttoned them and slowly slid the zipper down. Her hands were so close to my pussy I had to clench my teeth to keep from bucking up. I could feel her slick arousal on my thigh when she pressed against me. That undid me. I flipped her so her back was flat on the couch and my hips were pressed between her thighs.

"I like this much better," I said. Her dress was scrunched around her waist. When her legs hooked around the back of my thighs, I took control. I pushed her arms above her head and straightened her legs out with mine. I didn't want to stop touching her. I kissed a path down to her beautiful cleavage and gently pulled down the dress to taste the sweet, soft skin of her breasts. She slipped her arms out of the dress so nothing was stopping me. "As much as I don't want to stop, can we take this to your bedroom?"

She nodded and slipped out from underneath me. She straightened her dress, locked the back door, and reached out for my hand. "Let's go upstairs."

I kept my other hand on her waist and followed her up the stairs. I turned her right before we reached the bed so she would be in my arms. "I've waited a long time for someone like you." I kissed her possessively while I fumbled to open her dress. I moved with the zipper, dropping to my knees and waiting for the dress to fall away from her beautiful body. For a moment she held it to her, but when our eyes met, she let it go. I held my breath at the beautiful woman in front of me, then placed a soft kiss on her stomach. "You are so beautiful." A switch inside me flipped, and I completely stopped my frenzied need. Every inch of her needed to be appreciated and loved. I ran my hands down her legs and back up when I stood. She pushed my shirt off my shoulders and traced her hands over my breasts and down to my shorts. I slipped them over my hips and kicked them away. I was down to my sports bra and underwear and entirely overdressed. I yanked my bra off and stopped moving when I felt her lips on my collarbone and the soft skin right below it. I placed my hands on her hips.

"I need you naked," she said. Her voice was low and commanding.

I pushed my underwear off and followed her onto the bed.

This moment was everything—our relationship from when she was only Thursday, to tonight when she was Sophia Sweet standing naked and proud before me. I kissed her slowly until her hips rocked against mine and her nails dug into my back, pulling me closer. I slipped my hand between us and moaned when I felt how wet and swollen she was for me. I sucked her bottom lip into my mouth and ran my tongue softly over it. Her soft, whimpering moans turned guttural when I slipped one finger, then two inside. She was tight and firm and pulled at me when I started moving my hand.

"Oh, my God. That feels wonderful, Nico."

I was going to spend the next several hours getting to know what she liked and what she loved. I slowed my hand and sped it up at different intervals. Sophia tossed her head side to side as her orgasm slowly began to build. I stopped moving my hand but stayed inside her. I needed to taste her. I ran my tongue down her neck, down her chest, nipping at the skin along the way. When I reached her nipple, I gently licked it before sucking it into my mouth. I felt her hand on the back of my neck, so I pulled harder until I heard her sharp intake of breath. I thought it was too much, but her growl only encouraged me. I moved my attention to the other nipple, biting, sucking, and soothing it with my tongue. When I moved my fingers inside her again, she jerked so hard I thought I'd hurt her.

"Are you okay?" I asked.

"Don't stop."

I worked my way to the junction of her thighs. The first time I tasted her I almost passed out from the rush of desire that flooded my senses. I had no concept of time. I massaged her, fucked her, and held her legs until she shook uncontrollably. Her clit was swollen, and my fingers were already covered in her juices. She was seconds away from an incredible orgasm. I didn't slow down, and when she finally came, it was the most beautiful thing I'd ever witnessed. Sophia didn't hold back anything. I held her while she rode every wave of ecstasy. She curled into me and waited for her breathing to return to normal before she spoke.

"That was incredible."

"You're incredible." I pressed my lips against her sweaty forehead.

"I don't think this is casual."

I looked down at her. "What?"

"Earlier. You asked if I thought this was just casual. I don't."

I rested my head on my arm and continued to stroke Sophia. "I didn't go into this thinking it was casual. Do you know how long it took me to even get your attention?"

Sophia looked up at me. Even in the semi-dark room, I could clearly see the desire in her eyes. "Tell me when you first noticed me."

"It was a Thursday."

She playfully pinched my arm.

"What? It really was. It was a Thursday, and I was on the L and heard you and smelled you before I even looked up."

"I'm not sure how to take that."

"Let's see. I've known you about six weeks, right? But I was aware of you six weeks before that."

"You're not making sense."

"The way you walk commands attention. It's slower than most people walk, so the clicking of your heels is off somewhat. You know how when you hear somebody and they are walking fast, you're aware of them and wonder who's in such a hurry? Well, slow works the same way."

"I never knew that about myself. I'll try to walk like a normal person."

I brought her hand up to my lips and kissed each finger. "No. It's sexy. I love it. You can never sneak up on me now."

"So, you saw me six weeks before you said anything to me?"

"Technically five, because by the sixth I yelled at you for parking in the wrong spot," I said.

She pulled me down for a sweet kiss. "You barking at me was actually kind of hot."

"I was in work mode. I'm sorry. Truthfully, I couldn't tell it was you because of the glare on the windshield. You could have been some icky sleazeball salesperson trying to cold-call us. I'm brutal with those people." I linked my fingers with hers. "And my favorite part was trying to figure out why you always smelled so sweet. One week you smelled like frosting, the next like cotton candy, then chocolate." I playfully sniffed her neck. "Today you smell like a vanilla cupcake."

She hooked her legs around mine and flipped me. "Do you know what you smell like?"

I thought maybe chicken kebabs and wine.

She kissed me softly and moaned. "Do you?"

"Wine? A Chicago summer?" I prayed it wasn't bad. I'd been sweating profusely for the last hour.

She looked at me and smirked. "You smell like sex," she said right before her lips claimed mine.

CHAPTER EIGHTEEN

How are things going with Sophia?"
I'd come over to my mom's house to get her advice about Sophia, but as soon as she asked for specifics, I didn't want to tell her what I'd done. I only wanted her to tell me everything was going to be okay. "We're doing well. It's nice to be in a healthy relationship."

She lifted her eyebrow at me. "I'm happy for you, honey. Are you bringing her to your exhibition so we can finally meet her?"

My excitement fizzled. I knew I was going to have to tell Sophia, but how could I do it without jeopardizing everything? I should have come clean weeks ago. I was being selfish and taking everything she gave me without giving her the simplest and purest thing. Truth. "I hope so."

"Nicole. What's going on?"

My mom took my hand and pulled me down on the couch next to her. I rested my head on her shoulder.

"I fucked up."

"First of all, watch your language. Secondly, what did you do? I thought she was perfect. And I'm not just saying this because you're my kid, but you're pretty great, too. What happened?"

I let out a deep sigh. "So, remember how all my exes wanted different things or tried to change me?"

"I hated all of them."

"I know you did. With Sophia, I left out some important parts of my life. I wanted her to want to get to know me."

She turned to me. "What did you do, Nicole Briar?"

Fuck. I hated when she used my middle name. "I wanted Sophia to like me for me, so I didn't tell her I own part of Tuft & Finley."

"Well, who does she think you are?"

"Someone who works in the warehouse."

My mom rested her head against the couch cushion, as though suddenly the weight of everything on her shoulders was too much. "What exactly does she know about you?"

"What's inside. My likes, dislikes, my personality. The real important stuff. The stuff you want somebody to like you for, not the superficial things."

"Does she know you're an artist?"

I leaned back with her. "Nope."

The cushion moved as she shook her head. "Has she been to your place?"

"Nope."

"She hasn't been to your condo? How is that possible?"

"Easy. I didn't take her there," I said.

"Why not?"

"I just hated how my two 'all in' relationships were shit. They either wanted me to be somebody else or to use me for my money. I know I took it too far, but now I'm stuck, and I don't know what to do."

"You have to tell her. Now. Immediately. No sugarcoating. Beg for her forgiveness."

I groaned. "I'm such an idiot. We're doing so well."

"I don't understand. How do you date somebody and not take them back to your place or drive them to restaurants and dates?"

I couldn't sit any longer. I stood and paced in front of her. "She's been to my studio."

"How can she not know about your art then?"

"I kept the door closed."

"Nicole, that studio makes you look like a pauper."

"Really, Mom? Pauper. Nobody says that." I was lashing out. We both knew it. "I screwed up. I know that."

"When are you seeing her next?"

Tonight was the first night in five nights I wasn't at her house. I had to finish *Thursday* and get all the sculptures ready for transport, but I needed the advice of my mother right now more than anything else. I was hoping for a pass from her. I wanted her to say that it wasn't as bad as it sounded, but it really was. I was a jackass. "Probably not until Sunday. I have things to do, and she's busy filling orders."

"How's her line doing? Her chocolates are delicious."

"Really well. She's making enough to buy more equipment to increase her output. We're giving her a big order for the show." I hid my face in my hands, totally embarrassed for duping a woman I was falling for.

"Do you want to bring her over for dinner and break the news to her that way?"

I was still covering my face with my hands. "No. I need to do this on my own, and privately, so she can rightfully get mad at me." I looked at my mom. "I can't believe I've screwed this up so badly."

"If she's as wonderful as you say she is, then she'll listen to you, be angry at you, and eventually forgive you. Maybe once she knows your history, she'll be more understanding."

"Do you really think she'll forgive me?"

I watched my mom's shoulders slump and a sad smile appear. "I hope so, baby. I haven't seen you this happy or tormented in a long time. What does Patricia think about all this?"

"She told me from day one to correct the misunderstanding, but I didn't."

We were so engrossed in the conversation, we didn't hear Trish enter. "I brought over a bottle of wine because I could hear you crying all the way down the street."

"Liar. I'm practically whispering. You saw my car, didn't you?"

Trish shrugged. "Or that." She opened the bottle and poured three glasses. "I'm here to swoop in and save the day. Where are we in this soap-opera mess of a life?"

"Right at the part where I was giving you credit for being a great older sister and trying to get me to tell Sophia the truth," I said.

"The truth shall set you free."

We all toasted that sentiment.

"You missed the part where I told Mom I've been at Sophia's place the last five nights."

My mom's jaw dropped. "You didn't tell me that. You just said things were really good."

"Oops. Well, now that it's all out there in the open, I need details," Trish said.

"She cooked dinner last Friday, and I ended up staying most of the weekend. Tonight's our first night apart."

Trish started shaking her head before I could finish speaking. I frowned, knowing I wasn't going to like what she was ready to say. I took a large swallow of wine and braced myself.

"Mom, please tell your daughter that, if she wants that relationship to work, she's going to have to beg Sophia for forgiveness. And for the record, I know this woman, and it's not going to be easy."

"Maybe I can ease her into my life. And maybe the art thing won't pan out, and then that will be one less lie I have to clear up."

"Or maybe it won't work out with you two, and you'll never have to confess anything." My mom was turning on me now that Trish was here.

"Did you just really say you wanted your show to fail to avoid telling your girlfriend the truth? That's fucked up," Trish said.

"Language."

I sighed heavily. "I don't mean that. I'm just confused and in a tough spot. Of my own doing." I quickly held up my hands before the onslaught continued. I took another drink. "I really like her. A lot. I haven't felt this way in a long time. I'm not going to say the word 'love' yet, but I can see it happening."

"The sooner you tell her who you really are, the stronger your relationship will be. Trust me." After I emptied my glass, Trish held the bottle of wine out of my reach. "Listen to me. Your number-one focus is to finish *Thursday*. I've given Rian the labels to be engraved. You have to send me information on *Thursday* so I can finish." Trish had a great idea to use one of our recyclable products for the show. She squeezed my hand. "This is going to be amazing. In just three weeks, you're going to be a world-famous artist."

I rolled my eyes at her theatrics, but my heart thumped faster at the slight possibility. "Yet I can't get help in the art department of my own business."

My mother raised an eyebrow at my sister and was rewarded with a blush of embarrassment. She never gave us business advice. She stayed out of it completely unless asked. The eyebrow-raise spoke volumes. I gave a mental high five to my mom.

"We'll start interviewing after Labor Day. Anna and I've already talked about it," Trish said.

The timing was awful, but I couldn't complain. We needed help, and everyone knew it. Interviewing would be hard because I would have my mind on getting the sculptures to the gallery. Ben had offered his help with the overhead crane, but Lindsay said we probably wouldn't need it. They moved hundreds of pieces a year without a single problem. None that I knew of at least. I'd asked Ben to oversee the project, because if I was there and saw somebody mishandling my art, I'd probably puke.

"What do you want me to do?"

"Nothing. We're having recruiters look for somebody

qualified, and when they send over resumes, we'll bring you in. Unless you have any ideas?"

I shook my head. I didn't know a lot of creative directors in Chicago. I figured they would branch out to neighboring large cities. We found Shelby at the Art Institute of Chicago, but we needed someone with more experience. "I can't think of anybody. Just send me over resumes and portfolios."

My mom kissed my cheek. "I'm sorry you're having a stressful time right now, but hopefully everything works out. I want to meet this woman."

"Before it all blows up," Trish said.

"Patricia. Be nice."

"Yeah, Trish. Be nice."

I was desperate to hear Sophia's sexy, sultry voice again, so I called her. "What are you working on?"

"I'm trying to figure out my schedule and when I can fill this order for Equity Finance Insurance," she said.

"Oh, is it a big one?"

"They just placed an order for fifteen hundred boxes for Labor Day weekend."

"Holy shit! Can you do it?"

"I'm pretty sure we can. The only thing that throws me off is that they want a chocolate with their logo on it. We can do an edible overlay, but that will have to be done by hand."

I was confused. "Like an iron-on thing?"

"Yes, but without the heat."

"But everything is by hand anyway, right?"

"Yes, but the logo will be challenging. We've done it with Sweet Stuff chocolate before, but not for an order this big. It's pretty exciting."

"I can help if you need me. Hell, I'll drag helpers from the warehouse to stuff the boxes if you want. Gently, of course."

"That's so sweet. I'll let you know, but I think we can handle it."

"If helping you is the only way we can see one another over the next few weeks, then consider me a volunteer." I didn't have a minute to spare, but I needed to have the talk with her.

"I'm sure I can squeeze you in."

The huskiness of her voice made me shiver. She was teasing me. "Sophia Sweet, are you propositioning me? Because if you are, I'm in."

She laughed quietly. I assumed her chocolatiers were within hearing distance. "Tonight's bad. How about Thursday?"

"Ah, my favorite day." That reminded me to call Lindsay and have her place the order now. My exhibition was less than a month away, and with all the new business Sophia's Collection was getting, I didn't want to miss out.

"I'll call you tonight."

I was going to tell her Thursday. I smiled at the irony of the situation. I'd found her on a Thursday and could very well lose her on one, too. "That would be great." I ended the call and sighed. So much was going on right now my chest was tightening. I took a few deep breaths to relax. We had to make a major design change with an existing client, Clean Breeze. And with school already in session, Shelby wasn't available to give the project all her time. I wouldn't say she was panicked, but the changes had obviously overwhelmed her. I jumped in to make the ones they wanted and promised to have them back by the end of the week. The changes were extensive, but I had an idea. I explained that this happened all the time, and she shouldn't take it to heart.

"Kelsey, hold my calls this afternoon unless it's Clean Breeze."

"Yes, Boss."

I used to think her voice was flirty and fun. Now it grated on me. I gritted my teeth and hung up. It wasn't her fault. She was immature, with very little drive. Her life centered on going to the bars and gaining Instagram followers. I pulled up Shelby's files and started making the necessary changes. I would have stretches of long days and nights ahead, and I was already exhausted. I wasn't going to be able to see Sophia for a few days, and I hoped that, by then, I could work up the nerve to tell her the truth.

CHAPTER NINETEEN

I was only a few minutes late to dinner. We were going to meet at Sophia's house, but at the last minute, she asked me to be at a restaurant in the opposite direction. I was slightly miffed, only because I was dying to make love to her again, and the restaurant was forty-five minutes from her house. It was closer to my studio, but I wanted to avoid taking Sophia there again until after I told her the truth.

"Hi, how are you?" It was amazing how just looking at her energized me. The weight of all my deadlines faded away. My heart pounded at the sweet smile she gave me.

"I'm great. I bet you're wondering why we're here and not at my house?"

I didn't want to be the jerk whose mind went straight to sex. "I figured you really liked the food here and wanted to share it with me."

"I want you to meet somebody."

I froze. "Really?" The only person in her life was her grandmother. "Is it Grammy?"

She pulled me closer to her. "Grandma, and yes, it is. I want you to be your charming self." She followed that request with a sweet kiss.

I was excited at getting to meet her family but then upset because I was bringing another person into this lie. "I'll do my best."

"Wait. Are you nervous?"

I pasted on a smile. My sudden dry mouth made it hard to talk. I shook my head and cleared my throat. "Not at all. Let's go meet Grammy."

Her voice grew softer as we walked over to the table. "Behave." When we approached, she squeezed my hand and pulled me in front of her. "Grandma, I want you to meet my friend Nico. Nico, this is Hazel Sweet, my grandmother."

I took her hand between both of mine. "It's so nice to finally meet you, Hazel." I flipped on the charm switch and switched into my Tuft & Finley persona. I sat next to Hazel and gave her all my attention.

"I've heard so much about you, Nico. I understand you've helped Sophia a lot. Your company makes the new chocolate boxes."

"Yes. It's an excellent company. I'm glad Sophia's doing business with them." I hated every word that came out of my mouth, but at least I was being truthful.

"I think the design is perfect for Sophia. She was so excited when she showed me what your company came up with. How long have you been with it?"

"Twelve or so years now. Since the beginning."

"Have you tried the chocolates Sophia's making?"

"They're so delicious. And I've had your chocolates as well." Even though Sophia classified her grandmother's chocolate as candy, it was what I always thought chocolate was. Sophia scoffed about every brand I mentioned to her. Real chocolate was an art. And after tasting her artisan collection, I didn't disagree. It was a whole different world.

"Tell me what made you want to date my Sophia." Hazel, her eyes the same blue as Sophia's, stared at me with such intensity I knew this woman had substance.

I didn't hesitate. I didn't even blink. I looked Hazel straight in the eyes. "She's the first woman in almost two years who takes my breath away."

Hazel tapped the table. "I like you. You're honest. I can see it on your face."

Cue the guilt trip. I smiled and took a drink of water. "Did Sophia tell you how we met?"

"She said you met at the company that made the pretty boxes."

The flush on Sophia's cheeks was adorable, and I touched her hand. "Technically, she's right, but that's not when it all began. I noticed her on the L on her way to visit you one afternoon. It took me six weeks to work up enough nerve to say hello."

"And apologize for being a jerk at the company," Sophia said.

Hazel laughed. "She did tell me the part where you yelled at her." She stared at me intently. "You know, you look familiar to me."

I froze again. "That's interesting. I'm certain we haven't met before." I sat back in my chair and ran my fingers through my hair. She made me nervous. The waiter returned to take our orders, and I ordered the special. The thought of eating right now made my stomach lurch, but I had to keep the pretense going. Hazel knew something was off with me. I needed to redirect. "But enough about me. Tell me about Sweet Stuff. How did the business come about?" Hazel's eyes lit as she recalled meeting Jacob Sweet and how his big dream was to open a candy store.

"With a name like Sweet, it was his destiny, he said. Not only did he make candy and chocolate, but he was the sweetest man. He would always make new things and ask my opinion."

"Sophia does that with me as well. Never in a million years would I have thought strawberry balsamic and dark chocolate were a great mix, but it blew my mind." I rested my hand on Sophia's knee. I loved it when she asked if I liked a new flavor. It was adorable that she was just like her grandfather. "My palate is that of an eight-year-old. Sophia has shown me the differences in chocolate from various parts of the world. Who knew there was a certain way to eat dark chocolate?" The first time she gave me a piece of dark chocolate, I crunched it in my mouth and nodded at her. She looked at me with complete disdain and gave me another piece, but this time with instructions.

"You have to let it rest on your tongue and allow it to melt. You can't eat it like it's candy."

"Who taught Sophia how to taste chocolate?" I asked Hazel.

"Oh, that's all her grandfather. From his side of the family. When they came to live with us, Sophia jumped right in and offered suggestions. Most of them were pretty good, as I recall."

As predicted, I barely touched my food when it arrived. My anxiety was on a whole new level. "Why aren't you eating?" Sophia pointed at my plate with her fork.

I leaned toward her and whispered, "Tonight was a surprise, and I'm a little nervous. I mean, I'm meeting the most important person in your life."

"I'm sorry to spring it on you like this. Grandma called out of the blue, and I wanted my two special ladies to finally meet," Sophia said.

"It's been a pleasure." And it was, aside from the burning sensation in the pit of my stomach. Hazel was nice, and under any other circumstances, we'd be having the time of our lives right now. When the check came, I automatically reached for it, but Sophia grabbed it first.

"My treat. I'm the one who changed the plans." She put her hand over mine and surprised me by brushing a kiss across my lips.

I avoided looking at Hazel because I didn't want to see her reaction. My face swelled under the heat of being caught off guard. It was a sweet kiss, though, and kick-started my need for more. Even though it was almost nine, I wasn't done with the night. I needed to tell her the truth and hopefully spend some quality time with her. I walked them to Sophia's car.

"Why don't I meet you back at your place? It's closer."

I nodded, even though I told myself we needed to avoid my

studio. "Hazel, it was so nice to finally meet you. I'm looking forward to getting to know you better."

"It was nice to meet you, too, Nico. Watch out for this one. She's a spitfire." She pointed at Sophia, who gave an angelic smile.

"I believe you. I really do."

"See you in half an hour," Sophia said.

I watched them pull into traffic and sighed. The studio was clean, but I felt really uncomfortable there. Sophia wasn't going to take the news well, and I didn't want her to get behind the wheel angry. I made my way home and lit a few candles—not for ambience, but to get rid of the smells. I wasn't the only one working on things. Ben's shop was busy, and the scent of oil and exhaust managed to worm its way under the door. I slipped the doggy bag that contained most of my meal into the refrigerator and changed into a T-shirt and jeans. I hadn't planned to stay here tonight, but now I was. Sophia texted that she was waiting on the stairs.

I opened the door. "Did you park on the street?" I was greeted with a kiss that left me breathless.

She slipped her hands under my shirt and moaned when she touched my skin. Instant chills. I wasn't expecting her to be so open and immediately in the mood. My need exploded, and I tugged at her clothes. I was afraid we would both be naked within thirty seconds, so I quickly ushered her inside my living space. She locked the door and started unbuttoning her blouse. I quickly held up a finger, moved the coffee table out of the way, and unfolded the sofa bed. She jumped on me the second it was in place. We didn't talk until both of us were naked.

"I've missed you," she said.

I cocooned us under the sheet. "I've been waiting for tonight for a long time."

She put her hand right on my heart. "It's beating so fast."

My answer was a soft kiss on her lips. No way could I tell

her right now. I kissed my way down her, stopping when I heard a sharp intake of breath as my tongue circled her nipple and the soft skin right below her breast. I let myself get lost, desperate to taste her. She rose to greet my mouth, and I devoured her. This was not sweet, first-time sex. This was passion-fueled, fast sex. I entered her fast and hard. She cried out and reached for me.

"More, Nico. I need more."

I slipped a third finger in and waited for her to adjust to me. She was so tight and wet, and I became weak as my heart grew strong and filled with emotions I didn't want to sort out. I wanted only to think about physically pleasing Sophia, not about why my heart threatened to burst at how trusting she was with me in bed, or how gorgeous she looked flushed with passionate heat, her hair tousled on the pillow.

"Yes, like that." She hissed through clenched teeth.

Ordinarily, I would be mentally patting myself on the back, but something had shifted. I don't know if it was the guilt coupled with meeting her grandmother, but I slipped down a slope I wasn't prepared for. I had fallen in love with Sophia Sweet, and I didn't want to. Not this way. Not under a lie. Watching her move with me was overwhelming. I slid down her and ran my tongue softly over her clit. Her pussy clenched my fingers, and she moaned with appreciation. Sophia knew exactly how to have an orgasm. I wanted to drag it out and make it last forever for both of us, but she had other plans. She came hard and beautifully. Twice. After the second time, she stopped me. Her legs quivered, and she closed them. I pulled her into my arms and closed my eyes at my predicament. Fuck.

"I love how you're all in during sex."

She leaned up and looked at me. "What do you mean?" I kissed her fingertips when she touched my lips. "By the way, you have an amazing mouth."

"Thank you. I mean, you don't hide what you like, what you want, and you aren't afraid to tell me what you want me to do."

"That's because you're an amazing lover."

The last time we were together, Sophia had given me a massage I'd never forget. It had started with a bubble bath and ended with both of us having orgasms in the bathtub, but only one of us was naked. Our sexual dynamic was interesting. She wanted fast and hard, but when she made love to me, she took her time. "I think we have amazing chemistry. I told you so."

She laughed. "Oh, you did, did you?"

"Don't you remember? On the L? Telepathically."

"I did notice you several times." She paused when I tilted my head to look at her. "Notice you looking at me several times."

I laughed at her playful honesty. She was so adorable right now, I just couldn't tell her the truth. Not here and not tonight.

❖

"How do you not have any food here at all? Like not even condiments. No cereal, no bread. Who doesn't have bread?"

I opened one eye to find Sophia straddling me, wearing one of my T-shirts. Her beautiful long hair enveloped us, and I threaded my fingers in it. "I eat out."

"Yeah, you do."

I opened my mouth in surprise. "Sophia, did you just make a dirty joke?"

She sat back and laughed. "I can't remember when I've laughed this much. What are you doing to me, Nico Marshall?"

Everything about her body language seemed relaxed and comfortable. The smile, the soft touches. It took me a full minute before I realized Sophia was falling in love with me. She had the same look in her eyes that I'd had in mine the last time I looked in the mirror and thought of her. But she didn't seem to know yet.

"So, let's talk about that."

She rolled off me and leaned up on her elbow. "Talk about what?"

"Nico Marshall. The real me."

"What don't I know about you?"

The solemn look, the pouty lips, and the fact that she was wearing my favorite shirt made my brain turn to mush. I didn't want to destroy this beautiful moment. This was our first sleepover at my place. Not a great decision, considering that she was digging around for food and also barely found anything she could wear in my clothing stash. "You don't know that breakfast is my most favorite meal. I could never do it justice, so I grab a bagel sandwich at the corner. Plus, they usually have stuff at work."

"Where are all your clothes? Not that I was snooping, but this is kind of a small space. I did find a locked door. What do you have behind it?"

I hated that we were at my studio. This place had the warmth of a two-star hotel room. "I stash all my love slaves behind that door."

"But what do you feed them? Ketchup packets? Soy sauce?"

"My love. I feed them love. And my body."

She slid out of bed. "Come on. Take me to breakfast. I'm sure we're both late for work, so at this point, what's another hour?"

I checked the time. Shit. It was already seven thirty. "Want to take a quick shower?"

"Together? We'd never fit in your shower."

I frowned.

She mistook my lack of time management for getting my feelings hurt. "I didn't mean anything by it. Don't frown." She touched my face and made me smile. "Just that it would be hard to turn around in there with you and with these hips."

"Your hips are beautiful. And I was frowning because of the time. At least it's Friday, and we have the weekend."

"I'm going to be working. We have two massive orders to fill, and I just got another order for an art gallery. They're exhibiting a new artist and are going all out. Do you want to go? I'm not that into art, but it might be fun to see peoples' reaction to my chocolate."

If my heart wasn't fluttering in my chest, it would have crashed and burned at my feet. Her statue was just on the other side of the door. I could unlock the door and show her the truth, beg for forgiveness. "I don't know. We've been pretty busy at work."

She messed up my hair. "You just don't want to."

I opened the bathroom door and turned on the shower. "I didn't say that. I love art. I believe I asked you the art question several weeks ago."

"How do you even remember that?" she asked.

Only that it was my one true passion and meant everything to me. "I remember everything about us." I kissed her quickly and jumped into the shower. "Join me if you want." What a night. I wasn't expecting to come here, let alone sleep here. She didn't join me, which I was actually thankful for. I was out of it in five minutes.

"That was fast," Sophia said. She was already dressed in last night's clothes, with her hair pulled back and clipped at the neck.

"Look who's talking." I dressed in two minutes and ran product through my hair. I was a disaster, but I no longer smelled like sex. Trish would be happy about that. I looked at the time. "We'd better get you fed and me to work."

"I can drive you to work if you want," she said.

"That's sweet, but traffic sucks right now, and it's only a few minutes on the L."

"I'd do that, too, but I really need to change my clothes, so I guess let's have a quick breakfast, and then I'll head out. Seriously, Tuft & Finley is on the way," she said.

"Okay. I'd like that. Let's go." I held her hand and pulled the door shut.

"You're not going to lock it?" Sophia asked.

"You've met Ben, and you know he'd scare off any intruder. Besides, we have cameras in the hall, and I have nothing to steal."

The street vendor was literally just down the street.

"I recommend the egg-and-cheese croissant sandwich. You

can get it with any kind of meat, but it's good just like that." I could have yelled out our order to Anthony from my front stoop.

"Nico, welcome back. I haven't seen you in weeks," Anthony said.

"You're exaggerating. I was just here."

"How's work?"

God, I didn't want work to come up now. I shrugged and ordered for us. "Give me two sandwiches and two coffees." I turned to Sophia. "Coffee's okay, right? How do you want it?"

"Lots of cream and lots of sugar."

Shit, that's right. She drank tea. "I'm sorry. Anthony doesn't have any tea, but his coffee's the best." I smiled at him, and he rewarded me with an extra splash of cream, something he didn't do even when I begged. I nodded at a bench across the street. "We can have breakfast there real quick, before it gets too hot out here."

"Isn't your boss going to get mad at you? I'm worried about your schedule."

I waved her off. "No worries. Ms. Anderson is pretty forgiving."

"Do you seriously call her Ms. Anderson?"

"No. I usually call her Trish, but I like to make her feel important by referring to her by her last name. She hates it."

"You need to be nice. You know how bosses can be." She gave me a sexy look that made me weak. "Thank you for buying me a very delicious breakfast."

"You're welcome." I was done eating my sandwich in no time. Since most of last night's dinner sat in my refrigerator, I was starving. I hoped my mother made something more substantial this Friday. Cookies were great, but a good banana-nut bread would really hit the spot.

"Come on. I'm late, so that must mean you're super late." I pulled her up from the bench and kissed her. "Although staying in bed all day with you sounds much more appealing."

"Maybe when all this craziness is over, we can have a nice

weekend in bed somewhere," she said. She pulled me in the direction of her car, and I playfully sulked the entire way. "Come on. Get in. I promise to make it up to you." She wagged her eyebrows at me.

"I'm holding you to it."

"Deal."

CHAPTER TWENTY

"How are you holding up, baby sis?"

I jumped and threw my pen at the door out of sheer surprise.

"That well, huh?"

Today was the day they were coming for my sculptures. I thought they'd planned to take them the week leading up to the exhibition, but Lindsay needed them earlier for promotional purposes. I wasn't done with *Thursday* and told her I would bring the sculpture by the end of the week. Nothing like a little more pressure.

"Ben's texting me about their progress," I said.

"You should be there to oversee the pickup."

I shook my head. "Absolutely not. I'd be a wreck."

She sat in one of my guest chairs. "Yeah, because you're so chill here. How are you doing? Need any help?"

I put my head down on my desk like a child. "I'm okay. I'll have something for Windy City Beer by tomorrow. I finished Jet Pen, Sophia's new box design, and I've reviewed Shelby's Instant Unicorn can design." For some reason, toy and novelty companies loved working with us. Word of mouth awarded us a lot of business.

"I've got some good news."

"I'm all ears."

"We're starting to get resumes for the creative-director spot."

I sat up in a panic. I couldn't imagine putting one more thing on my plate before the exhibition. She held up her hands.

"Anna and I are weeding through some people. I'm going to do the initial interview and narrow it down for you. You trust me, right?"

"One hundred percent. You know exactly what we need. I promise not to be a snob about things." Trish and Anna had a knack for picking the right employees. I just sat in on interviews because I was part owner, and if they ended up being horrible, I had a license to bitch. We were lucky, though, and most of our employees were a great fit. The idea was to find somebody who would take over this job so I could devote my life to my artwork and slow down and travel. Maybe even settle down. I would step away from this job but still have an executive position, which meant showing up for board meetings and important functions.

"How are things going with Sophia?" She seemed hesitant to ask, which was fair, because the last time she brought up the subject, I got angry. Not at her, but at the situation.

"I'm going to see her this weekend. She's been super busy with orders."

Trish twirled a pen on my desk as though we were talking about something simple like the weather. I knew she wanted more. Truthfully, I hadn't shared with her like I had other relationships in the past. Before, I would call or text with juicy information, but I hadn't with Sophia because of my guilt. She stared at me.

"And no, I haven't talked to her."

"I figured as much. You'll tell me. How about we go to lunch and gossip about family stuff?" She suggested meatball sandwiches.

I stood because, for the first time in days, food sounded good. "Perfect. We have to discuss Ethan and Starr."

Trish's eyes widened. "Is everything okay?"

"Remember when we got tipsy and offered to pay for the baby's college? Let's go to lunch and talk about that."

Trish laughed. "Oh, shit. Let's hope all our other cousins don't know about our drunken promises."

I grabbed my wallet and keys and offered to drive. I didn't use the Audi much, but whenever I got behind the wheel, I told myself to drive it more. The air-conditioned seats and steering wheel made the blistering heat tolerable.

"Are you ready for your trip?" I asked.

Trish slid into the passenger seat and sighed. "I'm ready to relax, but Rob has all these plans for us. White-water rafting, horseback riding, and I'm like, it's only three days."

Trish valued alone time. Her idea of a vacation was a hot bath, sex, and a plush hotel room away from her everyday life. Rob liked physical activity like snowboarding and hiking.

"I'm surprised you agreed to participate."

"Well, marriage is about compromise, and you know how little I like to do that. Even I have to cave from time to time."

I found a parking place in front of our favorite sandwich spot. That never happened. We joked about playing the lottery because of our good luck. We ordered, Trish paid, and we sat at an empty table near the soda dispenser.

"Let's talk about Ethan and Starr," Trish said.

"Even though we probably won't be held accountable, it's a good idea to at least start a fund." Tuft & Finley offered small scholarships that employees and their families could apply for, but we didn't have anything for our own family.

"We can check with Anna about legalities. That's not what I meant. I just meant about how they're pregnant and expecting after the first of the year."

"At least Starr isn't super pregnant now, because I couldn't imagine being in that condition in this heat." I finished my water and went back for another one.

"That's what I wanted to talk to you about."

"Starr's luck at not being pregnant in summer?" Weird, but okay.

"No. Rob and I were talking, and since I'm almost thirty-five, our window for having kids is closing, so I think we're going to try to have one. Or maybe even two."

I stood. "Holy shit!"

She pulled on my hand to get me to sit. "It's not public knowledge. We don't even know if it's going to work."

I hugged her. If they were only talking about it now, I was going to lose my mind when she actually got pregnant. "I'm so happy for you. I'm going to be an aunt. Someday. This is big. Huge news."

"Keep in mind, this is about me being a mother, not about you being an aunt."

"I know, I know. We'll talk about dividing the responsibilities, but know up front that I'm going to be the best aunt in the world. The best presents, toys, trips, cars, dresses, clothes."

"Who said we're going to have a girl?" Trish asked.

"Who said I said it's going to be a girl?"

"Touché, sister."

"Do Mom and Dad know?"

"No. Rob and I've been discussing it ever since Anna got pregnant. It's now or never."

"You have time for two kids. Or go for twins right off the bat."

"Only if you move in and become the nanny," Trish said.

"The idea has merit, if I have to hide from the world." I took a bite to stop talking.

"Stop feeling sorry for yourself. Your exhibition will skyrocket you to fame, and we'll have to call your assistant to schedule family time."

I smiled. Family was always first. "Wouldn't that be great though? Not about having to call my assistant, but if I was that busy doing something I loved."

"It's crazy how Tuft & Finley just kind of took over our lives in the best way possible, even though we all had different ideas in college. Nothing like a twelve-year detour," Trish said.

"I'm not complaining. Most people have to work harder and longer for what they want."

"Don't sell us short. Remember the super-long days and nights just trying to get Tuft off the ground?"

I leaned back in my chair as the weight of the last twelve years finally hit me. "It'll be nice to finally breathe."

"And we're still relatively young. I mean, I'm going to try to have a baby, and you should try to have one, too. At the same time. That would be so much fun."

"That's a very big no from me. I'll pass."

"I'll be Mom's favorite." Trish folded her arms and smirked at me.

"For the first time ever."

She laughed. "Come on. Back to work. Hopefully I kept your mind off your sculptures."

I'd completely forgotten about the move. I shot Ben a quick text message.

How's it going?

Closing the truck right now. It went off without a hitch. Ben actually used the thumbs-up emoji.

"It's done. They're out of the studio." It was happening. In less than two weeks, I would know the fate of all my hard work.

Trish grabbed my hands and squealed. "I'm so excited for you. I really am. Do we need to swing by the gallery and check in with Lindsay?"

It's like she'd read my mind. "Definitely. Then we can visualize along with her."

Trish called Lindsay. We were only fifteen minutes from the gallery. "Okay. She'll unlock the door for us, but nothing will be set up, so be prepared," Trish said.

The gallery was on Chicago Avenue, and parking during the day was a nightmare. After circling for what seemed like forever, I was so anxious I started to sweat.

"Just park in the garage across the street." Trish pointed to the *Space Available* sign still out on the sidewalk.

I swung around and zipped into a spot on the second floor. I laughed nervously. "I mean, the sculptures aren't even here."

"I know, but let's just check in."

We crossed at the light and knocked on the door. I peeked into the window and saw a smiling face staring back at me. I took a step back and laughed.

"Come on in." Lindsay unlocked the door for us. "We have a show this weekend, so I won't set up yours until after Sunday. But I can at least share my vision."

"That sounds great," Trish said. She clearly knew I was struggling.

We walked around the gallery. "We'll have *Thursday* in her own room over here. You'll still get me the video this week, right?"

"Video? What video?" Trish looked at me in surprise.

"Since we don't have time to engrave the label, I wanted to do a video explanation of the piece," I said.

"It's a fabulous idea. We'll have a little display for it," Lindsay said.

Lindsay pointed to a map and showed us where each sculpture would stand or be placed on a pedestal. "I'm really looking forward to your exhibition. There's so much interest. I bet we reach full capacity. Oh, the postcard's here. You're going to love it."

I died when Lindsay handed me the postcard they'd mailed out. Luckily, it wasn't just a photo of me. It was a photo of me standing in front of *Broken*, but it still showed more of me than was necessary.

"You look amazing," Trish said. She held it up to admire the entire postcard. "When did you get this photo taken?"

"Last week, at her studio," Lindsay said.

I covered my face with my hands. "Ack. It's so real." I had to admit, I looked great. I wanted to look the part of the artist with the welding helmet and work clothes, but Lindsay recommended wearing a black blazer with a white button-down. She said it was an industry standard, and I believed her. "I'm starting to get pumped about this," I said.

Lindsay touched my elbow. "You should. We're going to have a great turnout. By the end of this, you'll be the name on everyone's lips."

I blushed. Not only was I embarrassed, but adrenaline rushed through me at the thought of this exhibit being my breakout. It was everything I'd dreamed about since I was a kid. "I hope so."

"You will," Trish said.

Lindsay left us alone with the map, and I was impressed with how well she'd organized the space. She'd left enough room that people would be able to take in the art without bumping into one another.

"This all looks perfect. Now let's get out of here before I have a panic attack." I found Lindsay and returned her map. "I'll call you when *Thursday* is ready."

"I'll send the art movers as soon as you call."

I smiled, even though lunch threatened to make an appearance. I held my stomach all the way back to the car.

"Are you going to be able to survive this?"

Trish offered to drive, but I waved her off. "I better survive this. I'm a mess right now, but I'm sure that next Friday I'll be fine and relaxed."

"After a glass of wine, perhaps?"

I was already way ahead of Trish. "I was thinking more like two."

Sophia opened her door. "Thank you for agreeing to date night. As much as I love spending quiet time with you, I think it's important to get out and be a couple."

I rested my shoulder against Sophia's doorway casually and handed her a bouquet of flowers. "A box of chocolates just seemed like a bad idea. Unless they're yours, and that would just seem like I'm trying too hard."

She kissed me. "You're already in, so you don't have to try too hard."

"I'm not in yet," I whispered and kissed her neck.

She giggled and pulled me into the foyer. "I've missed you. A lot. When are things going to slow down for you?"

I loved how she played with the buttons on my shirt. When she put her hand below my collarbone, I melted. I put my hand over hers. "Soon. Give me two weeks and I'm all yours."

"I'll hold you to it. Come on. Let's go before I change my mind," she said.

I stopped her and gave her a thorough look-over. "As much as I love seeing your legs in dresses, I adore your ass in jeans. I can say that, right?"

She slid her arms around me and pulled me close. "You're just saying that because I agreed to go out on your motorcycle again."

"I owe you big for this, don't I?" I was happy Sophia had agreed to ride Gerty again. It was monumental.

"I haven't decided how I want you to repay me. Maybe a long massage? Another amazing bubble bath?"

"Anything you want. Come on. Let's go before traffic gets worse." I handed her a helmet and steadied myself while she straddled the bike. She circled her arms around my waist and gave me a quick squeeze. It was a gorgeous evening with a nice breeze. The lights of the city always made me smile. I loved this town.

"I notice so much more of the city on your bike," Sophia said.

"I was just thinking that. The lights are brighter, and you hear all the noises that make our city great."

"Thank you, Nico."

"For what?"

"For being you."

"Thanks, babe." It was the first time I'd used a term of endearment with her. I wanted to say so much, but I had to concentrate on driving. I was extra careful because it was Sophia. I found parking a block away. While I was locking up the helmets, I felt her hand on the small of my back. When I turned around, she walked into my arms and stood there longer than a hug. "Are you okay?" I brushed a piece of hair from her cheek. She was so beautiful, and my heart tumbled in my chest as I looked into her eyes.

"I'm fine. I'm in a sappy mood tonight."

"Sappy is good, right?"

"I meant what I said. Thank you for being you. You've opened up my world the last few months, and I'm just grateful for you."

I kissed her softly and slowly. She molded herself against me, and another shift happened between us. That final wall was trying to crack. "Thank you for trusting me. I mean that. I know it hasn't been easy, so thank you for opening up to me."

She put her hand on my chest again. "You're making me feel things I haven't felt in a very long time." Her voice was shaky, and I knew she was so close to a confession. I kissed her again because I was afraid of what she'd say next.

"I think we have an audience. Let's go inside."

She nodded and slipped her arm around my waist. It was sweet how she leaned into me. I kissed her head and walked into the comedy club. The show was starting in fifteen minutes. I handed the usher our tickets, and he took us to a high top to the left of the stage. A waitress swooped in and took our drink and appetizer order.

"Nicole? Hey. Nicole!"

I turned and scanned the crowd. I laughed when I saw my parents two tables back. My mom waved and walked to our table.

"Mom. Hi. What are you guys doing here?" I waved to my dad back at their table and stood to hug my mother.

"Mom, this is Sophia. Sophia, this is Sherry, my mom. My dad, Alan, is over there waving at us. Why isn't he coming over?" I was completely fine for him to stay over there, but it seemed polite to ask.

"He's probably afraid he'll lose the table or that this is woman time or something like that." My mom shook Sophia's hand and smiled at her appreciatively. "It's so nice to meet you. We've heard so much about you."

"Likewise. I've heard nothing but wonderful things about you and your husband. Nico has a lot of respect for you."

"We're pretty proud of her." My mom and Sophia talked until the lights dimmed. Thankfully, my mother kept the conversation light and easy and mainly about Sophia. She kissed my cheek on her way back to her table. "She's lovely, Nicole."

My chest swelled with pride. I didn't think she'd ever said that about somebody I was dating, not that she'd met many of my girlfriends. "Well, that went better than expected."

"Your mom is so nice. Did you know she was going to be here?"

I shook my head. "Not at all. Total surprise."

The first comedian was a local guy that I'd seen before. We were there for Kit Weston. I hadn't seen her in a couple of years, so I knew she had new material. The opening act was entertaining and a decent crowd warmer, but Sophia didn't even know who Kit was, and I was excited to introduce her to her comedy. When the opener's act was done, Sophia excused herself to go to the restroom, so I headed over to my parents' table. "Where's Dad?"

"He went to stretch his legs." Mom straightened my shirt. It probably didn't need it, but my mother was always coming up with ways to coddle us, and it was endearing, so we humored her. "I really like Sophia. She's so sweet and smart. She seems so confident."

"She is. Especially about her job. She's definitely a keeper."

"Have you cleared the air with her yet?"

"Not yet, but soon."

She touched my cheek. "How are you holding up? Trish said you had a moment at the gallery."

"I'm okay. Everything's just overwhelming right now. I'll be fine the night of the exhibition. Or maybe several hours after it."

"You'll be fine, baby. Your art is beautiful. I couldn't be prouder of you."

"What are you ladies talking about?" My dad slid into his chair and took a swig of his longneck.

"The art show. Nicole is nervous, but I told her we're proud of her and know she's going to do well."

"I was surprised Sophia didn't know about your show," Dad said.

I went cold all over. My mom and I stared at one another. "What?" I slowly turned to face my dad. "You talked to Sophia?"

"Yeah. I introduced myself to her, and we chatted. I asked her if she was excited about your show and how you were so cute when you were nervous."

Of all the fucking luck. I stood and tried not to panic. "What did she say?"

"She said she didn't know about your show and asked when it was. I told her. I even shared the QR code with her." He looked back and forth between me and Mom. "Was I not supposed to? Are you bringing another girl to it instead? I screwed up, didn't I?"

"Shit." I looked for Sophia, but she wasn't in the room. "I'm going to look for her."

"What did I do?" I heard my dad ask my mom as I walked away. After that, I couldn't hear words, just buzzing. I slapped a few twenties on the table and waved at my waitress to let her know the money was there. Something told me that Sophia wasn't in the bathroom or loitering in the foyer. I could feel that she was gone. In my heart, I knew the worst possible thing had just happened. She'd found out the truth, and it wasn't from me.

CHAPTER TWENTY-ONE

"Come on, Sophia. I know you're home. Please answer the door." I'd been knocking on it for the past twenty minutes. I'd seen a light extinguish upstairs when I pulled up, so I knew she was home. "I want to talk about this. I need to explain myself. Please open the door." I texted her the same thing and got no response.

Nothing. Not a word. Barely a sound. I stayed there for two hours, until one of her neighbors shushed me and threatened to call the cops. I pushed Gerty down the driveway. When I started her up, Sophia's bedroom curtain moved. What a total fuck-up. It was completely my fault. I drove to my condo because I needed comfort, and the condo had everything I needed.

Can we please talk? I shot her a text the second I walked through the door. *I know you don't want to hear me out, but it's important that we talk.*

I watched my phone to see if bubbles would pop up, but they never did. I checked it periodically, and after two glasses of wine and a bundle of nerves in the pit of my stomach, I called her. I didn't care that it was three in the morning. It was rude, but I had liquid courage. When her voice mail popped up immediately, I knew her phone was off. I stretched out on the couch, and for the first time in months, I cried.

When I woke the next morning, I vowed to kill the construction crew who was pounding this early. Opening my eyes seemed impossible, but I cracked one eye open and blinked until the other one cooperated. The pounding continued, and my anger exploded.

"Shut up!" I yelled at whatever was making that noise. I didn't know if my voice was loud enough, but it made me wince in pain and grit my teeth.

"Nico, open up."

I leaned up when I recognized Trish's voice. "No." I flopped back down and put a pillow over my head. When I heard a key in the lock, I growled. Giving Trish a key had seemed like a good idea, but now I was questioning all my life's decisions. "Go away."

"You don't mean that. Do you want to tell me what's going on?"

"No."

"That's not going to work. Come on. Talk to me. I know shit went down last night. It's not like you to miss work, at least not without phoning me."

"What time is it?" What day was it? Memories of my horrific night flooded my brain, and I groaned again. "Sorry."

"It's noon. I had to leave work to drive around town and try to find your sorry ass."

"There are only a few places I could be," I said.

"I heard what happened. I figured you needed your big sister."

"I smell coffee." That got me to scoot over and scrub my face.

"You want to talk about it?" Trish handed me the coffee and rubbed my back.

"You were right. I should've told her. Did Mom call you?"

"This morning. She phoned the office, figuring you needed the night to straighten things out. She said Dad told Sophia about the art show. Don't be mad at him."

"It's not his fault at all." I took a sip of coffee. "I don't blame anybody but myself."

"Tell me what happened."

I relayed all the sweet moments that led up to the instant my life fell apart, and then I told her about the aftermath. "I didn't even talk to her. She wouldn't answer her door or her phone."

"She left you at the club?"

"Yes. She grabbed a cab or Lyft." I ran my hands through my hair and stood. I was wobbly, but I needed to pace. "I pounded on her door until the neighbors threatened to call the cops. I texted and called. No response. I fucked up."

"First of all, you need to calm down. Give her time to digest the information. And truthfully, she knows only half. She isn't even aware that you're part owner of Tuft & Finley."

I looked at her in disbelief. I hadn't even thought about that. I found my phone wedged in the couch cushions—dead. "Where's my charger?" I raced to the bedroom and plugged my phone in. I waited until it launched. No texts or phone calls from Sophia, but several from my family and work. I called Sophia's phone and listened to unanswered rings until her voice mail clicked on. "Sophia, it's Nico. I really need to talk to you. Please call me back." I had to find her today. I needed to shower and change.

"I'm guessing you won't be in today." Trish was sitting calmly, watching me lose my shit.

I stopped. "Sorry. My life's imploding, so I need to try to salvage it."

"Do you need me to do anything?"

"Just rule me out for today. I'm sorry I didn't call. It was a rough night." Trish pulled me into a hug and held me for a bit. "Thank you for checking on me."

"Go shower. You smell like a winery."

"I feel beat up inside and out."

"I'm not even going to give you a hard time. Call me if you need me. Keep your phone charged. I don't want to have to chase you down." She grabbed her coffee and looked at me over her shoulder. "Okay?"

I nodded. "Thanks, sis."

I stripped and jumped into the shower after she left. My first stop would definitely be Sweet Stuff. I knew Sophia was too dedicated to her work to allow her emotions to prevent her from going. I found a white button-down, slim-fitting shirt, a pair of skinny jeans, and oxfords. I looked casual and exactly who I was: Nicole Briar Marshall, business owner, artist, and somebody who liked nice things. I spent a few minutes on my hair and gave myself a pep talk. I didn't expect Sophia to respond to me today, or tomorrow, or even next week, but I was determined to try.

I grabbed my wallet, the keys to my Audi, and headed to the garage. I waved to the parking-garage attendant and cruised into traffic, trying hard not to replay last night in my mind but failing miserably. I didn't even try to call her again. I zipped in and out of traffic and pulled up outside Sweet Stuff in record time. I rolled my sleeves, checked my reflection in the flip-down mirror, and exited my car. The same blonde stood at the counter.

"Is Sophia in today?" I asked.

She blinked at me and shook her head. "No. She's out of the office."

"Her car's out front. Can you please let her know that Nicole is here to see her?" I crossed my arms and stared at the clerk. She turned to the left, then to the right, then back to me as if she suddenly remembered the script she'd been given. I held my finger up to stop her before she started. "Please. At least let her know I'm here."

I walked around the store, inhaling deeply. I smiled at how I could identify each scent now. My phone dinged twice. I was going to ignore it, but the blonde cleared her throat.

"Excuse me, but can you check your phone?"

Please leave. I have nothing to say to you.

I wanted to yell and push my way to the back of the store, where I knew she was hiding.

I'll leave if you give me five minutes. I need to explain several things to you. Please.

I can't right now. Please just go.

Tell me when we can talk. You're too important to me. I was groveling, and I didn't care.

Not any time soon.

I wanted to push and make her understand, but I also knew she needed time to process. At least we were communicating. Not exactly what I wanted, but it was a start. This was going to be a marathon, and I was used to sprinting.

❖

"Hi, Hazel. It's Nico. Do you have a moment to talk?" It was Labor Day, and Sophia hadn't spoken to me in five days. I had reached a new level of desperation.

"Oh, hi, Nico. Do you think that's such a good idea?"

"I'd like to think so. Are you telling me no?" I held my breath and pressed harder on the intercom button while I waited for her answer. She buzzed me in. I stumbled in surprise and almost missed the door handle. I climbed the stairs to her apartment and smiled sheepishly at her. "Thank you for seeing me."

She stepped back. "Come on in."

How did her apartment smell like chocolate? "Are you baking?"

"I'm making fudge." She walked into the kitchen, slipped into her apron, and started cutting pieces out of a soft cylinder of chocolate she pulled from the refrigerator. She offered me a piece, and I didn't hesitate.

"That's the one thing I didn't buy at your store and have always regretted it. It's delicious."

"This is my own special recipe. Sophia doesn't like fudge to be creamy, but I think that's what makes it perfect."

"I'm going to have to agree with you. This is the fudge I grew up loving. I mean, I love what Sophia's done with her artisan line, but this is the chocolate of my childhood."

Hazel pointed at me and smiled. "This is why Sweet Stuff will still be in business. Sweet Stuff is more for children, and people who want to remember their youth."

That gave me an idea. "If you're ever in the market to upgrade Sweet Stuff, you could get an updated logo and a catchphrase like 'your youth remembered' or 'chocolate of your youth.'"

"Well, I've already passed the business down to Sophia and her brother, so it's up to them, but I like the way you think." She sliced the fudge and wrapped the pieces in waxed paper. She finished by tying each with a red bow.

"Where are these gems going?"

"Just to my book club and some friends in the neighborhood."

"Sophia said you stay busy during the week."

She motioned for us to sit at the kitchen table and poured an iced tea I didn't ask for. I appreciated both the gesture and the indication I could stay. "Thank you."

"I heard a little bit from Sophia, but for the most part she clammed up when I asked questions. I knew she was upset, but she didn't really say why. Or if she did, I didn't understand."

I took a sip of tea and a deep breath before I confessed all the things I'd done wrong. "Let me start off by saying I didn't mean to hurt her. I really like Sophia. It took me forever to even work up the courage to talk to her."

"I remember the story about the train. Tell me who she thinks you are."

"I need to tell you a little bit about my past." I launched into my company and the beginning of Tuft & Finley. I mentioned my exes, Samantha and Mandy.

"Your company is successful?"

I nodded. "It gives me a very comfortable life. When Sophia saw me on the L, she guessed I was a welder, and I didn't hear any judgment in her voice. I knew I wanted to get to know her better, but I wanted her to know me for me, not my money and success."

"You are a welder, though, right?"

"I'm an artist. I'm the creative director at our business, and I weld sculptures. My first big art show's coming up next week." I tried to keep the pride out of my voice, but it was hard.

"Sophia's doing chocolates for your show."

"Yes. I asked the gallery owner to reach out because I love Sophia's new line."

"I think that's sweet, but she thinks you pity her."

I gasped. It had never occurred to me that she would take it that way. "Wait. That's not true at all. There's so much I need to tell her."

She held up her hand. "I understand. You wanted Sophia to like you for you and not your money. You've been hurt, and you want to make sure Sophia is in it for the right reasons."

"I want to explain myself, but she won't talk to me. At all. I don't know how to get through to her. I know I f—messed up."

Hazel stood. "Walk with me. I need to deliver these."

Okay. I guess we were done talking about that. I sighed, because she was my last hope. "I have my car. I can drive you. It's warm out there."

"Oh, no. I'm delivering just around the neighborhood."

I held a canvas bag open while she stacked the waxed packages inside. We walked slowly around the block. Hazel told me stories about the neighborhood and what it had been like fifty years ago, when they moved here.

"We used to spend time outside and got to know our neighbors. Now I barely know any of them. We're getting a lot of younger families who spend most of their time inside," she said.

Smiling faces greeted us every time a door opened. Hazel hugged her friends and handed them fudge. Sometimes she introduced me as a local artist, sometimes as a friend, and once she slipped and said I was dating her granddaughter. I hoped that was still true. When we finished, I found myself smiling. I hadn't smiled in five days.

"Thank you for asking me to join you. It was a pleasant distraction."

"I like you, Nico. You have a good heart. I hope Sophia forgives you because I think you're good for one another."

"Do you have any advice for me? How to get Sophia to talk to me?"

"Give her time. If it's meant to be, then she will reach out to you. Patience, Nico. That's all you need."

I almost rolled my eyes. I didn't want to hear that. I wanted to hear the magical solution on how to win Sophia back. "Thank you for talking to me today. I will be patient and wait." I gave her a quick hug and got into my car. At least she was willing to give me the time to talk today. I drove to the studio and parked, saying a quick prayer that my tires had stayed inflated.

I didn't have time to go back to the condo and switch out cars because *Thursday* was due early next week. I had four days to finish her, and my heart was in a horrible place. I needed to concentrate harder than ever. It was important to finish, not just because I had a deadline, but for Sophia. Not that I expected her to be there, but hopefully one day she would see it.

CHAPTER TWENTY-TWO

Trish knocked on my door and, when I opened it, handed me a bottle of champagne. "Are you ready, superstar?"

"It's four in the afternoon. I don't think I want to start this early."

She gave me a quick hug and tried not to wrinkle me. "I'm at your service for the next twelve hours. And you look gorgeous."

I placed both hands on my stomach. "Thank you. I can't handle being this nervous for that long. Let's hope it wraps up early."

"Oh, I'm sure it will, but the afterparty will be off the hook!"

"Do people say that anymore?"

She shrugged. "I don't care. You know what I mean." Trish had rented a hotel suite for the weekend across from the gallery and hired a bartender for tonight to pour drinks until we ran out of alcohol. "Did you pack a bag?"

"No. I'll be too excited to sleep."

"Get one. In case you spill something on you or need to brush your teeth or style your hair." She tried to touch it, but I dodged her.

"Don't mess it up. I paid a lot of money for this cut." My stylist, Bastian, had just left my condo. Since it was such a big day for me, he had cleared his afternoon, and his makeup artist joined him. I didn't like to wear makeup, but since my tan was fading and there would be a ton of photos, I gave her some allowance. They both did a fabulous job. I looked amazing. I just hated that it had to be done so early in the day.

"Don't cry or get emotional because your mascara will run."

We both laughed because we knew I would cry several times tonight. They used waterproof mascara for that reason and left me a cleanser for when I was ready to take it off. I couldn't forget to pack that. "Okay. Let me put together a small bag."

"We need to get going. Lindsay wants you there by five, and you know what rush-hour traffic on a Friday is like."

I found a small piece of luggage with wheels and packed more than I would wear in a weekend. I grabbed hair product, my favorite soap, and my brush. I wouldn't call myself high maintenance, but I did require a fair amount of time in the morning to prep for the day.

"Hurry up."

"Ack! Don't stress me out more than I already am." I grabbed my phone, wallet, and keys. "Okay, I'm ready."

Trish turned and opened the door. "Superstar coming through. Everyone back away."

I pushed her shoulder playfully and shushed her. "Not everyone knows."

"They do now." She grabbed my hand and locked fingers with me. "It's really happening. I'm sure you're nervous, but I want you to know I'm so proud of you. Tonight is going to be a success." She dropped my hand to hit the elevator button and turned to look out the window.

"If you cry, I'm going to ruin this perfectly applied face, and then I'm going to be mad." Her back was to me, so I realized she was trying to keep it together. She waved me off and kept her distance until the elevator dinged, and then she finally turned back around. Tears sparkled in her eyes, and I immediately started blinking back my own.

"I'm okay. We can't ruin your face. Come on. I told Tommy I was going to be five minutes. It's been fifteen."

The Crenshaw Gallery was located on Michigan Avenue, and parking wasn't available anywhere.

"Oh, my God. Wow. Look at this place." Trish grabbed my knee and squeezed. "This is for you, sis."

"Don't be an idiot. It's not even five. My show doesn't start until seven. This is normal downtown traffic on a Friday night."

A cop flagged us to keep moving, but Trish waved him over. "This is the artist for the show at Crenshaw. We should have a spot in the lot." She pointed to the side lot by the gallery. "Can you let us through?" He stepped aside and let us park in the only available place. A sign announced it was reserved for me.

"I'm going to text Lindsay and tell her we're here. How cool is this?"

Seeing my name on the sign gave me confidence. "I'm feeling a little better about things." We got out of the car when we saw Lindsay's assistant, Ashton, wave to us from the back door. I was already starting to sweat. I needed air-conditioning and a drink.

"Welcome. Come on in. It's good to see you again." Ashton ushered us in and locked the door. "We just heard *New York Magazine* is sending a reporter."

"Is that normal?" Trish asked.

"If it's a popular artist or if there's a lot of interest, yes."

I laughed nervously. "See? I'm normal."

"Oh, we've had a lot of interest in your work, Nicole." Ashton led us to a small room in the back that was chilly and full of food. "Help yourself. Lindsay will come join you in a bit and tell you what to expect when the doors open."

Trish poured us each a glass of wine the minute Ashton closed the door. I stripped off my blazer and hung it on the back of the chair. "I should've brought my clothes and changed here. I'm going to be a hot mess before it even starts."

"It's freezing in here for a reason. Most people are stressed, and they keep it cold so they don't panic-sweat like you're doing right now," Trish said.

"I picked the wrong day to wear tight clothes," I said.

"It's cool in here, trust me. You'll be fine." She handed me a glass and raised hers. "I feel like we've shared a lot of toasts about this already, but here's to your success tonight."

I clinked my glass against hers and took a sip. The wine was drier than I liked, but I drank it anyway. I nibbled on a cracker with cheese and watched as Trish nervously ate her way around the room.

"Aren't these Sophia's chocolates?" Trish held up an almond marzipan and a beautifully designed, spiced chocolate ganache.

I confirmed those were hers. "Thankfully, she didn't cancel the order."

"She's not going to turn down good business, no matter where she is emotionally."

I snorted. "Her heart is fine." It seemed Sophia wasn't broken. Apparently, I was just another girl and what we had was in the past. I hated that the days had slipped away from us, from any kind of reconciliation. She had never responded to my calls or text messages. I thought visiting Hazel would stir some emotion in her and she would reach out, but she never did. I took a deep breath. Tonight was my night. It belonged to me, not to my past. I finished my wine and grabbed a cold water. "When is Lindsay coming? Didn't Ashton say soon?"

As if on cue, Lindsay knocked twice and peeked in. "Hi. I'm here. How are you?"

I motioned for her to enter. "I'm good. I'm ready. Tell me what you want me to do. What's my role?"

Lindsay sat down and smiled. "I want you front and center. Don't greet people, but be available if they want to introduce themselves. I will introduce you to people who are either interested or have the potential to be interested."

"People with deep pockets."

She nodded. "Very deep pockets."

"I'll work the room the best I can." Talking to new people wasn't a problem.

"I'll make sure she doesn't ramble," Trish said.

That was the problem. I was too anxious to control my mouth. It was going to be hard to sit back and listen to criticism or try to explain my creations. I didn't know what to expect. Were people going to be rude? Supportive? I checked the clock. Doors were opening in thirty minutes.

"I'm not worried at all. Nicole is charming and full of life. This will be a successful exhibition, I can tell." Lindsay stood and shook our hands. "Showtime in thirty minutes." She gave my hand a squeeze and winked at Trish.

"Apparently you're in charge," I said.

"Duh. And just so you know, Mom and Dad are parking at the hotel and checking in. They'll be here right at seven. They didn't want to stand in line."

"I'm sure Lindsay would have let them in. We have plenty of room in here." I slipped my jacket back on because my adrenaline was flatlining. I shivered at the sudden chill in the room.

"You want to walk around for a bit? Oh, you know what? I want to see your video. The one you made about *Thursday*."

"Are you going to make fun of me?"

"Of course I am." Trish led me around the gallery to the back, where *Thursday* was. "Oh, Nico. She's beautiful."

"You can see her?" Sometimes Trish told me what I wanted to hear.

"I can't tell you if I like *Thursday* or *Broken* best. Can I watch the video?"

I hit the play button. I'd recorded the message five days ago when I was in an emotionally raw place, but Lindsay assured me it was great. It was thirty seconds of me explaining the truth about a beautiful woman on the train whose heart I won and lost in the blink of an eye. I didn't make excuses or interpret what had happened. The recording just ended. Trish looked at me in disbelief.

"You didn't include an ending."

I shrugged. "I don't know the ending yet."

"It's edgy and powerful. And it breaks my heart, but I think people will understand this a lot better than a label. I like that it adds a different dimension to the work." Trish rolled her shoulders and cracked her neck—she was as nervous as I was.

"Fifteen minutes. Want to grab a drink?" I looked around for the bar.

"How do you feel? Would another drink put you over the edge?"

"I'm so nervous I don't feel anything." Except random flashes of heat.

"You need to take deep breaths and settle down. Tonight is your night. This is all about you, and you're going to kill it." Trish put both hands on my shoulders. "Lindsay said to expect up to three hundred people, but I'm calling it now. People will have to wait outside just to get in here. You made it. Thank you for having me here by your side."

I looked away. "I told you not to make me cry." I didn't have makeup with me, and even though Stefan said they planned to be here, I didn't expect them to work.

"Okay. Quick. Let's find something else to talk about." She looked me up and down. "I love the boots. They add a rough sexiness to the whole look." She gave me a thumbs-up.

I looked down at my outfit. It was somewhat boring, but I was advised to dress in a simple manner, since the art was supposed to speak for itself. I wasn't a flashy dresser anyway. I was wearing a black suit, a light-blue V-neck T-shirt, and my black boots. Trish had suggested a blue shirt instead of my standard white because the blue made my eyes pop. She handed me a shot of tequila. "Nice and smooth, just like tonight's going to go."

I welcomed the burning sensation as it coated my throat and gave me a quick burst of energy. "I'm fucking ready. Let's do this." I high-fived her and headed to the front of the gallery. Trish positioned herself behind me and Lindsay and promised to walk the room and report all the news, good or bad. I could see people gathered near the entrance but didn't recognize anybody.

Lindsay looked at the clock. "Are you ready?"

With a dry mouth and my heart in my throat, I nodded.

"Smile," Lindsay said.

I smiled and rocked on my feet until Trish tugged at my blazer.

"Settle down."

I immediately stopped and smiled at the people who walked into the gallery. A few shook my hand, but most of them just smiled and nodded. It was so hard not to squeal with excitement when my friends piled in and even harder not to cry when my family showed up.

"Baby, look at you. This is amazing." My mom glanced around the room as if seeing my work for the first time. She kissed my cheek and moved on at Trish's encouragement.

"Mom, you have to see how *Thursday* turned out." Trish took her by the arm and directed her away from me.

My dad kissed my temple. "I should follow them before we both break down."

"Thanks, Dad." I was emotionally stronger by the time the rest of my family filed in.

When Ethan and Starr arrived, he picked me up and hugged me.

"This is amazing," he said. I could see the pride on his face. He hugged me again. "I'm so proud of you. My cousin, the artist."

Starr thumbed behind them to the group of people waiting to meet me. "We'll find you later." She kissed my cheek and steered Ethan away so other people could introduce themselves.

Lindsay moved me around the room and introduced me to Harrison Kemper, who, according to her, was riveted by *Broken*. I shook his hand, and we spent at least ten minutes discussing the technique before we dug into the emotions behind it. My heart was on display for the world to see, and the only thing I could do was sit back and watch people react to it. I apologized when Lindsay swooped in to steal me away to meet another potential buyer, Gwendolyn Meehan, a board member of Center on Halsted. We'd met before at a few fund-raisers Tuft & Finley helped sponsor.

"Nico, I didn't realize this was your exhibition," she said.

"Hi, Gwen. It's good to see you again." I hugged her like I would a distant friend. Although we were friendly enough, we were never in the same circles. Gwen was in her mid-fifties and organized several events I'd attended when I was a baby dyke.

"This is gorgeous." She circled *Thursday* several times.

I wasn't sure if I needed to walk away or if she had questions. Thankfully, Lindsay turned me around to meet another person. And another person. I was about fifteen feet from the sculpture, talking to Harrison again, when Trish got into my line of vision. I quirked an eyebrow at her. She responded by shaking her head, indicating nothing was wrong. She waved over Ethan and Starr and chatted with them.

I blew her off and returned my attention to Harrison, who was telling Lindsay he was interested in three of my sculptures. I wasn't going to get too excited, but his interest made me smile. He asked me again about my techniques. I was explaining the processes of manipulating different metals when something caught my eye or, rather, someone. I recognized her long honey-color hair. Sophia was here.

Trish moved again to block my view, but it was too late. I'd seen Sophia's face. She was watching the video. My heart soared. She was here. And it wasn't just because of her chocolates. I squared my shoulders and was about to leave Harrison Kemper without a second thought, but Trish shook her head. I stopped. She slowly moved to the side, and I saw my mother and Sophia talking. That was everything. Unless Mom revealed more about me than Sophia knew, her comments could only help my case. Through the crowded space, twenty feet apart, my eyes locked with Sophia's. I couldn't look away even when I heard Lindsay say my name twice.

"I'm sorry?" I turned back to the conversation, having missed the last minute of it.

"How did you get into sculpting? Do you dabble in other media?" Harrison wanted all my attention, and I was desperate to get away. "I draw and paint, but welding sculptures is my favorite." I went into an elaborate rehearsed spiel about working with metal until he seemed satisfied. When I was able to excuse myself, I looked for Sophia in the crowd, but I couldn't find her.

"Did she leave?" I interrupted Trish's conversation.

"Excuse me for a moment," Trish said. She pulled me away by my elbow and lowered her voice so only I could hear. I smiled apologetically at the couple she was conversing with. "I don't think she left, but you need to stay focused."

I put my hand on my heart. "You should feel how fast my heart is beating right now." I took a deep breath and exhaled it softly.

"Quit being weird. Go find her, but don't ignore people along the way. Remember, tonight is about you, not about her."

I searched everywhere, but I couldn't find her. She'd left before I even had a chance to say hello.

CHAPTER TWENTY-THREE

I didn't know how she did it, but Trish managed to get us onto the roof of the hotel. We watched the sunrise with mimosas and croissants and a great view of the city we loved.

"Last night was amazing," Trish said.

"Best night ever," I said. Not really, but definitely top five. I pulled the blanket tighter around my shoulders. It was cold but I didn't care.

"I wonder how many sold? I bet everything does. I was totally right about the ladybug. She was one of the first to go."

I grabbed a croissant and tore into it. The mimosa was hitting my stomach hard. Or maybe it was the endless amount of alcohol at the hotel gathering after the gallery closed. Even our parents, who were still asleep, got tipsy. It had been a good night for the Marshall family. I felt encouraged after I knew Sophia was at the event. Her presence gave me hope, and once I had that, I was invincible the rest of the night. "I doubt they all will, but I already know two people who want to commission me to sculpt something for their properties."

"Time to get a lake house."

I toasted her. "Time to get a lake house. Or a Maserati."

"Cars are boring. And don't even say motorcycle. You have plenty of those. Maybe you can find a better studio or buy the second floor of the lofts."

I knew Ben had knocked out part of the second floor on our

side of the building because he needed room for the overhead crane, but I didn't know what he was using the rest of the space for. Honestly, I didn't care. "No. I love my studio. It's so easy to get there."

"At some point, you're going to have to get some sleep. You wowed them all last night with your art, but tonight you have to answer some tough questions," Trish said.

I had agreed to an Artist Talk, where I would discuss my artistic practice with some of the crowd from the exhibition. It gave people a chance to ask questions they weren't able to last night because I was being pulled in every direction. "I don't think so. It's going to be easy and fun, hopefully."

"Well, not too shabby a weekend for you. And you can sleep all day Sunday. You're going to need it." The high we were riding was going to end. Trish had been right there with me the entire time.

"Hey, listen. I want to thank you for always supporting me. I mean, you have a lot going on in your life, and you give me so much time. I appreciate it."

"I love you and am proud of you, and I expect a seventy-five percent commission."

"Lindsay's fifty percent is heavy enough. You get fame associated with our name." That word felt good to say. Fame. Even if Lindsay got a hefty cut, it was worth it. I could put any price on a commissioned piece. When Lindsay told me she was putting *Thursday* at thirty thousand and *Broken* at thirty-five, I'd almost fainted. Even the ladybug went for three thousand.

"I don't care. I'm just so happy your dream came true and I was here to see it happen."

"You helped make this happen. Without your encouragement…" I paused for the perfect words.

"You mean pushing you?" Trish said.

"Yes, that. Without you pushing me, I would still be in a destructive relationship, angry at the world, with no direction, so I owe you."

"We're family. That's what we do," she said.

We drank our mimosas and smiled at the sounds of the awakening city. Weekend traffic was picking up. People were trying to hang onto summer that was turning into fall. I had lost summer to my art and a girl.

Trish stood. "Come on. Let's get some sleep. We can't have you looking exhausted and hung over."

I grabbed our empty glasses, and we headed back to our floor. I slipped into my room, stripped, and barely made it to the bed, exhausted. This night could have been better only if Sophia had been next to me and not just a face I saw between twenty other people, like on the afternoon train.

❖

"I'd like to thank everyone for joining us this evening. Thank you, Nicole, for sharing your art with us. During tonight's Artist Talk, Nicole Briar will be discussing the techniques, visions, and inspiration behind her art. Everyone, please welcome Nicole."

For whatever reason, Lindsay had me wait in the hallway. My sculptures flanked the rooms, and eighty chairs were placed in the open area of the gallery, with standing room available. Judging by the buzz I heard, the room seemed at least half full. When I rounded the corner, I couldn't hide my surprise at how many people had returned to the gallery tonight.

I wore my dark jeans, a white button-up, and my wingtips. I felt more comfortable than I had the night before, but that could have been due to the reception I'd been given. I sat across from Lindsay and looked out at the crowd.

"Thank you so much for spending another evening with me. As you saw when you came in, my welding clothes are displayed up front. Welding and bending metal is difficult, and there's always an element of danger when you work with fire." I was getting nervous looking around the crowd, so I turned to Lindsay. "I work with three different welding machines and all types of metal. Like with any art, whether paint, or clay, I had to learn how far I could push different metals without cracking them and how to fix them if I did."

"How did you get started?"

I found my dad's face in the crowd. "My dad and I rebuilt a car, frame and all, when I was in my early teens. It was a 1980 Datsun 280Z. He showed me how to weld. It was so much fun and so challenging, I knew I'd make art that way. It was my favorite car for that reason—a project I did with my father, plus I got a lot of dates out of it. We painted it cherry red. I drove it in high school and most of college. When it ran its course, I parked it in one of my parents' garages, and my dad sold it for parts."

"Can you tell us what inspires you?" Lindsay asked.

"Life inspires me. Pain inspires me. I do my best work when I'm overwhelmed with love or anger or sadness. The energy that's bottled up inside me needs to come out, and I try to release it in a productive way."

Lindsay turned to the audience and pointed at someone who'd raised their hand.

"What's your favorite here?"

"I have so many favorites for so many different reasons. It's like picking a favorite child." That remark got a chuckle from the audience.

Trish put her hand up. "Tell us about *Broken*."

I took a deep breath. "A few years ago, I went through a terrible divorce. The relationship wasn't healthy, and I had to step away in order to save myself. We all do what we can to cope and process our feelings, and I chose art."

A voice at the back of the crowd spoke up. "Tell us about *Thursday*."

I looked around but couldn't find who said it. She stood, and I automatically put my hand up to my chest when our eyes met. Sophia was here. My Thursday. She stood tall, and her gaze didn't waver as she challenged me to answer the question. She was angry and beautiful.

"Thursday is the woman who got away."

"How did you lose her?"

A few gasped at her forward questioning, but I blocked the reactions out. "I lied to her. I kept a big part of myself hidden, and when I realized I should have told her everything about me, it was too late. She left."

"Why did you lie?" Her voice broke, but her gaze didn't.

I looked around the room as people started realizing this was more than just a simple question-and-answer session. "To protect myself. I was already broken. I needed to make sure she wanted me for me."

"Did you try to get her back?" an oblivious man in the audience asked. He obviously had no idea what was going on, but I appreciated the question. Almost everybody else appeared to have realized the woman standing was Thursday.

I took a deep breath before I answered. "I'll never stop trying."

She nodded and sat back down. I took a deep breath and blinked back the tears. The last thing I needed was to lose it.

Trish jumped in with a question she knew I wanted to answer. "What are you working on now? What can we expect to see in the future?" She stared at me and nodded encouragingly for me to focus and answer the question.

"I finished my last sculpture just this past week. I've been practicing a new welding technique that allows me to create complicated and very intricate pieces. Everything here is so large, and as much as I enjoy huge sculptures, the little ones are just as challenging." I smiled gratefully at Trish.

Throughout the entire session, I kept looking for Sophia. She was still there. Even at the very end, when the crowd gave me a standing ovation, she was there. I had to smile and talk to so many people, but I always knew where she was in the room. When she looked at her watch a third time, I knew my window of opportunity was closing. I excused myself and walked over to her.

"Thank you for coming. I mean that." I reached for her hands and almost wept when she didn't pull away. "Will you wait for me? I should be done in fifteen minutes."

Sophia nodded. God, I wanted to kiss her, but I couldn't jeopardize this tender moment. She was here for me, for us.

"I'll try to hurry," I said.

I found Lindsay talking to my parents and kissed them both. "Hi. How's it going?"

"I was just telling your parents that this was such a successful exhibition. I can't tell you how many phone calls we received about it today. And tonight's turnout is amazing."

"What time are you closing the doors?"

Lindsay checked her phone. "I'll make a final announcement that we're closing up in ten minutes. Is that good?"

I nodded. She excused herself and got the attention of the patrons still there. It was Saturday night in Chicago, and people were excited for the weekend. I shook hands and thanked attendees for giving me their time. When just the staff and my family remained, I said my good-byes and found Sophia sitting on a bench in front of *Thursday*. I sat next to her and leaned back in my chair. "What do you think of her?"

"She's lovely. Your work is beautiful."

"Can we go somewhere? Get away from here so we aren't constantly interrupted?" She closed her eyes for a few moments. I was afraid she might say no, but she nodded and stood. "Did you drive?" Since Trish picked me up, I had no mode of transportation.

"I did. Where do you want to go?"

"I'd like to take you somewhere."

"Your studio? It would be nice to see where you created this art."

Guilt hit me hard and my shoulders sank. "I want to take you to my condo. I have a lot to tell you. I want you to see where I live most of my life and get to know all of me."

She handed me her keys. "I'm parked a few blocks away." I followed her and asked her about Sophia's Collection, her grandmother, everything I could think of to keep the conversation going.

"Even though traffic sucks, I'm not too far from here." Out of my peripheral vision, I saw her nod a few times. It took twenty minutes to get to my building, the longest, most stressful stretch of time in my adult life. She didn't talk at all. Instead, she stared straight ahead. I had to be buzzed into the garage and make small talk with the night attendant. When I finally parked, I handed her the car fob. "Thank you for letting me drive your car." She walked with me to the elevator, and I punched the fourteenth floor after swiping my card. The elevator ride was quiet, too.

"You have a nice place." She walked straight to the floor-to-ceiling windows and looked out at the Chicago skyline.

I turned on lights and kicked off my shoes. I wanted to shower and change, but time with Sophia was precious, and I refused to waste it. "Can I get you anything to drink?"

"A glass of water, please."

I nodded and poured two ice waters. After I handed her one, I sat in the chair opposite her, took a deep breath, and looked straight into her beautiful blue eyes. I'd missed seeing them. "Hi. I'm Nicole Briar Marshall, part owner of Tuft & Finley and the creative director there. Trish Anderson is my sister. Anna Finley is our other partner. We started Tuft & Finley in college. I live here, and I also have a studio apartment where I work on my art in my spare time. I'm single, I've had some really horrible relationships in my past, but I'm working on myself and learning to trust people again."

"Did you leave out anything?"

"I do most of the designs at Tuft & Finley. I designed Sophia's Collection."

She stared at me in clear disbelief but didn't say anything. Her silence was killing me.

"I really want you to say something to me. Anything. Or throw something."

She leaned forward and put her hands on her knees. "Wow. That's a lot to process."

I stayed as still as I could, afraid to move, breathe, or say anything. She was teetering, and I needed her to fall back on my side, to fall in love with me again. "I did what I did because I've had two long-term relationships with horrible women. They wanted my money. I vowed that the next woman I had a relationship with would want me for me—not for my money or my cars, but for my heart."

She looked offended and rightfully so. "That's not who I am. And besides, you've had several opportunities to tell me the truth," she said.

"I know, but things were so great between us, I didn't want to ruin our relationship. Every time I planned to tell you, I chickened out. I was just so happy that a beautiful, smart, independent woman wanted to be with me."

"Why didn't you correct me when I thought you worked in the warehouse? I feel like I was part of an experiment or a joke."

She wasn't wrong about the experiment part. "Definitely not a joke. Everything I said to you and felt for you was real. And not that I'm making excuses, but I work everywhere at our business. I pride myself on being able to do anything there. I can drive a forklift, design a logo, close large deals, and work in a production line. Some days I have to do it all. We all work hard for the money we earn there. But you're right. I should have corrected you."

She walked to the windows and leaned against one. "And now you're a successful artist."

"Well, that remains to be seen, but hopefully so. That's always been my dream."

"You know, I didn't plan to go to your art show, but my grandmother thought I should at least hear what you had to say and see your art."

I joined her at the window, silently thanking Hazel the entire time. "Your grandmother's a smart lady. I'm sure you know that I visited her last week."

For the first time tonight, I saw a smile on her face. "She told me you showed up at her apartment and were very persistent."

I shrugged. "What can I say? The Sweet women make me do crazy things." I touched her arm. She didn't pull back. I could tell she was struggling. "Can we have a fresh start?"

"Maybe we're better off as friends."

Those words crushed me. I clutched her hands. "You don't mean that. After everything we've been through, all the good and the fun times we've had. Now that you know everything about me, we can conquer anything as a couple."

She pulled away and took a step back. "You've processed this mess. You've been living this life, this lie for months. I'm going to need time."

I nodded. "I understand. Whatever you need from me, just ask. I'm here. This is the real me. I'll do anything you want."

She picked up her purse and walked to the door. "Let's stick with being friends. New friends."

I nodded and suppressed a smile, because that was something. I'd been down this road with her before. "I can live with that." I opened the door for her. "For now."

CHAPTER TWENTY-FOUR

The L was more crowded when the weather turned. It always surprised me how quickly it changed from summer to fall in the upper Midwest. I kept my blazer on and found a seat in the back of the car, holding a white box tied with a red ribbon on my lap.

Sophia and I had texted some since she visited my condo. I initiated every time, but she never ignored me. We even had coffee one night after work, but she was extremely guarded. I needed to make a move, and that's exactly what I was doing right now. The closer we got to her stop, the straighter I sat up.

When the doors finally opened and I caught a glimpse of her, every emotion fluttered up from my chest and clogged my throat. I swallowed hard so I could breathe again. She was beautiful and unaware. I smiled when I saw her heels. Damn, I loved those shoes. They stuttered on the ribbed walkway, and I raised my head. She saw me. I pointed to the empty seat next to me and gave her a weak smile. Today she smelled like dark chocolate and marzipan, my new favorite.

"Happy Thursday," I said to her when she sat down. She put her own white box with a red ribbon on her lap and looked at me.

"Hi. Are you taking Hazel some chocolates, too?"

"No. These are actually for you."

"You made me chocolates?" She seemed impressed, and for a split second, I doubted my choices.

"Not really." I handed her the box.

"Should I open it now?"

"If you want to."

"You aren't dressed for welding." Her voice softened. "You look nice."

"Thank you. I'm required to dress up for work when I'm in the office." I was trying not to read too much into the compliment. Our newfound relationship was slow, but I was willing to wait forever if I had to. I ate every crumb of attention as if I were starving. "Please open it."

She took her time untying the bow and placing it between us. When she opened the box, she put her hand to her throat and looked at me. "You made these for me?" I nodded. She held up a metal version of her lavender bonbon. "How did you get the metal to look purple? It's not paint. How did you do these?" I smiled as she cradled each piece in the sample box. I'd made versions of my favorite Sophia's Collection chocolates.

"I'm trying a new welding technique so I can work on miniatures and thought I'd make replicas of your chocolates." I played it like it wasn't a big deal, but the amount of cursing during production told a different story. Not to mention a few new tiny burns on my hands. I handed her another small package. "I wanted to see your reaction before I gave you this."

"You're spoiling me."

"You deserve it. Go ahead, open it."

She opened the seal and pulled out a metal version of her logo.

"I know it's cutesy, but like I said, I'm practicing on—" I never finished my sentence because she kissed me. The moment her lips brushed mine, I reached for her out of instinct. It didn't matter that we were on the L surrounded by strangers. The only thing that mattered was that she was in my arms, that she had knocked down the wall that kept us from being together.

"Everything is so beautiful. Thank you." She looked at the

tiny artwork and smiled. She touched each piece over and over. "I can't believe you did this for me. When did you have time?"

"Let's just say that during the last three weeks I had one thing on my mind." I tried to smile and joke, but the gravity of the moment rested heavily on my heart, and I almost let out a sob. I looked away as I gathered my thoughts and felt her hand on my forearm.

"Do you want to visit Hazel with me?"

I nodded before I looked at her. "I would like that very much."

She handed me Hazel's box so she could look at hers again. My heart swelled as I watched her admire my work. "I can't believe you made swirls and even got the splatter look. Amazing."

"It took a lot of trial and error, but I'm happy with the results. Nothing is as good as the real thing, though."

Her blush gave me hope. By the time we reached the stop, our conversation had picked back up, and I was excited about the future and what was in store for us.

"How did you know where my grandmother lived?"

Fuck, really? I'd forgotten about that one small, tiny detail. "The night we had dinner. She mentioned her neighborhood and the street, so I just took a walk one day." That wasn't a total lie.

"She said really nice things about you. I'm glad she encouraged me to attend your art show. It was incredible. She was sorry she missed it."

"It's sweet that she wanted to go." I stopped walking and put my hands on her shoulders when she turned to see why I wasn't beside her. "Seeing you there was everything. I want you to know that. I realize we're trying to get to a comfortable place, but I miss you. I miss us."

She stopped me. "Let's have a quick visit with my grandma, and then we can go somewhere and talk. Not here, okay?" My heart sank, but I nodded. She touched my face. "As much as I hate to admit it, I've missed you, too."

And just like that, I was back on cloud nine. Back to opening my heart and letting the good feelings in. I wanted to hold her hand, but since we both had boxes, I would have to wait until we were done visiting with Hazel. Sophia called her when we were standing outside Hazel's greystone.

"I brought a friend." Sophia looked up at Hazel and waved. I waved, too.

"Nico, it's so good to see you. Come on up, both of you. It's cool outside." She rubbed her hands on her upper arms to ward off the chill when she opened her window.

Since I was in Sophia's company, I didn't notice the weather. I was warm from stress and from her confession.

"Grandma thinks anything below seventy is cold." Sophia grabbed the door when it buzzed and held it open for me.

"Whoever divided this greystone into three apartments did a really nice job."

"She can afford to live somewhere nicer, but she loves the neighborhood and has spent most of her life here."

"Oh, I love it. I really do."

Hazel greeted both of us with welcoming hugs. She gave me an extra squeeze and a wink, and my smile grew exponentially. She was on my side.

"It's great to see you both. Two boxes? What did I do to deserve two boxes?"

"Sorry, Grandma. One is for me. Nico made me something."

Hazel looked at me in surprise. "Are you getting into the chocolate business, too?"

Sophia and I laughed together. "Not really," Sophia said. She handed Hazel the box. "Go ahead and peek inside."

Hazel opened it and put her hand to her chest. "Oh, my. Nico, is this your art? It's so detailed and beautiful."

I beamed like a kid who'd just won a prize. I welcomed Hazel's praises for about five minutes, and then I got antsy. Making small talk while the rest of my life vacillated between happiness and another round of depression wasn't my strong suit. As if reading my mind, Sophia relieved my agony.

"I'm sorry, Grandma. Nico and I have to be somewhere, so we can't stay long."

Hazel held up her box and thanked Sophia. "Thank you for bringing these to me. Give me a call over the weekend. We can catch up then."

After we left Hazel's, I was unsure of her intentions, but I knew she wanted to talk. "Do you want to go to a coffee shop or for a walk in the park?"

"Can we just go back to your place, where it's quiet and I can think?"

"I'd love that." I considered the best way back to my condo, but she handled that problem as well.

"Let's go back to Sweet Stuff and grab my car."

She seemed calm but guarded, so I was nervous about what it all meant. I didn't know if she was going to tell me that being friends was too much or that she wanted more. I couldn't read her, but I was hopeful. Why would she want to go to my place if she didn't want to move our relationship to the next level? "That sounds good."

❖

The quiet car ride back to my condo was punctuated with honks and a few times of me clearing my throat. The elevator ride was even quieter. When I unlocked the door to my place, it was so hard not to nervously pace. "Can I get you anything?"

She shook her head. I excused myself to get rid of my blazer and slip on a warm sweater and fuzzy socks. I couldn't get warm. Then I turned on the fireplace and poured myself a glass of whiskey. I sat on the couch next to her, with enough space between us to not make her uncomfortable. "Tell me what you're thinking."

"In every situation I can think of, what you did was inexcusable. You made me into an experiment," she said.

I wanted to jump in and tell her all the reasons why she was wrong, but I sat there quietly.

"Just when I opened up and started trusting again, I find out that everything about you was a lie." She stood and walked over to the window. It took all my will to stay seated and wait my turn. "Tell me how I'm supposed to trust you after everything?"

I joined her at the window. "Our relationship is one hundred percent real. What I feel for you, the love that continues every day, is real. I started this relationship under false pretenses. I've never felt this way, and it scared the shit out of me. That's not an excuse, just me being honest."

She looked at me in what seemed like confusion.

"When it started, I was broken. I couldn't risk giving my heart to someone who would take advantage of me again. But then it was too late to tell you. We were doing so well, and deep down, I was terrified I would lose you if I told you the truth."

"Did you really think I would be after you only for money?" She sighed. "I'm a proud person. I wouldn't be after anyone for that, regardless of my circumstances. Sweet Stuff was slipping, so I decided to do something about it. Hell, I paid for college, my house, everything. I created Sophia's Collection to save Sweet Stuff, and my efforts are working. I don't need anyone else's money."

"Now I know you aren't that kind of person, but I had to be sure. And then when I was sure, I was in too deep, and I couldn't lose you."

"But you did."

I stepped closer. "But you're here now, and that means everything." I gently tucked her hair behind her ear, afraid to be in her personal space. She didn't step back. "I want to be with you, Sophia. We have fantastic chemistry, and it's so much fun when we're together. You're perfect for me. I'm so very sorry." I moved my hand to her cheek. The slight pressure against my hand gave me the confidence I needed. "I love you, Sophia Sweet. I love the way you smell, the way you taste, the sounds of your heels anywhere. I love how much you care about chocolate and your grandmother and Walter and your obsession with *Lord of the Rings*. I love your dry sense of humor and how you hate bananas, but love anything banana flavored."

She put her hands on mine. "I don't like the texture."

I half laughed and half sobbed. "What?" Nothing made sense.

"I don't like the texture of bananas." She didn't sound angry or hateful.

"That's what you got out of everything I just said?" I didn't know if I should be offended or just go with it.

"I was so angry at you." She put her hands on my chest as if to push me away but never did. "I felt stupid and used. I tried to stay mad at you, but I can't. I want to hate you, but I can't. Understanding your past, I know why you did what you did. But no more lies, Nico. I miss you and want you back, but no more lies."

My knees felt weak, and I threatened to drop as I processed her confession. It was time to confess everything so we could start clean. "I used your paperwork at Tuft & Finley to figure out your grandmother's actual address, even though I had a good idea of the general area from our dinner. That's how I knew where she lived. Doing that was invasive and an abuse of my position. And that's the final thing between us."

"So, you did sort of stalk me. On paper." She stepped closer and dropped one hand but kept the other one right under my collarbone. Her spot. "Don't even tell me that you hate chocolate. I couldn't take that."

I placed my hand over hers as if protecting and swearing on my heart. "I love chocolate so much, now that I know what real chocolate is. I have no other secrets. I promise I will never lie to you or keep anything from you unless it involves surprise parties or birthday gifts."

When her eyes met mine, I knew I was forgiven. My chin quivered as I fought for control over tears I knew would fall. I kissed her softly, hesitantly until I felt her press against me. She put her arms around my neck, and our gentle reconciliation kiss turned passionate in a matter of moments. I pulled back.

"Am I forgiven?" She nodded and reached for me.

That was all it took. I led her to my bedroom and pulled off the sweater I'd desperately needed minutes ago. She reached for the buttons on my shirt, and I slipped off her blazer. "I've missed you so much."

"I've missed you, too," she said.

I wasted no time getting her naked and into my bed. This was how it was supposed to be. Sophia here in my home, with no secrets between us. Touching her was the most important thing. I missed the softness of her skin, the curve of her hips, and the sharp breaths she took when my lips or my fingertips hit a sensitive spot. "You're so beautiful." She arched her back as I worked my way over her body, kissing and touching her everywhere. "Marzipan and dark chocolate."

"What?" It was more of a moan than a question.

"Today you smell like marzipan and dark chocolate." I didn't get an answer. Nor did I expect one. This was my Sophia—warm, sweet, and giving.

I worked my way down her body, eager to taste her again. I ran my fingers up and down her slit, watching her writhe with pleasure. I knew she trusted me again. I slipped inside her tight warmth and moved in a rhythm we knew well. I ran my tongue over her clit and pressed harder when her orgasm seemed close.

"Oh, Nico. Nico." Her heels dug into the mattress as she climbed higher and higher until she came. She grabbed my shoulders and pushed into me. I moved my fingers faster and harder until she came again. The second orgasm was always her favorite. "I love you. I love you so much."

I almost stopped because I wasn't sure if I'd heard her correctly, but my heart fluttered rapidly, and I knew I had. "Tell me again." I raised up on one elbow so I could see her. She opened her eyes and said it again without wavering.

"I love you."

Her words broke me. I covered my face so she couldn't see the tears, but she obviously knew exactly what was happening. I felt her hands in my hair soothing me.

"I love you, Nico. I couldn't walk away from you. From this. You made me have fun and live again."

I wiped away my tears and crawled up to kiss her. "I'm so sorry. I never ever want to hurt you anymore."

She pulled me close and kissed my cheek. "I know you won't. Today is a new beginning for us. Only love, life, and laughter from here on out."

I smiled when her hands wandered down me, touching all the places I called my Sophia Sweet spots. "And really amazing sex."

She bit my earlobe playfully and whispered in my ear before sliding down my torso. "And chocolate. Don't forget chocolate."

EPILOGUE

"Don't let her get away," Ethan shouted.

I turned and grabbed Lilah right before she raced by me. "Where are you going, sweet baby?" She threw her arms around my neck and gave me an awkward toddler hug.

"Man, she's fast. Thanks for grabbing her. I'm nervous there might still be nails around." Ethan scooped Lilah out of my arms and placed tiny kisses all over her until she squealed with delight. He looked at the recently painted front of our home. "This is a beautiful house, Nico." Starr echoed his appreciation and gave me a hug.

"It has everything we could possibly want." Sophia and I had moved in together over a year ago. With the money from the sale of the condo and my sculptures, we'd decided to build the perfect house.

Now that Sophia's Collection was booming, she was able to hire more chocolatiers and not work so many damn hours. I still had the studio, but Sophia had decorated it. She spent a lot of time there with me when I sculpted. Most of what I was designing and creating was commissioned work. I collected a paycheck at Tuft & Finley but delegated most of the projects. I worked remotely most days and showed up on Fridays to eat baked goods and check in.

"Have you seen Trish today?" Ethan asked.

"I'm headed there next. She's tired of seeing my face."

He laughed. "It's day three. Give her some time. She'll want you sooner than later." He followed me to the front door. "When do you officially move in?"

"Next week. We have a final walk-through, and then the cleaning company is going to make everything beautiful. I don't want to have do anything other than direct movers where to put things," I said.

"Let's see the place." Starr's excitement ramped up my own.

I unlocked the door and let everyone in. "Welcome to Home Sweet Home."

"Clever, but you can do better."

"Briar Patch?" I asked.

"That's not very welcoming," Ethan said.

"I don't want people to get too comfortable here," I said.

"It's beautiful, Nico," Starr said. She ignored our ribbing and went on her own tour with Lilah in her arms.

"I can't believe she's so perfect," I said.

"Which one?" Ethan asked.

"Both. And you know what?" I looked at my watch. "It's almost time to go see another perfect baby."

Everly Nicole Anderson had been born three days ago. They were home from the hospital, but Trish's husband, Rob, had asked that we wait until the afternoon to visit. I was beyond excited about Everly. I was more nervous than Rob. I'd wanted to be in the delivery room, but my mother had talked me out of it. She said there were some things I shouldn't see. I paced the waiting room instead. Eight hours and five cups of coffee later, we welcomed Everly into the world. I couldn't even hold her when Rob issued me into the room. I sat in the chair and wept. She was perfect. Trish finally had to tell me to stop crying and hold my niece.

"I can't even tell you how loved you already are," I said. She opened her eyes for only a minute as if to say hello and fell promptly back to sleep. I nuzzled the soft black fuzz on her head and kissed all her perfect fingers.

"Honey, put her hat back on. It's cold in here." Mom was eager to hold her, so I carefully placed Everly in her hands. Sophia reached for me, and I pulled her close.

"I can't process everything I'm feeling." Later that night we discussed starting a family of our own. I was scared but thrilled at the idea of having children with Sophia.

"Is Sophia meeting us here or at Trish's?" Ethan asked.

I checked my watch. "There. She wanted to stop at the warehouse first to make sure everything was moving along smoothly."

"I'll have to thank her for hiring my two boys for the warehouse and see how they're doing," he said. Ethan was involved in the Second Chance program that gave troubled teens and young adults an opportunity to change. Sophia had hired two of the boys Ethan worked with to help in shipping at Sweet Stuff. She'd told me they were doing a great job.

"They're doing fine. Let's get out of here and go see the new cherub." I followed Ethan and Starr over to Trish's house, which was two neighborhoods away. It was a longer drive to work, but work was no longer the most important thing to me. Family was. Parking was difficult because everyone was there to see the baby. I didn't see Sophia's car yet, so I shot her a text and went inside to see my family and our friends.

"Hey, Grammy." I kissed my mother on the cheek.

"I still don't know what I want Everly to call me."

"We have time. Maybe Nana?" I called her mother Nana and thought it was a fitting tribute to her side of the family.

"I can't possibly cry anymore. Nana's a great idea. Thanks, baby."

The house was packed with people downstairs dropping off gifts and eating snacks. I sneaked upstairs and found Trish breastfeeding Everly.

"How are you feeling?"

"I'm sore, tired, and hungry. Tell me you have food."

I held my empty hands up. "I can run down and make a plate of food."

She waved me off. "It's okay. I need to burp her and maybe give you two quality time while I shower. Who's downstairs?"

I lit up at the prospect of having alone time with my niece. "The question is who isn't downstairs. I guess nobody wanted to wait on a party for you."

Trish waved her hand around Everly's room. "We have everything we could possibly need or want."

"I saw a lot of diaper cakes. Those will come in handy. And other things, but I don't want to ruin the surprise. And I can burp her while you get ready." Who had I become? I'd avoided babies like the plague before. Suddenly I was thinking of children of my own and offering to burp babies.

"Okay. Grab one of those towels and put it over your shoulder."

I did as instructed and melted into the chair when Trish gave me Everly. "Go shower," I whispered.

She disappeared, and I was finally alone with Everly. I gently patted her back and told her all about her upcoming life. "You're going to be older than your cousins, so you're going to have to help them out. But before they come into this world, it's going to be you and me, kiddo. We're going to have so much fun. Sleepovers, pizza parties, shopping sprees. Oh, and all the parks. Don't tell your mom, but I'm going to get you a puppy. Yes. A real fluffy one. One you can snuggle with at night. And we'll get you on a skateboard or in dance class when you're three."

"You're probably going to have to get Trish's permission on the dog," Sophia said. She slipped in the room and kissed me quietly before kissing Everly's soft head.

"How did you know where to find me?"

"Oh, please. Your mother didn't even have to tell me you were up here." She knelt beside me, and we stared at Everly. "She's so round and perfect."

"I hope her eyes stay this blue."

"She'll be a heartbreaker, like her aunt."

I put my hand up to my chest. "What? Me? Never. I'll teach her all the right things to do."

"You look good holding a baby," she said.

The words still didn't make me panic. I knew Sophia was my soul mate and we were destined to start a family together. We just had one more thing to clear up.

"So, will our babies be Marshall-Sweet or Sweet-Marshall?" I asked.

She paused. "That's a good question. Both have a nice ring to them."

"I know this isn't really the time or place and that the idea scares you, but I really want to marry you, Sophia Sweet. I want us to have tiny babies together and have our dream life. We're on the right path, but I want to do this legally. Will you—" I didn't get to finish. She kissed me so hard I clutched Everly for fear we'd topple backward in the rocker.

"Yes, Nico. I want to be your wife and have a family with you and be part of the Marshalls, because you're the best thing that's happened to me."

Tears instantly sprang to my eyes, and I had to let them fall, because in one hand I held my niece and in the other the woman who'd just agreed to marry me.

"I'm so happy, babe." I cupped her cheek and wiped away her tears with my thumb.

"I'm so happy, too," she whispered.

I was the luckiest woman in the world. All my dreams came true because I never gave up. I never gave up on Sophia, I never gave up on us, and I never gave up on love.

About the Author

Multi-award-winning author Kris Bryant was born in Tacoma, Washington, but has lived all over the world and now considers Kansas City her home. She received her BA in English from the University of Missouri and spends a lot of her time buried in books. She enjoys hiking, photography, spending time with her family, and her dog, Molly (who gets more attention than Kris does on Facebook).

Her debut novel, *Jolt*, was a Lambda Literary Award finalist. *Forget Me Not* was selected by the American Library Association's 2018 Over the Rainbow Book List and was a Golden Crown Finalist. *Breakthrough* won a 2019 Golden Crown Award. *Listen* was an Ann Bannon Popular Choice Award finalist and won a 2020 Goldie for Contemporary Romance. Kris can be reached at krisbryantbooks@gmail.com, www.krisbryant.net, @krisbryant14.

Books Available From Bold Strokes Books

Secret Agent by Michelle Larkin. CIA Agent Peyton North embarks on a global chase to apprehend rogue agent Zoey Blackwood, but her commitment to the mission is tested as the sparks between them ignite and their sizzling attraction approaches a point of no return. (978-1-63555-753-4)

Journey to Cash by Ashley Bartlett. Cash Braddock thought everything was great, but it looks like her history is about to become her right now. Which is a real bummer. (978-1-63555-464-9)

Liberty Bay by Karis Walsh. Wren Lindley's life is mired in tradition and untouched by trends until social media star Gina Strickland introduces an irresistible electricity into her off-the-grid world. (978-1-63555-816-6)

Scent by Kris Bryant. Nico Marshall has been burned by women in the past wanting her for her money. This time, she's determined to win Sophia Sweet over with her charm. (978-1-63555-780-0)

Shadows of Steel by Suzie Clarke. As their worlds collide and their choices come back to haunt them, Rachel and Claire must figure out how to stay together and, most of all, stay alive. (978-1-63555-810-4)

The Clinch by Nicole Disney. Eden Bauer overcame a difficult past to become a world champion mixed martial artist, but now rising star and dreamy bad girl Brooklyn Shaw is a threat both to Eden's title and her heart. (978-1-63555-820-3)

The Last First Kiss by Julie Cannon. Kelly Newsome is so ready for a tropical island vacation, but she never expects to meet the woman who could give her her last first kiss. (978-1-63555-768-8)

The Mandolin Lunch by Missouri Vaun. Despite their immediate attraction, everything about Garet Allen says short-term, and Tess Hill refuses to consider anything less than forever. (978-1-63555-566-0)

Thor: Daughter of Asgard by Genevieve McCluer. When Hannah Olsen finds out she's the reincarnation of Thor, she's thrown into a world of magic and intrigue, unexpected attraction, and a mystery she's got to unravel. (978-1-63555-814-2)

Veterinary Technician by Nancy Wheelton. When a stable of horses is threatened, Val and Ronnie must work together against the odds to save them and maybe even themselves along the way. (978-1-63555-839-5)

16 Steps to Forever by Georgia Beers. Can Brooke Sullivan and Macy Carr find themselves by finding each other? (978-1-63555-762-6)

All I Want for Christmas by Georgia Beers, Maggie Cummings & Fiona Riley. The Christmas season sparks passion and love in these stories by award-winning authors Georgia Beers, Maggie Cummings, and Fiona Riley. (978-1-63555-764-0)

From the Woods by Charlotte Greene. When Fiona goes backpacking in a protected wilderness, the last thing she expects is to be fighting for her life. (978-1-63555-793-0)

Heart of the Storm by Nicole Stiling. For Juliet Mitchell and Sienna Bennett a forbidden attraction definitely isn't worth upending the life they've worked so hard for. Is it? (978-1-63555-789-3)

If You Dare by Sandy Lowe. For Lauren West and Emma Prescott, following their passions is easy. Following their hearts, though? That's almost impossible. (978-1-63555-654-4)

Love Changes Everything by Jaime Maddox. For Samantha Brooks and Kirby Fielding, no matter how careful their plans, love will change everything. (978-1-63555-835-7)

Not This Time by MA Binfield. Flung back into each other's lives, can former bandmates Sophia and Madison have a second chance at romance? (978-1-63555-798-5)

The Found Jar by Jaycie Morrison. Fear keeps Emily Harris trapped in her emotionally vacant life; can she find the courage to let Beck Reynolds guide her toward love? (978-1-63555-825-8)

Aurora by Emma L McGeown. After a traumatic accident, Elena Ricci is stricken with amnesia, leaving her with no recollection of the last eight years, including her wife and son. (978-1-63555-824-1)

Avenging Avery by Sheri Lewis Wohl. Revenge against a vengeful vampire unites Isa Meyer and Jeni Denton, but it's love that heals them. (978-1-63555-622-3)

Bulletproof by Maggie Cummings. For Dylan Prescott and Briana Logan, the complicated NYC criminal justice system doesn't leave room for love, but where the heart is concerned, no one is bulletproof. (978-1-63555-771-8)

Her Lady to Love by Jane Walsh. A shy wallflower joins forces with the most popular woman in Regency London on a quest to catch a husband, only to discover a wild passion for each other that far eclipses their interest for the Marriage Mart. (978-1-63555-809-8)

No Regrets by Joy Argento. For Jodi and Beth, the possibility of losing their future will force them to decide what is really important. (978-1-63555-751-0)

The Holiday Treatment by Elle Spencer. Who doesn't want a gay Christmas movie? Holly Hudson asks herself that question and discovers that happy endings aren't only for the movies. (978-1-63555-660-5)

Too Good to be True by Leigh Hays. Can the promise of love survive the realities of life for Madison and Jen, or is it too good to be true? (978-1-63555-715-2)

Treacherous Seas by Radclyffe. When the choice comes down to the lives of her officers against the promise she made to her wife, Reese Conlon puts everything she cares about on the line. (978-1-63555-778-7)

Two to Tangle by Melissa Brayden. Ryan Jacks has been a player all her life, but the new chef at Tangle Valley Vineyard changes everything. If only she wasn't off the menu. (978-1-63555-747-3)

When Sparks Fly by Annie McDonald. Will the devastating incident that first brought Dr. Daniella Waveny and hockey coach Luca McCaffrey together on frozen ice now force them apart, or will their secrets and fears thaw enough for them to create sparks? (978-1-63555-782-4)

Best Practice by Carsen Taite. When attorney Grace Maldonado agrees to mentor her best friend's little sister, she's prepared to confront Perry's rebellious nature, but she isn't prepared to fall in love. Legal Affairs: one law firm, three best friends, three chances to fall in love. (978-1-63555-361-1)

Home by Kris Bryant. Natalie and Sarah discover that anything is possible when love takes the long way home. (978-1-63555-853-1)

Keeper by Sydney Quinne. With a new charge under her reluctant wing—feisty, highly intelligent math wizard Isabelle Templeton—Keeper Andy Bouchard has to prevent a murder or die trying. (978-1-63555-852-4)

One More Chance by Ali Vali. Harry Basantes planned a future with Desi Thompson until the day Desi disappeared without a word, only to walk back into her life sixteen years later. (978-1-63555-536-3)

Renegade's War by Gun Brooke. Freedom fighter Aurelia DeCallum regrets saving the woman called Blue. She fears it will jeopardize her mission, and secretly, Blue might end up breaking Aurelia's heart. (978-1-63555-484-7)

The Other Women by Erin Zak. What happens in Vegas should stay in Vegas, but what do you do when the love you find in Vegas changes your life forever? (978-1-63555-741-1)

The Sea Within by Missouri Vaun. Time is running out for Dr. Elle Graham to convince Captain Jackson Drake that the only thing that can save future Earth resides in the past, and rescue her broken heart in the process. (978-1-63555-568-4)

To Sleep With Reindeer Justine Saracen. In Norway under Nazi occupation, Maarit, an Indigenous woman, and Kirsten, a Norwegian resister, join forces to stop the development of an atomic weapon. (978-1-63555-735-0)

Twice Shy by Aurora Rey. Having an ex with benefits isn't all it's cracked up to be. Will Amanda Russo learn that lesson in time to take a chance on love with Quinn Sullivan? (978-1-63555-737-4)

Z-Town by Eden Darry. Forced to work together to stay alive, Meg and Lane must find the centuries-old treasure before the zombies find them first. (978-1-63555-743-5